EVIL AMONG US
Species Intervention #6609
Book 5

J K. Accinni

E.K. Publishing
Lakewood Ranch, Florida

www.speciesintervention.com

This is a work of fiction. Names, characters, places and incidents
either are the product of the author's imagination or are used
fictitiously and any resemblance to actual persons, living or dead,
business establishments, events, or locales is entirely coincidental.

EVIL AMONG US
SPECIES INTERVENTION #6609
Book 5
J.K. Accinni

An E.K. Publishing book published in arrangement with the author,
Lakewood Ranch, FL
Copyright © J.K. Accinni

ISBN: 978-0-9899769-3-0

Dedication

I am happy to dedicate this book to all of the wonderful readers who have taken valuable time from their day to leave reviews for my books on Amazon.com or Barnes and Noble. I know how difficult it can be to express yourself with the written word. And God knows, who has an extra minute to spare in their complicated lives? I read every review and find myself delighted with the varied perspectives readers take of my books. Reviews to authors are like dollars to Donald Trump . . . so precious!

I cannot forget to thank three special people who gave me an unselfish helping hand when one was needed. Ms. Wanda Hartzenberg of South Africa, Aileen Aroma of Miami, Florida and fellow author RaeBeth Buda of Fairchance, Pennsylvania. I truly believe these women are unaware of the magnitude of their efforts on behalf of Indie authors. The world we live in is filled with takers. These three ladies are givers. I will always be impressed with their efforts on my behalf and that of my fellow authors.

I would also like to recognize the cover design by GraphiczxDesigns and the editing by Karen Perkins of LionheART Publishing House.

Prologue

The brown sky rained dirty ash onto soundless trees denuded of life and flattened as if a giant fist had descended to pummel them from the gray and wintery sky. The horizon was blank; the most famous skyline in the world gone, leaving devastation, twisted metal and death.

There was a complete absence of color, life or warmth. The crushed horizon smoldered with a palette of black and leaden barrenness; benumbing and bone-crushing godforsaken loneliness.

The crumbled remains of the Bronx Zoo flinched under the sight of its once-proud sign, bent and misshapen. Precious wildlife reduced to ash. Minute bone fragments of the Womb's proud creations scattered in the wind.

Yes . . . the premonition directed to a naïve Abby by the transformed Netty Doyle as an Elder of the Womb came to pass over six months ago. No longer just a premonition but a cold ugly reality. Bloody reality. Hopeless reality . . .

The evil death that rained down on the Earth from the very hands of man that had been entrusted to protect it had done its job effectively. Just as man had idiotically planned while stupidly believing the time would never come. What was the old cliché? Man plans, while God, the Womb, laughs?

No one laughed now. Those who survived the early bombings found death at the hands of the next waves of horror, mass hysteria, depraved lawlessness and disease. If the plague, revisited from the Middle Ages, didn't get you, then dysentery, dehydration or starvation did.

Now that the population existed only in miniscule numbers that huddled deep in rare, clever concealments, human feces no longer littered every landscape. The smell of raw human sewage no longer carried on the perpetual wind that harbored its own invisible death to man and beast.

Yes, the wind that struck terror in the hearts of even the strongest, the most psychotic, and the most resourceful, carried invisible radiation along with the powerful spawn of dirty bombs. Even the most infectious microbes searched on the wind for unlucky hosts, the final death knell for the hapless humans and creatures in every corner of the once green planet.

What did the leaders of the most powerful countries in the world think would happen if one of them were foolish enough to hunger for absolute supremacy through the means of nuclear power? Did they think the world would come rushing to their feet in supplication? Only Homo sapiens would conceive of such a barbaric maneuver.

Yes, Homo sapiens: the species that, unlike any other creature, harbors a conscious ego. The ability to manipulate its environment and the complete disregard for the balance of nature and the other creatures that shared the formerly glorious planet.

And where now were the exalted leaders from the United States that bled their constituents so readily into poverty over the last 245 years?

Where were *any* authorities for that matter? How long would the politicians survive in their hunkered- down, taxpayer-funded concrete and steel monoliths in the ground? How many years would pass before their food ran out? Five years? Ten? Fifty? Could they hold out for *one hundred years*? If they could, what shape would the Earth be in? Questions, nothing but questions: long answered and prepared for by the most expensive experts taxpayer money could buy. For all the politicians in all the countries that assumed they would survive . . . the Womb laughed again.

Chapter 1
2057 AD

Five-year-old Suzy lay on the dirty cot with her leg chained to a metal spike embedded in the cold ground, muddy from the drizzle and constant footfalls of the men who came to confer with Doc Benjamin. Many attempted to catch a glimpse of the now notorious young captive who promised salvation for all from the devastation closing in on them as they maneuvered around the poisonous cities like army ants, ducking and weaving, destroying and obliterating everything in their path.

Their numbers now counted in the hundreds. For every man there were five to ten women, all young, most under the age of twenty. And all owned by an individual man. Virtual slaves.

They did the work during the day, setting up the extensive camp and cooking the meals, and were forced to extend comfort at night. If they refused they were beaten, starved and left without shelter, such that it was. It didn't take long for a young girl to be broken. Most were still mourning the loss of their families who had been robbed and murdered by the very men they were now forced to view as their protectors. Some existed in a state of perpetual shock, unable to answer questions or respond to threats as they were repeatedly raped or beaten. But they were alive. They were amongst the lucky few; if you could count their existence as living.

The only things that kept them from going over the edge were their sister captives. The strong and resilient ones knew their best chance of survival was to nurse the weak ones on the off chance they could increase their strength enough to overcome their captors.

It was a hopeless plan, doomed from the onset. The strength of the men only increased as they gathered food from their victims, stray livestock, and indispensable salvage in their march across new territory, pushing further and further east to their destination. But it was this trifling spark of defiance that the girls nursed, unwilling to let the fledgling ember of purpose be extinguished and so threaten their tenuous hold on thoughts of independence and freedom.

Suzy cringed as Doc Benjamin approached with Avery at his side. Avery claimed to be a veteran of the last few wars the United States had been sucked into by conservative politicians who hungered for the international conflict that enriched the pockets of the multinational corporations; in turn enriching their re-election coffers. He claimed to be an expert in electronics, rigging up a communication system between the men that rivaled anything the few rag tag groups of authorities had in the beginning.

Now, most in authority were either part of Doc Benjamin's group or dead. Stupidly, the principled ones had failed to adjust quickly enough to the new rule of eat or be eaten. Not literally, of course; it hadn't come to that yet. But unfortunately, their ethics didn't have room for flexibility, leaving their stripped corpses ignobly and anonymously behind in the dirt with the rest of Doc's victims.

Suzy tried to keep her eyelids squeezed tight as Avery approached. He was a lumbering giant of a man. His shaved head with its knobby protrusions and his dead, flat eyes that glittered as he watched the young girls laboring around the vast camp did nothing to dispel the aura of restrained violence. He hadn't touched her, but his excited grunts and the soft sobbing that were usually accompanied by sharp slaps and occasional screams could be heard around camp. That alone convinced Suzy that even though she didn't understand what was happening, she knew it was only a matter of time before she was the recipient herself.

"When ya gunna let me have the little one? You promised it was my turn the night we took her." Avery eyed Suzy's thin form, apparently asleep on the ramshackle cot, his voice unexpectedly squeaky and high pitched. The whining tone made Doc Benjamin cringe with annoyance. He turned to eyeball Avery. With the long suffering patience of a mother who's close to being on her last nerve with a beloved child, he sighed.

"Avery, you know she's our ticket to the bomb shelter her

grandfather has. We need to keep her happy and cooperative. How long do you think that would last if I turned her over to you? Didn't you get the last two women we liberated?"

Doc sidled up to Avery. A quick glimpse of steel flashed in his eyes, unseen by the giant. He playfully slapped Avery on the cheek; his hand stinging while Avery remained unperturbed, still caught up on what he felt was an undeserved slight.

"Yeah, but Doc, they both didn't work out. I had to dispatch the mother the first night when she tried to claw my face after I broke her kid's arm. And you know that was an accident. She just didn't get it when it was her kid's turn to be my bed warmer."

The whine in Avery's high-octave voice was trying Doc's patience. He snaked his arm around the giant's waist. "It's time to break camp and get a move on. Why don't you see what's keeping my breakfast? Tell the women to send a sweet for the girl. I need to have a talk with her when she wakes up." The giant's face sagged.

"But—"

"No buts. We don't have time to go over the inventory right now either. It'll keep. Just check on the livestock and make sure the men eat before they start to round up the herd again. We need them to keep up with us. What good does it do us if they get lost on the way to Lily Pond Road? It took us a long time to make it here to Sussex County. I'm not about to lose them after all this." Slapping Avery on a thick, meaty cheek a second time, he turned him around and sent him on his way, patient resignation in the slump of Avery's huge slabs of shoulders.

As he waited for his breakfast, Doc leaned back on the vehicle he and his men had confiscated from Suzy's grandmother and the worm, Seth. *What was the woman's name? Laura? No Lorna . . . yeah. Seth and Lorna.* He stewed over his error in letting them go. He should have killed Seth on the spot, but something about the old lady had made him pause. Not to mention the comatose young teen in the back of their car. There was no telling what illness she might have been carrying.

In his haste to get away, he had let the one person who could save them all slip through his fingers. His fists tightened in anger. How was he going to keep his horde under control if he continued to make bad judgment calls like that? His decision to follow Seth and the grandmother to Sussex County was called into question continually. He'd heard the whisperings.

He glanced over to Suzy's sleeping form. *Too bad the kid doesn't remember where her grandfather's bomb shelter actually is. It must be huge if they're growing crops inside.*

And she said they had medicine and something that cures people. At least they'd pulled the name of the road out of her. Now they just had to figure out where Lily Pond Road was. He absently fingered the ugly sores with their hanging scabs on the underside of his arm. No matter what he did to treat them, they refused to heal.

Doc peered up at the gray sky through a gap in the lean-to, wondering how long it would be before they saw the sun again. It had taken them months to get this far and they never did catch up to Seth and the grandmother. It made him suspect they had wandered off the route or been killed on the way. Perhaps the tribe had arrived before the twosome. After all, Seth and the old woman were on foot, dragging the sick teen. His horde had many vehicles. Even slowing for the multitude of stops to scavenge for gas supplies, females and anything else they might find useful at some future date, they had made decent progress.

When they had traveled off Route 15, the main artery leading into Sussex County, he had quickly established camp in a town called Franklin, just to the east of Sparta. They had decided that going further northwest to the town of Andover, which had at one time been nothing but rich farmland, was the wrong direction. There was no point in going further. He cursed under his breath as he remembered entrusting the map they had liberated from Seth and Lorna's car to one of his most reliable men.

Thompson had passed it on to his wife, one of his only men to have a spouse in the tribe. Unfortunately for them both, she'd lost the map during a mad scramble out of a town in Pennsylvania after they'd discovered dead bodies covered with bulbous growths and dried blood. They'd dropped everything they'd just scavenged where they stood and bolted, with Doc threatening to shoot anyone who held on to their tainted bounty. He didn't know what disease had struck the hapless inhabitants of the town, but he knew it could be most anything. His forethought regarding the issuance of collapsible breathing masks months ago had kept them safe . . . so far.

That night he had been forced again to make an example of a member of the tribe who had faltered and placed them in jeopardy. He had forced everyone to watch as he'd placed the woman on her knees, head over a log and had one of the strongest men in the tribe strike her neck with an axe, removing her head. He'd hated to do it because of the effect it had on the other women in the tribe. For the next day or so they had become less malleable. But things would eventually settle back down. It had served its purpose, keeping everyone on their toes.

He was at a complete loss as to what direction to go in from here. He knew they couldn't be more than two hours from New York City. The once great metropolis had taken a direct hit, followed up by a series of secondary hits once the other psychotic leaders of third world powers decided to pile in. When all communication was lost, he could only speculate as to who had done what to whom and why. Did it really matter now anyway? He knew the only thing he had to worry about was where the hell the bomb shelter was. And keeping everyone healthy, of course. That's what gave him his power.

That had never been an easy job even before the bombs. As he'd had told Suzy's grandmother, he wasn't a real doctor. Not like the doctors of his grandparents' era. The general public, like so many other issues, were completely unaware that the profession of physician no longer existed. Those that wanted to be *doctors*, simply studied to become what used to be called physician assistants. That was the doctor of today. It wasn't that the government had tried to hide it, although they had done so quite successfully, it was the fact that no one had paid attention. Their own lives were so all-consuming that few had the energy or inclination to pay attention, allowing the government to slowly strip them of most of their rights, fostering a new reality that few took the time to call into question. *Don't worry, the government will handle it, the government will solve everything, the government will take care of us.*

It also allowed interesting gentlemen like himself to slip into the ranks of the revered medical profession. Men with questionable ethics. It wasn't that he was such a bad guy. He just believed in different things. Like the fact that he was destined for greatness. He'd known that from the time he had discovered that a wide engaging smile could charm even the hardest bitten parent or superior.

His wandering mind thought about Avery and his many talents. Was there any wire, tool, or inanimate object that guy couldn't put to good use? It almost made up for his volatility when it came to dealing with flesh and blood. Before too long, Doc's eyelids drooped and he found himself nodding off to sleep.

Suzy concentrated, straining for sounds, hearing only the distant clatter that meant morning departure was not far off. She tested the silence by softly clearing her throat. Doc remained quiet so she finally relaxed for a few minutes to say her daily prayer to her grandmother to come find her. She swallowed a soft sob, gulping it down her throat as her little-girl perceptions wondered why it was taking so long. Her undeveloped brain warred with her treasured fantasy of rescue. No matter how many times she told the girls who fed her and attempted to comfort her that she would be rescued, they only shook their big heads that sat on emaciated rag-covered bodies with huge sad eyes and looked away. All were silent, not wanting to hurt the little girl with the truth of her reality. A few even envied the special treatment the five-year-old received.

Poor Suzy, not an ounce of fat remained on her bones. She refused to eat and often found herself in the arms of some of the men from the tribe as Doc directed her to be force-fed. It was the only thing that kept her alive; that and the delusion of rescue by her beloved grandmother. In the last few months, the reality of her captivity and the circumstances in which she lived had served to erase any trace of the happy, joyful child, along with most of the memories of her five years. She no longer remembered her mama and papa, her sister Jennifer, Seth, or even where she was from. The only probable reason she was still alive was her agonized screams for her grandmother to rescue her and take her to the magic bomb shelter when she was first captured. After she screamed and cried herself out, Doc was able to get enough monosyllabic answers out of her to convince him that the sanctuary was real.

Suzy shuddered as she felt Doc place a heavy hand on her thin shoulder. She began to tremble instantly. He turned her over, glancing down at the hardened crust of last night's gray gruel that decorated her hand-me-down shirt. The infinitesimal spark that was actually Suzy receded from her eyes to take refuge in the primal part of her mind that protects us all from facing horror. The only thing that Doc could see was an empty husk. She instinctively knew he had exhausted all hope of finding a way to reach her and extract even a morsel of information that would guide them further.

"I'm sorry, little one. But maybe it's better this way. My men will leave you alone." Taking her in his arms, he did an uncharacteristic thing. He hugged her and held her close. The spark that was the child Suzy flared, burning bright before receding back to its place of refuge.

From outside the lean-to came shouting. Men converged from everywhere, departure forgotten as everyone waited to hear the news brought by their advance team. The woman caught each other's eyes, glances of terror shared by all, as they wondered what new fate lay before them with the obvious urgency of the news.

Doc laid Suzy back on her broken cot and stood as his men approached. He ran his fingers through his lank, greasy hair and secured it with a band, allowing it to drape down his back like his men, then stepped out to meet them. The stench of the camp's unwashed bodies hit him in waves as the crowd around his lean-to thickened.

"Well, gentlemen, it appears you have some news for me?" He listened intently to the report from the scouts who stayed at least half a day in front of the tribe. Yes, there was a discovery. Not the bomb shelter they were hoping for, but maybe something else that might save them; something that would shelter them from the poisonous winds that were surely bound to catch them eventually in their hot indiscriminate soupy grip.

"Well, for God's sakes, gentlemen. Would one of you kindly get to the point?" From the ranks of the scouts a young man in his mid-twenties stepped up. He held a piece of sun-worn plastic in his hands. A sign, its letters faded, but still readable. The young man's fetid smile split from ear to ear even as he brushed at the flies that swarmed over the open sores on his forehead.

"And there's water too, Doc," he exclaimed as the rest of the tribe hugged and slapped each other on the back. For in his hands lay what they would view as their temporary salvation, little knowing they would be fated to call it home for as long as most of them would survive. He stepped closer to Doc, holding up the sign for all to see. It read simply: The Franklin Mine ca 1910. The zinc and mineral fluorescence capital of the world.

Little did they know they were only ten short miles from the Hive.

Chapter 2

Lorna pulled hard on the contraption that Seth had fashioned after the converted wagon had given out for the last time. Who knew an eighty-five-pound teenager could feel so heavy? But it was a miracle that she still lived.

Lorna glanced back at the pile of bones in the two-wheeled sled, not even recognizing Jennifer anymore. She stopped counting the times she had fought with Seth over leaving her behind. *When was that?* she wondered as flakes of cold, wet gray ash fell from the ominous gloomy sky. *Was it a month ago? No, I was warm then. Maybe last year . . . I think Suzy was a baby then. Nah, that can't be right. I need Clyde. He can help me. I need to get to Clyde. Then I can pick Suzy up at her school. Yup, can't forget to pick up Suzy.* She shuddered as she thought about Suzy waiting for her at school. "Can't leave my baby doll alone," Lorna muttered as she brushed ineffectively at her blood as it continued to drip from her nose, a constant occurrence these days.

Her finger caught on the rags that adorned her, holding together her own emaciated frame that kept moving forward beyond all reason.

"Ahhhh." She bent over in pain, dropping the bar that enabled her to pull Jen as another paper-thin fingernail ripped off her hand. She fumbled to untangle it from its nest of rags, forcing her unbalanced form to fall to the ground.

"Help meeee . . . Seeeth." Her voice whispered its forlorn plea; a refrain that repeated itself every day in response to any deviation from their long journey.

The easily distracted Lorna no longer saw Seth as an enemy in her delusion. Small comfort to Seth who had the responsibility of keeping them safe and keeping Lorna moving forward to Sussex County, where they now traipsed after skirting the not so greater metro area of New York City in an attempt to avoid the fallout from the bombs.

"Seeeeth." The empty whisper came at him again. He felt too weary to answer. Not that she would respond with anything like a cogent reply anyway. He picked up a stone and lobbed it at her as she lay disoriented on the ground, trying to get back on her feet.

"Get up, old woman." He swallowed his distaste. *The stupid fool. I can't believe she's got me this far.*

Seth had only one concern now: that he would be able to find the big granite rock in the woods. He watched as Lorna crawled on the ground like an animal, grunting and blubbering his name through the blood and snot that ran down her chin.

He wasn't much better off himself as his ear, butchered by Avery, refused to heal, leaking an odorous fluid. He hoped fervently that medical care would be available once they found the sanctuary. Eyeing up Lorna, he wondered how long she would last. They must be somewhere in the vicinity of the sanctuary now.

It was a delicate balancing act with the water. He needed to keep Jen alive if he wanted Lorna to cooperate. And he needed to keep Lorna alive long enough to talk their way into the sanctuary. Such a dilemma. He couldn't really let Lorna live past the moment they gained entrance. He watched her frantic moaning and struggles to stand, blood from her nose now splattered all over the wretched heap that was all that they had left of Jennifer. *Well, they can't blame that on me.*

Seth wondered if he would be able to pull off his plan. He hoped that in the surprise of their sudden appearance, he would be able to distract the people there enough with cries of help for Jennifer for him to give Lorna's neck a discreet snap. She was the only one who could rat him out. Even though she was a burnt-out husk of microbes and radiation sickness, he worried about how responsive she might be after some good medical care. Seth grinned, his heart racing as he contemplated how he would kill Lorna.

Ambling over to her in his own feeble fashion, he gripped her under her arm, the flesh feeling loose and unconnected to her bones.

The smell of urine assailed his nostrils. With a grunt, he strained to bring Lorna to her feet so they could attempt to get up the hill that led to the forest perched at the edge of what looked like a deserted neighborhood of tiny ranch houses and a few split levels.

He heard the squeak and rendering tear of metal as he glimpsed a child's swing set tumble to the ground behind a modest home that had collapsed on itself. This was Lily Pond Road.

Turning back to Lorna, he just hoped they would have the strength to drag Jennifer up the hill and through the woods.

"For Christ's sake, Lorna. You have to help yourself a little. I can't do it all." Lorna looked at him as if she didn't recognize him. Seth sighed. He could see Lorna was blanking out again and going to be next to useless, just when he needed her the most. How the hell was he going to find the trail to the rock without her directions? She said *to follow the trail* a few months ago when he had pressed her for specifics. *What the hell is that supposed to mean?*

He knew she wanted to get there as much as he did, but he had to be careful. She might be looking to pay him back for losing Suzy. He had yet to come up with a story to explain that debacle. He reached up to feel where his ear should have been, wincing as the throbbing pain kicked up a notch from his clumsy touch. He cleaned the pus and fluid from his shaking hand, his ragged drawers the only place to wipe.

At least he knew they were in the correct place. He scanned the empty tractor trailers that sat around a small ranch house which no longer featured windows or a front door. The dwelling appeared to mock him with its vacant window eyes, daring him to come inside.

Tearing his gaze from the empty house, he renewed his efforts to get Lorna and Jennifer up the hill. He silently assisted Lorna to her feet, placing her hand back on the metal pull bar. He scrambled to the rear of the makeshift wagon and shouted, "Come *on*, Lorna . . . Pull!"

She turned to look at him, a momentary morsel of clarity flowering in her bloodshot eyes. "Seth, are we on Lily Pond Road?"

Seth trod carefully, not knowing how long Lorna's mental state would stay anchored in the present, or what kind of new trouble she would give him. He grimaced as Lorna's face crumpled and she began to wail. She sank to the ground on her knees, dragging Seth down with her. The sled that supported Jennifer slid a few feet down the hill then halted.

"We didn't go back for Suzy. How could I ignore her?" Lorna squinted at Seth. "She's not at school, is she? We left her behind."

Seth could see the wheels of her mind turning in her eyes, trying to connect the events of the last five months. Lorna's eyes widened as she stared blankly at Seth. Her voice hissed venom, slow and painful. "You low life *scumbag*. You actually think I'm going to have my husband save your pathetic ass after what you did?"

Seth drew his shoulders together as he rose off the ground. He bit down hard on his lip, restraining himself from punching her in the face. He'd been through this many times. If he kept his mouth shut, Lorna's moment of clarity would pass. He reached under her arm to yank her up as she struggled against him.

"Take your bloody hands off me, *you insect*."

Seth raised his hand in the air, stopping a mere few inches from her face. Her red splotchy face leaked blood from her snotty nose as she defiantly stood her ground. Just as he decided to go ahead and slap her anyway, he witnessed the light fade from her eyes to be replaced with pliant confusion.

"Seth, what are you doing? We need to get to the school. I promised Suzy we wouldn't be late. Now help me pick up my bags." Seth lowered his fist as Lorna slipped out of his grasp to scrabble after the wagon.

Sighing with relief, Seth helped her retrieve the rickety wagon and they resumed the trek up the hill to the woods amid breathless grunts; the neighborhood homes mocking their progress with their shouts of death and silence.

"Hold on Lorna . . . hold on." They were having trouble with the wagon. The ruts on the floor of the woods refused to give way as they pulled the wagon behind them, forcing their meager strength to dissipate rapidly. Lorna struggled, flailing ineffectively, creating another obstacle for Seth to deal with.

"Seeeth, it won't . . . it won't."

"It won't what? For Christ sakes, Lorna, you think I can't see?" He stopped to scan the trees, denuded of all life: no leaves, no birds, and no squirrels. He rubbed his sore back, feeling his bones flex like rubber and his muscles quake and chatter. As he watched Lorna mutter to herself, he scanned the faint pathway that disappeared into the barren woods.

"Lorna, we need to talk."

She continued to mutter and pull ineffectually at the wagon.

"*Lorna.* I want to talk to you." He stood in front of her, removing her hands from the wagon's iron pull bar. When she showed some vague sign she was listening, he pointed into the woods. "We can't go any further with the wagon. We need to leave it here while we go look for the boulder." She immediately shook her head and muttered louder. He grabbed her by the hand and dragged her away from the wagon. Lorna's pathetic wail turned to a shriek as Seth pulled her away and deeper into the woods, the two of them stumbling along like drunken barflies.

As luck would have it, they quickly came to the granite boulder. Seth dropped Lorna's hand to wrap his arms around the almost mythical stone, tears of relief coursing from his red-rimmed eyes.

"Oh my blessed Lord, it's here. It's here. I'm saved!" He slapped the boulder with the palm of his hand. Turning with his back resting against the boulder, he found Lorna standing motionless, just staring at him. His happy grin clearly confused her.

"So, Lorna, what do we do next?" He sounded like a puppy that had just been promised a thick juicy steak. "Where's the shelter?" He swiveled his head around, looking high and low around the boulder. "Where's the door?" He glanced back at Lorna and noticed her blank expression, unnaturally quiet. He could see her start to weave and ran to catch her.

"Oh no ya don't. Not when we finally got here." Wrapping her thin arm around his neck, he dragged her around the enormous boulder to search from another angle. He stopped in surprise to see the rise of a hill behind the boulder.

"Well, what do we have here?" Before he could do any further investigation, he heard the rustle of dried bushes. Turning from the hill they confronted the sickly sight of an emaciated feral fox. Dried blood soaked her once fluffy henna fur that decorated her ears. Her eyes flashed wildly, clearly out of her mind with hunger and disease. A low growl deep in the throat of the fox snapped Lorna out of her trance.

As the fox crept closer, froth at its mouth dripped to the ground. It crouched low and tense, ready to attack when Lorna decided to join the growls with her choking and guttural scream. Seth leaned into the hillside, forcing Lorna to shield him as he cowered behind her. The fox sprang to Lorna, clamping its teeth down on her flailing hand.

Chapter 3

As Kenya and Kane shuffled into Netty's kitchen followed by the rest of the inseparable group—Chloe, Scotty, Echo, and Barney—Caesar poked his head into the room. Chloe gave him a quick pat on the head as Scotty ran for the ubiquitous tiger's water dish. All hungry voices waiting for dinner stopped as Kane lowered Kenya with her big belly into a chair that had been specially made for her. Netty and Abby came rushing over. Abby knelt at Kenya's chair, her arms around the distressed teen, while Netty stood stoically, an unreadable expression in her eyes.

"Oh, you poor sweet child. How in the world did you get to the fields today? I thought we agreed you would stay off your feet? What if something happened? You need to stick close to us."

Kenya rolled her eyes at Abby, her voice impatient. "I'm about going *crazy* here, chickey. This baby doesn't wanta come. And I feel healthy as all get out. I can't just sit around all day. *I'm gunna go nuts.* I want to be with my friends if this damn baby is going to give me such a hard time. Have you figured out *something* to get it out of me yet?" Kenya swiveled her head around to see Netty watching her. She glanced down to see the winged woman quietly wringing her hands.

"What the *f'ing* Lord is the matter with me? Netty, I know you know something. *Why hasn't my baby come?*" A slow rise of hysteria sounded in her voice.

Johno detached himself from his seat at the table next to Crystal, who reached out to drag him back. "Johnny, you know you ain't gunna be able to do anything. Why do ya even bother?"

Johno gave her a gentle quiet motion with his hands and knelt down in front of the anguished teen. He took her hand in his, calmly stroking in a methodic fashion. "Shhhh. There you go, little Miss Kenya. Now we have all been through this before. Do you think anything has changed since yesterday?" Kenya looked into his impassive eyes, finding a calm reassurance. She took a breath, ready to expel all the pent up emotion from the inconvenience of lugging her big belly around all day. The steady pressure of his stroking soothed her. All that came out of her mouth was a whimper.

"But, I . . ." She sniffed.

"Shhhh, I know. We all know, young lady." He continued to stroke her arm, not taking his eyes off her face. "Why don't I have Miss Salina fix up some of that special tea you like?" Kenya's mouth opened, then glumly closed again. She hung her head and whispered, "I don't know how much more I can take, Johno. I want to have a normal life."

Kane's hand found its way to the back of her neck. Her head fell to the side as she enjoyed the sensation of his work-worn fingers kneading her muscles. She managed to fit in a quick grateful smile, never one not to reward her admirers. Turning, she gave her attention back to Johno, whom she could tell was deadly serious, her histrionics clearly wearing down even the most patient man in the Hive.

"You will take exactly as much as it *takes*. This baby is the most important thing in the Hive. Apart from the animals," he added quickly. "It doesn't help the situation when we spend so much of our time beating up Wil and Netty because you haven't had the baby yet."

Kenya rolled her eyes. "I wasn't gunna say anything."

Johno hung his head as the rest of the crowd broke out in laughter because they all knew Kenya would do just that. She did it every day and would probably do it again tomorrow. The ritual was common place, but becoming tiresome.

Salina slid a cup of tea toward the teen, agitation on her face. "Johno, don't be so rough on her. She's just a baby herself."

"I ain't no baby, Miss Salina. Me and my baby can take darn good care of ourselves. And as soon as we get outa this place, Chloe and me are taking the baby and going back to *Sarasota*." Kenya's eyes broadcast the belligerence of youth as she followed Salina's figure back to a seat next to Clyde, her arm slipping around his with easy familiarity. "And Kane's coming too, aren't you, chickey?" She gave him a beguiling smile as Captain Cobby's voice rang out from his position at the head of a table next to the adoring Karen.

"My son isn't going *anywhere*, let alone back to Sarasota. Can somebody talk some sense into this girl? It's been six months, more or less. We know from Echo and Baby that the Earth is full of poisons now."

At the mention of their names, Echo and Baby tottered over to Cobby and stroked and prodded his face, their long leathery fingers soft and loving. He reached out to give the two minions quick hugs.

So much had changed in the six months since their hasty flight during the onset of Armageddon. The minions had begun to express themselves to many of the survivors, to their delight. It was considered an honor if Baby or Echo chose to single you out for attention.

As Johno tried to calm Kenya out of her daily crying jag over the fact she was *still* carrying her unborn child in her belly five months after her due date, Netty backed away from the crowd to search for Wil. Joining the animals by the fireplace, she lowered herself to the floor, exchanging a tense glance with Wil, burdened with meaning.

She quickly smiled as Bonnie welcomed her to join Chance and the dogs who were in their usual frolicking abandon, hoping the exuberant young lady hadn't noticed their exchange.

She pulled a fully grown Barney onto her lap, the happy dog not taking his eyes off Echo, who was working her way over to the fireplace after greeting her favorite people with Baby. Netty scanned the room, noticing the handsome vitality in the crowd.

No longer did the women sport wrinkles or gray hair. No chubby waistlines or ponderous energy levels due to the drain of obesity or chemical-laced food of a progressive population. No diabetes, asthma, allergies or headaches; just buoyant perfect health that they all attributed to the unusual food they ate.

And with perfect health came animal attraction to the other sex. Why not? They were living and working in close quarters. The adults looked younger than they had in ten years. It was only natural and helped pass the time. Many of the new couples had long discarded the secret nature of their budding romances and moved into quarters they could share together, announcing carefully to all that they were a couple.

Netty took in the happy black and white faces of Gloria and Billy, the trucker who no longer toted an inhaler everywhere. Gloria danced her days away, her work a joy, her diabetes gone with the emergence of a strikingly beautiful and youthful figure. And now she had the love of a man who thought she walked on water. What more could she ask for? Even her cache of mice was breeding up a storm, having been relegated to the growing fields to live their lives naturally.

The lean and surly Crystal with her momma pig, Tulip, could be found perpetually nagging at Johno. He, who had fast become a voice of reason in the early days of the frantic adjustments they all were forced to make. Who else could have turned the opinionated and critical Crystal into a quiet and simpering woman in love? Netty acquiesced to the adage that opposites really did attract.

The kids had paired up early. Scotty had Chloe, and Kenya had Kane, although since she had not delivered the baby, Netty could sense Kane's patience wearing thin. She had not failed to notice the tentative knowing smiles Emma and Kane tossed to each other when they thought no one was in the area. With a sigh, she prayed Kane would continue to support Kenya until she adjusted to her new reality, but knowing of the angry demeanor of Johno's man, Elias, after having been discarded by Emma, she thought Bonnie's sister was walking a thin line. It had only been five months since she'd cut him out of her life and he still appeared unwilling to accept the fact. Could be that they had some trouble brewing with the kids.

Ginger Mae had blossomed beyond all anticipation. The scars on her face had completely disappeared. Her bleached hair grew in, disclosing the blonde was really a brunette. When she'd decided to crop the blond ends of her hair, she was adorned with an elegant short pixie that left her closely resembling the old Hollywood movie star, Audrey Hepburn. She had also developed quite a deep bond with the cats and elephants. Netty guessed her favorite must be the matriarch, Tobi. But then the great gray goliath was *everyone's* favorite, wasn't she? Tobi's sensitive nature and remarkable intuitiveness to all that was animal and human made her a great comfort and distraction.

Netty glanced over to Ginger Mae to see her holding court with her remarkable daughter, Daisy, at her side. Dezi was horsing around with Bonnie, who had slipped over to join the hilarity coming from their table.

What surprising buddies they had turned out to be; bonding tightly with the responsibility of caring for the little piglet, Chance, who would have perished without their loving care. Who knew the irrepressible and cocky smart alec would develop into such a reliable caretaker of a piglet?

Chance was the only one of the litter that was allowed to come into the kitchen. He followed Bonnie around as if she were his mother. And if you tried to separate Chance from Dezi, the piglet made such a squalling that no one could bear it. Caesar was none too fond of the noisy piglet himself. So trying to tether him in the corridor with the big tiger had not been a solution. Besides, Chance clearly preferred the company of Echo, Baby and the dogs at dinner time.

"Yikes, let go of my arm, Dezi." Bonnie choked on her laughter as Dezi got her in a headlock.

"Are you going to sweep the floors in the men's dorm like you promised?"

"I don't remember saying that." Bonnie reached under his arms to try to tickle her way to a release.

"You don't remember the deal we made for my spice loaf in exchange for the chore? Babe, I'm gunna have to spank you. Maybe it will help you remember."

Turning the tables on her, Dezi reached down to tickle *her*, getting a shriek for his efforts. Daisy reached over to join the melee.

Netty turned her attention back to Wil, who was watching the elephant keepers arm wrestle at their table. Abby scurried around them, her arms stacked with plates as she attempted to finish setting the tables for dinner. Her tail accidentally brushed one of the wrestlers, causing him to lose his concentration and inadvertently bump a dish to the floor with a clatter. The entire room broke out with laughter and claps. Kimir stood on his chair to watch the unlucky victim of Salina's anger at the broken plate cringe under her admonishing glare.

"Gentlemen, if you insist on behaving like boys, I will have to send you to bed without dinner. One more broken plate and I will . . . I'll . . . hmmm." Her unlined face lit up. "I will make you wash the ladies' laundry for a week." The men booed and hissed at the offending keeper who had broken the plate.

"Wil," Netty whispered to get his attention away from the good-natured brawl that was sure to develop between the keepers and Salina. She heard a shriek as one of them picked Salina up off her feet and swung her around, depositing her on the counter near the sink.

Wil turned his attention back to Netty, the smile in his eyes disappearing as he sobered at the fright in her expression.

"Don't worry so much, Netty. It's going to be okay."

"I don't know how you can say that." Exasperation spat her hisses out like a gun shot. "We need to have a plan, an explanation that will keep them all calm."

Wil reached for her hands. Looking straight into her eyes he asked, "Why don't we just give them the truth?"

She recoiled at the suggestion, jerking her hands from his to worry over her flaxen hair that had tangled in her wing. "You know we can't do that. How do you tell that to Kenya? The poor girl is frightened and upset enough as it is. Some women might consider killing themselves when they hear news like that. You don't understand, Wil. We need to do this in small doses." Her voice became more than a whisper, drawing the attention of Baby by the fireplace. As he joined them, his aura pierced their mind.

"Sister, Brother, change is coming." From afar, Echo called to Barney, her aura lapping over Baby's. Barney ran to Echo who wrapped her arms around her furry love.

Scotty looked up at Netty and Wil, as if he had also heard Baby's pronouncement. From the corner of the room, Peter sat alone, watching and saying nothing as the innocent survivors, oblivious in their pleasure with one another and the good health they enjoyed, happily played on.

Chapter 4

Scotty grunted, sweat dripping from his forehead as he helped Kane turn over the rich red claylike soil. Echo lounged on a hillock with Barney and the gang, the stately pit bulls King and Queenie keeping pace with Scotty and Kane. Baby tottered behind, placing medium-sized fuzzy red pods in the ground. It was Chloe's job, but now and then Baby would slip away from Netty and Wil to join them in the planting. Chloe always took the opportunity to *supervise* the dogs as she relinquished her mundane task to the eager Baby.

Scotty glanced up as he heard the tinkle of Chloe's laugh. Tiny Teddy's antics with the posse as he tried to hump Penny's ear or dominate Tucker's big black standard poodle could keep her entertained all day.

He took in a deep breath as he scanned the horizon of the growing fields. The turned earth emitted such a vibrant aroma of musky life that Scotty felt renewed. Shaking his head at Chloe's antics, he realized that if he didn't love her so much, he would probably choke her.

"So, dude, you going to go over there and make her get back to work?" Scotty gazed into the healthy face of his best friend next to Echo. Kane's mocking grin already knew the answer to the question. Sheepishly, Scotty shook his head, staying silent. Kane knew what a sore subject Chloe's inability to take their situation seriously could be with Scotty.

As The One, he had responsibilities. He needed to be alert and prepared for what would be required of him some day. It didn't help that the girl he loved made a joke out of the title bestowed on him. Or that she refused to face reality about the conditions topside. Her insistence that they go with Kenya back to Sarasota drove him nuts. She just didn't *get* it. But then neither did Kenya.

"So how's it going with Kenya? You making any headway with her? She's driving the rest of us batty with her incessant whining at dinner time. Can't you make her ease up?" Kane straightened up, the long muscles across his back flexing and glistening with sweat, making the leaner Scotty green with envy.

"Any time you decide to trade those wings and your immortality for my muscles, dude, you just let me know." Kane's enormous grin reveled in Scotty's discomfort at getting caught admiring his muscles. Kane gave him a playful punch as Scotty grabbed him in a headlock. They both felt the excited aura at the same time.

Baby stood at their feet, his tiny hands opening and closing spasmodically. Scotty and Kane laughed out loud as the little guy demanded to be picked up. Baby's aura hit them harder.

"Okay, okay, relax, Baby. We're just playing." Kane lifted the little guy up.

"Brother Kane, my Sister Echo would not be pleased to hear you struck Brother Scotty."

"Baby, it's okay. It's just fun . . . horsing around? Don't you ever horse around?"

The aura quickened. "But I have no horse and neither do you. Are you trying to fool me, Brother Kane?"

"Now, why would I do that, Baby?"

The aura dulled. "So you could kill Brother Scotty and steal his woman. Then you would kill me. I saw you hit him and he tried to defend himself."

Scotty and Kane, dumbstruck at Baby's words, quickly put the confused creature on the ground. They sat him between their legs as they absorbed the impact of Baby's mind whispers. Scotty wiped the frightened look off his face and took Baby's thin, furry shoulders between his hands. "Baby, do you agree that Kane is my brother?"

"Yes, Brother Scotty. We are all brothers."

"No, Baby. This is a different kind of brother. This is the kind where you love one another. Where you promise to watch each other's backs. Where you are buddies for life."

Baby's neck swiveled from one to the other, his aura still dull. "Sister Netty and Brother Wil are buddies."

"No, Baby. They love each other in a different way. The way a man loves a woman is different from the way a man loves another man." Kane snorted at Scotty's feeble explanation. "Well, I mean . . . a . . . you know, like the way Kane and I are brothers."

"I do not understand why you are going to kill him. Did he *steal* your horse?"

"No, I don't *have* a horse. Where in the world did you get the idea I would kill Scotty? We're best friends. I would no more kill him than I would one of the animals."

Scotty's perplexed demeanor gaped at Baby who pronounced, "All human men are evil and must be exterminated before they can kill again."

Kane hurriedly scrambled to his feet at Baby's words. "Whoa now, Baby. I think you have us confused with some other men. I would never harm Scotty or anyone else for that matter. You need to understand that." Whispering to Scotty, Kane asked, "Exactly how damaged do you think this little dude is?"

"I am not damaged as you say, Brother Kane. I am different." The auras were coming faster now, the colors brighter. Scotty stepped in, sensing the conversational tone could rapidly decline.

"Kane didn't mean anything, Baby. We just thought you were . . . I mean . . . you have been through a lot physically. Landing on this planet while you were pregnant, getting hurt by some asshole . . . Gee, there's no telling how stressful that was."

Baby's aura stopped as he stared at Scotty. Then he turned to Kane. His aura lightened. "Is Kane an asshole, Brother Scotty?" The boys exchanged quick glances. A trick question?

"Well, to tell you the truth, he used to be." Scotty laughed, smirking at Kane. The auras flashed; Baby hopping from one foot to the other. Scotty reached out waving his arms at Baby. "No, no, not like that. Kane's not an asshole. He's one of the good guys."

"He has changed into *not* an asshole?"

Scotty could hear Kane breathing deep, attempting to humor Baby for his own good, yet finding it difficult to remain silent. Scotty gave him a shushing sign. "Kane was never the kind of asshole that hurt you, Baby. We all love Kane. There are no assholes in the Hive.

Everyone here is family: good people, not assholes. We're not perfect, but we are trying hard to be whatever the Womb needs us to be."

Baby settled down, his tiny neck swiveling to and fro. Glancing up, Scotty noticed Echo on the way over from Chloe and the dogs, her expression blank, her aura silent. She wobbled up behind Baby, placing her scrawny hand on Baby's spare shoulder. Baby turned to stare at Echo, reaching out in an exchange of face-touching. The moment was silent save for the distant laughter and yips of Chloe and the dogs.

Scotty caught movement in the corner of his eye as Caesar rose on all fours from his position in the grass near Chloe to stare toward the small tableau.

Moments passed, the silence growing uneasy. Baby then swiveled his mesmerizing orbs to Kane, slowly, tentatively reaching out to stroke his face. He dipped his head down, then simply turned and toddled across the field without a backward glance at Echo or anyone.

Scotty sent his own developing aura out to Echo. "Can you please tell us what the heck just happened, girl?"

Including Kane with her aura, Echo tried to explain. "Brothers, my brother is not the same minion he was on Oolaha. It is true he has been damaged, but he is in full control of his mental faculties. He will get better over time. A long, long, time. But he will never be the same. We need to respect his feelings and decisions." Perplexed, the boys exchanged glances.

"Has Baby made a decision about something we should know about?" Scotty peered after the disappearing figure.

"No, Brother Scotty; his affairs do not concern you. He loves you all, but remains what you would refer to as *sensitive to violence*. But do not fear . . . everything he does is with the permission or direction of the Womb. And you *know* the Womb only wants the best for us all; even as faith in your race has been terminated."

"Ewww. There's the word I didn't want to hear: *terminated*." Kane sprawled back on his butt, his expression warring with his fright. "Echo, just tell me. Do I need to stay away from Baby?"

The aura came soft and calming. "No, my kind friend, Brother Kane. Baby has examined your soul. He only does it to understand when he is troubled. He would protect you to his own death. You are one with him." Sensing their relief, Echo turned and hurried back over to rejoin Barney and the posse.

Tensions having dissipated, the boys leaned back to take a break. Kane shook his head. "When will the surprises stop? I much prefer the boring job of cleaning the *Lucky Lady,* Womb rest her soul, than the drama in this Hive. Grrrr."

As the boys resumed their digging, the dogs' excited barking announced the approach of another figure from across the field. In the distance, they identified the slight outline of the blossoming Emma.

"Oh, no. Here comes more trouble," Scotty mumbled under his breath, but the sentiment did not escape Kane.

"Come on, dude. You have Chloe, can't a guy have a little fun?"

"Sneaking off for a piece of tail is one thing. If Kenya or Mama find out, I'm going to get the blame right along with you. And I don't know how much longer I can cover for you with Chloe. She knows what Emma's up to and sooner or later, she's going to tell Kenya. And why do you want Elias on your back? Do you *see* the way he still looks at her?"

Kane brushed him off. "Nah, that's over and done with. Emma doesn't want anything to do with Elias. Dead, done, history. Besides, Johno keeps a good eye on all his keepers. Elias would be in deep shit with Johno if he started something. It's up to Emma anyway." Kane smirked and rolled his eyes. "And she has made *that* perfectly clear to *me*, if you get my drift."

"Yeah, I get it. I don't need the details, bro . . . ." Scotty continued to shake his head as Emma approached with a box containing their lunch. From a distance, he saw Chloe rise and follow the dogs and Echo as they ambled toward them, Caesar trailing his magnificent presence as usual.

Not immune to the charms of a young healthy female, he admired how the Hive seemed to agree with Emma, Chloe and Kenya. The three girls were bursting with good health, perfect specimens of happy, sexy, young womanhood: long lean muscles, trim waists, strong legs, gleaming teeth, and vibrant, clear eyes. All three were just filled with feminine hormones that knew exactly how to laser right in on charged male testosterone.

Kane stood up as Emma approached, helping her set the heavy box on the soft grass of the hillock.

"Hey Scotty, hey Kane." Emma simpered as Kane's name left her lips. Their eyes connected and a signal was exchanged. "Why don't you give me a tour around the fruit trees, Kane? They smell so fresh." As her words begged an innocent question, the intimacy in her eyes told Scotty that Kane would be missing his lunch again.

"Oh, don't run off. Sit down so we can talk for a while." As Chloe approached, she grabbed Emma's hand, dragging her down to the ground. "So what did you think of Kenya's latest tantrum last night at dinner?" The boys remained silent, squirming at the subject of Kenya's long overdue delivery.

"Babe, can't we talk about something more pleasant? Kenya's all fucked up now and there's not much we can do to help her except to cover her chores." They all nodded, Kane verbally thanking the Womb for Johno's calming intervention with Kenya every night.

"But I don't see why Netty can't do anything. Why doesn't she talk to the Womb? Have you noticed how quiet she gets when Kenya starts screaming about the baby?" Chloe's eyes narrowed as she turned to Echo. "Why do I think you must know what's going on, Echo?" Chloe and Echo had managed to find a way to coexist in Scotty good graces, but every once in a while Chloe found an excuse to jump on her. Perhaps it was because Echo still refused to send her auras and only spoke to her through Scotty. A slight everyone noticed as Echo and Baby began to open up and connect to others as the months wore on. Chloe threw an angry glance at Echo.

"Scotty, can you see if she could please answer the question?" Chloe asked.

"She already has. She said there's nothing wrong and the Womb need not be bothered."

Chloe wrinkled her nose, disbelief glowering from every pore. "Ha. I told you, Scotty. Something's up and that damn creature knows all about it. Who are you going to side with? Us or it?"

Scotty clenched his teeth, trying not to explode. Echo swiveled to him, her aura serene and relaxed. "My Brother, do not pay heed. Your young companion knows not of what she speaks and needs much time to gain wisdom. Be patient."

Chloe shook her short hair unpleasantly. "If the two of you are just going to talk behind my back, then I'm out of here." So saying, she picked up the remains of her lunch and took off down the hill, Teddy looking from her to the posse. "Come on, Teddy . . . *come.*" With his mistress's command in his tiny ears, Teddy sprang up and leaped down the hill.

Emma let out a belly laugh. "Still jealous of Echo I see. Some things never change." Turning to Scotty she asked, "Mind if we take off for a few minutes? Kane needs a break anyway." Without waiting for an answer, she pulled Kane to his feet and scampered off with him to find some privacy.

Scotty watched as they disappeared, disappointed with Chloe and envious of Kane. "Well gang, since everyone's deserted me, I guess I might as well catch a few zzzs myself.

Echo popped up with Barney, all attention. "My Barney and I will be quite happy to help you catch the zzzs, Brother Scotty."

He laughed tenderly at the innocence of Echo's loyalty. Wrapping them in his wings, he scooped them up and lay back against the warm grass to snuggle. They settled down to nap, the rest of the posse joining as Echo kept one luminous golden eye cocked to watch for the missing zzzs.

Chapter 5

As Wil and Netty tried to separate themselves from the grasping fingers, shrieks and sobbing that always accompanied their leave-taking from Father, they exchanged anguished glances. Running late, they prayed Abby and Jose would wait for them. Their meeting and difficult revelation was well overdue. The two winged Elders were not looking forward to imparting the news to the survivors, but they hoped to get a read on how to best approach the now fairly contented survivors through Abby and Jose.

They rushed through the many miles of corridors, using their wings for speed, a luxury normally frowned upon as they refrained from demonstrations of their unique differences in front of the completely human survivors.

Abby luxuriated in the warm water of the bathing caves, watching the glow of Jose's eyes bounce over the luminescent minerals and jeweled stalagmites. Their wings drooped wetly, but would soon dry and puff up luxuriously from the cleansing in the warm mineral waters. Jose slipped his arm from around Abby's neck to rub her forehead.

"Babe, did you notice these bumps on your forehead?" He squinted in the dim light.

"Ouch! Don't do that." She swept his hand away from her head. "It's been sore for a while, but I just dismissed it. Why?"

Jose smiled, projecting pride and love as he explained. "I think you just might be getting your horns."
She dropped her jaw. "You're kidding me."

"No, I really think you are. I wonder why I haven't gotten mine?"

"What makes you think you'll get them? Wil doesn't have horns."

Jose voice revealed his puzzlement. "I just assumed. We evolved from the cells of minions, and Baby and Echo have them. Netty has them. And you're getting them. Why shouldn't I? Maybe there's a *reason* Wil doesn't have them." Abby climbed out of the water to lie naked on the shore, waves lapping gently, tugging at her long, tangled hair, and trying flirtatiously to entice her back to the wet warmth.

"Netty and Wil should be here any moment. I wish you'd put on your clothes, Abby." Jose strode from the water to dry off and slip into his clothes.

"Oh Jose, lighten up. I'm sure they know what a nude woman looks like. They're the only two I feel completely comfortable around except you and Scotty. Sometimes I just need to relax and let down my hair. I still feel suspicion around some of the women and it makes me defensive."

"Is Ginger Mae or Kenya still giving you a hard time?"

"No, Kenya's a dear, poor kid. She understands the implants forced me to behave oddly toward everyone. I don't even remember a lot from those days. Kenya told me I actually slapped her on the *Lucky Lady* when we were fleeing from Sarasota. I can't believe I did that. Did you see me do it?"

"No, but I had my mind on Chloe, still shocked over discovering she's my sister. I must have missed that. So much has happened, I can't recall everything either. And I didn't have an implant." Jose reached out for Abby as she stood to dress.

"Ummm, you look so incredible." Kissing her, he ran his hands over her pliant skin like a starving teenager. As Abby felt a flame of desire, she reached down to discover Jose's readiness. She swallowed a laugh at the hopefulness on Jose's face.

"Come on, babe. You know I want you. Let's just slip back behind that big boulder over there."

Abby tilted her face to his and reached out with her teeth to give his lip a teasing bite. "Not now. You're right, Netty and Wil should be here soon. Don't look so sad. I don't want to get dirt all over my nice clean wings, anyway. You should have thought of that sooner." She danced away from his searching fingers, a laugh deep in her throat.

As she finished dressing, she remarked on the rest of the

survivors. "Have you noticed how Ginger Mae has blossomed? Her face looks almost normal now. I think she may be on the verge of forgiving me for my cold behavior, but I know she's beginning to harbor some mixed feelings about my relationship with Daisy."

"It's natural that she'd be jealous. Daisy's *her* daughter, not yours."

Jose's remarks stung. "I'm very fond of Daisy and I need to spend time with her on our project. She's the only one with the capacity to absorb the information from the library and keep it stored in her mind. Netty has plans for her. Her potential is limitless." Jose's raised eyebrow foretold his skepticism. "Don't give me that look."

"I don't know where either you or Netty thinks Daisy will be able to exercise this potential. Do you think the bears will care? Or maybe Tobi and the herd might care? And I still don't buy the assumption that the food is curing any ailment or imperfection the group has. That's just a fairy tale. I think it's time Netty and Wil clue us in to a few mysteries around here."

"That is just what we are here to do."

Abby and Jose scrambled up to face Netty and Wil at the entrance to the bathing cave. Her face flamed with hot blood as she realized they'd overheard Jose.

Wil beckoned them over to a mineral formation that would be conducive to comfort.

"Please don't be angry, Netty." Abby hurried to be seated next to her mentor. "Jose is just naturally curious about many of the unusual occurrences in the Hive."

Netty smiled widely, amusement coloring her words. She reached out to take Abby's hand. "Child, you don't need to apologize. We want you to feel you can come to us with anything. We are aware of your questions. We hear the speculation from the others. And Salina is becoming suspicious regarding Kenya's baby. Before we have an uproar, we thought it better to share information with you that may be upsetting to the others." Netty's eyes glanced toward Wil as he gave an encouraging nod. Abby noticed tightness in their faces, a wariness. *This isn't going to be good.* She clenched her hands, feeling Jose reach for her for reassurance.

After a pause, Wil cleared his throat. He looked them in the eyes, unencumbered by the force of the brilliant luminance of their combined presence. "This will not be easy."

Abby felt Jose tense, his grip on her fingers tightening.

Wil sighed, his tail swatting at imagined flies, another sign of distress.

Softly, Abby asked, her tremulous voice a mere whisper of fright, "Is there a problem?"

Wil grimaced. "No, not exactly. First, I want you to remember you are Elders now. You will live far beyond the life span of everyone in the Hive. Even Baby and Echo. Since entry into the Earth's atmosphere seems to have turned on the enzyme that neutralized the chemical block on their own eternal life, it appears they have a possibility of living as long as we do, but we cannot be sure."

Netty took over. "Both of you must realize that when we emerge from the Hive, the planet will be much different. There will be so much work to do. The wildlife must be acclimated to their new surroundings after living below the earth for so long." Abby caught a premonition with Netty's word, her chest compressing with anxiety. Netty's speech slowed as she searched their faces for a reaction.

Jose spoke up. "Please, go on. Just tell us what we need to know."

Netty continued. "We will not be leaving the Hive for at least a century."

Abby and Jose's blank look told the story. "A century . . . one hundred years." An audible gasp sounded from the two young Elders. A fast blink and Abby got it like a thunderclap. "But everyone will be dead. Except us."

Wil rose to his feet, pacing slowly as he continued to deliver the news. "Well now, that's not quite correct. As a matter of fact, everyone will be as alive as they are right now. Which brings us to the purpose of this meeting. It is time the rest of the group receives some answers to their miraculous cures and good health. As everyone has noticed, the healing of Ginger Mae's unfortunate knife wound to the face from the gentleman you refer to as Armoni . . ."

"*He was no gentleman.*" Abby's bitterness escaped.

Wil shushed her with his hands and continued, "As I was saying
. . . and Kenya's ungodly overdue delivery . . . it won't be much
longer before we have a revolt on our hands. They need answers."

Jose clapped his hand on his thigh. Raising his voice, he
demanded, "Just *tell* us, for Pete's sake."

"We need your help and advice to tell them. At this point, no one
will be able to accept what is happening to them if they know how
the Womb is doing it." At their startled expressions Wil added, "Yes,
it's the Womb, of course. No one will age a day more than they were
when they entered the Hive. The Womb is presently healing any cell
as it divides. Under normal circumstances, the cell of every living
creature on this particular planet would divide forever until enough
corrupted cells accumulate to cause a deleterious effect or a
mutation. It could be a wrinkle, a gray hair in time, or as serious as
disease and cancers. The Womb is healing those exact cells as they
begin to split and divide to grow more corrupted cells. As the Womb
heals them, or even corrects the ones that were already corrupted
when they got here, they will not age and will in fact improve as you
have witnessed."

Haltingly, Abby absorbed the information and spoke. "But that is
a good thing. Where's the problem?"

Netty took over from Wil. "They will question how it is done. I
do not think they are ready to handle that. We hoped you would offer
us a way to make the explanation more palatable." As Netty
described the process that happened every night as the entire group
of survivors and the creatures slept, Abby and Jose paled.

"I see. Maybe we better stick to the food theory for now," Abby
offered. "Can you give us a few days to think this through? It's not
going to go over well. We need to be ah . . . delicate with this
explanation."

As they all agreed, Jose spoke up. "Wil, I've been meaning to ask
you. Why is it that you don't have any horns like Netty? Abby is
beginning to grow hers, but Scotty and I have yet to start. And we

were changed by Echo years before Abby was."

Wil shrugged; his demeanor flippant. Netty rose to wrap her arm around his shoulders. His tail instantly curled around her waist as if seeking succor.

"The Womb is a wise and far-seeing creator. In that wisdom, it was clear that even a male Elder, having originated from Homo sapiens, could not be trusted to suppress what is left of the human lust for blood and domination. Therefore, it was decided only female Elders of human origins will grow antlers. It is a grave responsibility to wear the antlers and command their power. The Womb, with such infinite wisdom, could see that females put the lives of their children first and could be counted on not to dominate for the sake of domination."

At Jose and Wil's disgruntled satisfaction with the explanation, Netty shrugged her shoulders. "It is what it is. No offense intended, but I see the wisdom. That is how we got into this situation to begin with. Throughout history, if man was not fighting about women, land, or other riches raped from the Earth, it was about competing religions that gave men the permission to dominate with all forms of atrocities. Religions were manufactured by men as excuses for horrid behavior. Not that some religions were bereft of merit, but clearly you can see the truth of our Creator. The only religion the Womb would sanctify would be one of life, respect for the planet you have been given, and balance. As you all have been told before, when balance is lost, the Womb must intervene. Since this is not the first intervention on this planet, the Womb's patience is wearing thin. So much amazing life lived on the planet. It is well worth the effort to save as much as time allows."

Smiling, Netty turned to Abby. "We owe so much to you, my dear. The Womb is not without its benevolent side. As plans are interrupted, we adjust. We had many, many years to prepare for this life in the Hive." She grimaced. "Not as much for the others you brought along, but we are making the best of it and I am sure everyone will be quite happy here until we can surface." Netty clearly meant to end the conversation. "Any questions?" She waited as Abby and Jose absorbed the meaning of all Netty and Wil had trusted them with.

"No, I think you have summed up our future very well for now." Jose's voice contained an undertone of disbelief—*or is it hurt?* Sighing mentally, Abby knew he would get over it. *Time to deal with the practicalities.* Stepping forward to give Netty a hug, she spoke shyly. "I feel closer to you than ever, Netty. Thank you for trusting us with this information. And I agree, for now we should allow everyone to believe it's the food. I know you must get on to your afternoon errand and I must get back to the library." She gave Netty a sidelong glance. "Perhaps in time you might wish to share your afternoon food delivery with me. It could free up Wil to help Jose in the library. We have so much work to do there. I don't even know if one hundred years will be enough."

Netty ushered her protégé forward toward the bathing cave entrance. "In good time, my dear . . . in good time." Netty rewarded Abby with the fond loving smile she had hoped for as the men trailed disconsolately behind, unable to conceal their bruised egos and displeasure that the women were the favored ones.

Chapter 6

Bonnie sat high on top of Tobi's broad, coarse back, watching the babies tumble around in the shallows of their bathing pool. Fortunately, the floor of the pool was thick with sand instead of rock, enabling Tobi and the older juveniles to instruct the babies in the necessity of protecting their tender skin from the African sun by flinging sand in the air to cover their backs. When the sand dried, it tumbled harmlessly to the floor of the cavern.

In the wild it would be mud that baked on their backs in the hot, relentless sun, lasting from waterhole to waterhole. Here in the Hive, the mystifying light source failed to burn exposed skin. But the elephants didn't know that. It was important that they didn't stray from the habits and traditions that kept them alive on the savannas and lowveld that used to be their home. Sooner or later they would need to fend for themselves in the new world above.

"Hey . . . up here, Emma." Bonnie waved to her older sister, who was lugging a cardboard box that undoubtedly contained her lunch. Bonnie didn't mind that her eighteen-year-old sister got so much attention from the boys. *Who needs all the drama?* Besides, she had her hands full with Chance, the affectionate little piggy she helped Dezi raise, along with the other creatures that owned her heart.

"Down, Tobi." Tobi lowered her tremendous bulk slowly, bending to her knees so Bonnie could climb down carefully, stepping from her head to her shoulder to her knee and down to the water. As she splashed her way along the shore, Tobi swiftly and silently tagged behind. Bonnie noticed the anxious expression on Emma's face. With a laugh she turned to confront Tobi.

"You rascal. I know what you want." Reaching into the box of lunch items, she rummaged around until her fingers touched the hard crusty treat Tobi favored. Holding the treat behind her back as Emma scurried up a rock, she faced Tobi.

"Are you looking for something, girl?" She screamed in laughter as she played hide the treat with Tobi. The generous fifteen-year-old gave a wave to the iconic monolith of the world's most treasured and looted continent. Tiring of the game and hungry herself, Bonnie demanded a kiss as she always did from her favorite creature. Tobi raised her trunk to snake Bonnie's neck and wrap it round to her face. Softly, she blew air on Bonnie's cheek then gently pulled the young girl toward her mouth where her pink tongue waited to slop all over her face.

"Ewww . . . that's disgusting. Why do you let Tobi *do* that to you?" Emma asked. Bonnie's hands raised up to show Tobi the green, crusty treat and with one crunch from the elephant's huge maw, it was gone.

"Because I love her. And it's her way of saying she loves me. She knows I trust her completely." Bonnie laid her head against the upper part of Tobi's trunk. "I'd die if I ever had to give her up. I guess someday when we leave here, I'll lose her. I don't know how I'll be able to bear it, Emma."

"Don't be so dramatic, you silly nit. Now take your lunch before the keepers come back from their lunch. I don't want to run into Elias."

Bonnie rooted through the box, extracting enough for two people. Getting a raised eyebrow from Emma, she pretended not to notice, mumbling about hungry creatures under her breath. As she prepared to walk away to eat her lunch, Bonnie did a double take.

"What the heck is all over the back of your smock?" Emma appeared disheveled and dirty, her smock stained by grass marks and her hair knotted in clumps.

"Boy, Mom's going to have a fit. You better try to get something new from the supply closet. Mom will take one look at you and know what's up. You've been with Elias."

Bonnie's disapproving glare set Emma off. "Just because you like to roll in the stink of filthy creatures and don't get scolded means *I* won't get scolded *either*." Smugness radiated deep from within Emma's grin. "I'll just say Tobi dumped me in the grass and roughed me up."

Bonnie raised high on her tiptoes, her finger shaking in the air. *"Oh no you won't.* You're not blaming *anything* on Tobi. How could you, Emma?" Tears slipped from her eyes as she thought of the damage to Tobi's gentle reputation and the possibility that her mother and Johno would ban her from Tobi's company.

Emma relented, taking her sister in her arms. "I'm sorry, Bonnie. I didn't mean to hurt you. And I'm sorry I said I'd blame Tobi. It's not her fault. I'm just mad you think I'd be with Elias." She squatted down on the ground next to her sister as Tobi wandered off to supervise her herd. "Want to know a *secret*?"

Bonnie's suspicion grew as Emma cultivated her air of mystery. Narrowing her eyes, she studied the flush on Emma's cheeks. "What in the world are you talking about? Give."

"I'm in love." She beamed at her sister.

"Again? Who is it this time?"

Bonnie's quizzical face gave Emma a chance to preen. "It's for real this time. And he loves me too. I can tell."

"Who? Who is it, Emma?" Bonnie gripped her sister's shoulders, turning her face to face.

"You have to *swear* not to tell anyone. We have a few little things to work out."

Bonnie nodded.

"Kane." His name came out in a lovelorn whisper.

Bonnie didn't doubt Emma was in love with Kane, the guy was drop dead, spot in your eye, good-looking. "So, you think Kenya's big ole pregnancy is a *little* problem?"

Emma's face fell. "Yeah, I know. What the heck is *with* that? Kane can't just walk away from her in *that* condition. If the damn baby would just come all the other women would take over, giving her all the support she needs. Then Kane and I could let our relationship slowly come out in the public without anyone thinking he's a louse for leaving poor Kenya. *Ugh.*" She threw her hands up to shake out her snarled hair. "I just wish this pregnancy would be over."

Emma gave Bonnie a quick hug. "Now we have a secret. Kinda

nice, huh?"

Bonnie shook her head with a lopsided smile as Emma gathered the cardboard box to go.

"Well, I better scat. See you at dinner." And she was gone, dancing her way out the cavern entrance, clearly a young woman in love.

Still feeling hungry for her lunch, Bonnie made her way to an alcove she utilized to shelter her food from the elephants. As she turned the bend, she drew up smartly, discovering she had company.

"Oh, you startled me. Do you mind if I share this spot with you, Peter?"

As he glanced up, Bonnie saw Peter wipe away a tear. She rounded a boulder to perch next to him, gently placing her hand on his arm. He looked down, his glasses slipping down his nose to fall on the rocks, cracking the glass. He slapped his hand on his thigh. "Oh . . . sure, Bonnie. Whatever you want. I'll just get out of your way." He rose to take his leave. Bonnie reached down to pick up his broken glasses. She extended them toward Peter, gazing up at his perpetually sullen demeanor.

"I'm sorry about your glasses, Peter. Please . . . let me share my lunch with you. I have plenty." She spread the luncheon goodies on the rock. "Come on, Peter. You look like you could use some good food." A reluctant smile tugged marginally at Peter's lips, transforming his face into that of a young man. His defensive and suspicious posture straightened.

"You're a good kid, you know that, Bonnie?"

"Thanks. Come on, why don't you sit down and dig in?" Her infectious innocence soothed Peter's suspicious nature, allowing him to temporarily let down the guard he wore so aggressively, discouraging all overtures of friendship from the rest of the survivors. Even Abby had been unable to break through his newly acquired intractable exterior.

Bonnie fingered his eyeglasses as she separated Salina's delicious offerings for them to share.

"They look like they're shot. What are you going to do now? Can we fix them?"

Peter appeared to redden at her choice of the royal *we*. "You don't have to *help* me. It wasn't your fault anyway. I've become quite careless with them. They don't seem to work like they used to." He squinted into the distance at the elephants as they watched Chance, the now mature piglet, rush the babies, sending them squealing and then come racing back for more. "I can actually see fairly well without them anyway. My eyes don't appear to be as unfocused as they once were. Strange. But so much of what I see in the Hive is strange."

He reached for a piece of green cake, shot through with soft flecks of a strange and delicious spice that melted in your mouth then exploded with flavor. It crossed Bonnie's mind that she'd heard plenty of comments from the other survivors that *he* was the one who was a little strange.

"What do you mean, Peter?"

He turned to consider her question, temptation flitting across his face. Bonnie clapped her hands to the sides of her face. *"You know something.* What is it? Please, please *tell* me." Peter's facial expression shut down like the skirts of a Victorian miss caught with her pantaloons showing. Bonnie's enthusiasm was too much for the lonely and betrayed cuckold. Mumbling under his breath, he rose from the rocks. His round, pale face highlighted the roundness of his now exposed eyes. Bonnie noticed they were an unexpectedly vivid shade of green that telegraphed confusion and hurt.

"Wait, Peter." She quickly wrapped the piece of Salina's raspberry cake. Softly, she approached him. "I'm sorry you can't stay. Maybe we can try this again someday. I'm usually here when the keepers take their lunch break." She placed the wrapped cake in his hands. "This is my favorite, I want you to have it." Peter stared at Bonnie then looked at the cake in his hands. She could see some kind of calculation going on behind his brilliant green orbs.

"That's nice that you thought of me, Bonnie." He backed away awkwardly with the cake in his hands. His head bobbed as he turned and scurried away.

Hmmm, what a strange guy. Scanning the remains of her aborted lunch, she discovered his broken glasses nestled under the wrappings. She picked them up and like the good, sweet girl Salina had raised, tucked them away to return to him.

Later that evening at dinner, as the noises of Kenya's hot invectives rained down over Johno and Salina's attempts to console the freaked-out teen, Bonnie eased her way over to Peter's spot at the end of the long table, the furthest from the social interaction that fortified the rest of the survivors. He swiveled around as she approached, his green eyes unblinking and stoic.

"Hi, Peter. You left your glasses. I thought you might want to hold on to them in case we find a way to fix them." She withdrew them from her pocket to place them next to his plate.

Peter fingered his broken glasses then fixed Bonnie with a subtle tweak of his lips. "That was very thoughtful, Bonnie. It seems I have no trouble seeing now. But I'll hold on to them, just in case." He turned back to his plate, the conversation over.

"Ahem . . . ah . . . *okay* then." Puzzled at his abrupt dismissal, Bonnie backed away to locate Chance. Spotting the little guy over by the fireplace with Echo and Barney, she hurried over. As she practiced her aura-casting to Echo and Baby, with Chance on her lap, she promptly forgot about the enigma that was Peter.

The next afternoon, Bonnie set out down the long membrane encrusted corridors with little Chance trotting at her heels. As he stopped to nuzzle every clump of dung, she knelt to give him a goose and to laugh at his squeal of indignation.

"Come on, baby doll, Tobi and the keepers are waiting for us." At the entrance to the animals' bathing cave, she bumped into Dezi returning from the growing fields after delivering lunch. With his exposure to the animals now limited by his current proficient skills in the kitchen, Dezi had ripened into a funny, engaging man. Most of his bluster resurfaced during the dinner social hour as the men still riddled him about being relegated to the kitchen with the women, but for the most part, he felt the inclusiveness that came from Ginger Mae, Bonnie and Abby. And his darling Chance.

"Hey, babe, what's up with my two faves?" Dropping the food box on the ground, he squatted as Chance ran as fast as his tiny hooves would allow, standing on his hind legs for a hug and a scratch from his daddy.

"Hey, you little monkey. You staying outa trouble?" Chance snuffled, his tiny nose leaving trails of slobber on Dezi's face and arms.

Bonnie chuckled as Dezi planted a kiss on Chance's tender snout and stood to wipe his face with the end of his shirt. "Who let you out of the kitchen?"

Dezi threw her a conspiratorial glance, his face and form no longer the scrawniest in the Hive. His well fleshed-out profile now reflected a sweet, becoming effect with a thick beard to replace the wisps of chin hairs, his formerly slight build sporting added muscle and weight, enhancing the miraculous transformation. Little did anyone know of the hyperthyroid and metabolism condition that no longer ravished the brash trucker-turned-kitchen-aide.

"Your mother asked me ta do the deliveries today. She needed Emma to stick closer to the kitchen. I think she plans to have a heart to heart with her. Something 'bout a certain boyfriend of Kenya's?" Bonnie's hand flew up to clamp over her mouth as she sniggered in astonishment.

"I guess the cat's out of the bag. Mom's going to *kill* her if she gets pregnant."

Dezi raised an eyebrow as he scooped up the food box and followed Bonnie into the animal's bathing cave. "I think she asked Jose to stop by to talk to her too."

Bonnie shook her head. "Emma always looked up to Jose as we grew up. He was a great big brother to have around, up until he got his wings and tail and fell for Abby. Now we hardly see him anymore. If he's not working in the library with Wil, he's with her. I don't think he's going to have the same influence on her. Besides," Bonnie's eyes rolled at Dezi, "*she's in love.*"

Dezi threw his head back with a snort. "She's not gunna listen. You don't tell a girl her age ta leave a boy alone when she's *in love*. You'll see what I mean, shrimp, when you fall in love the first time."

Bonnie shrieked.

"Don't laugh. Someday you'll get tired of making goo-goo eyes at that big elephant in there and pick yourself out a man." He gave her a quick wink. "The pickins around here are a tad slim if ya ask me." The keepers gave them both a wave as they funneled out into the corridor for lunch.

Johno stopped for a quick word. "Hello, Miss Bonnie . . . Dezi. She's searching for you, young miss. Don't keep her waiting. She is not afraid to express her displeasure." His jovial grin animated his dark face, amusement dancing in his rich brown eyes. Dezi reached over to pull Bonnie's hair then left amiably with his arm around Johno to leave Bonnie to her elephants.

Feeling on top of the world, Bonnie dragged her food box toward the rocks for later. Slipping a treat into her pocket, she ran toward the small herd to claim her friends, her heart suffused with warmth as the big beautiful matriarch Tobi trumpeted an impatient welcome.

After a while, the exhausted Bonnie tore herself away from the herd to claim her lunch. Rounding the outcrop of rocks, she discovered Peter.

"Hello, Bonnie." Peter rose, a loaf of Netty's crusty green bread in his hands. "I brought you something." He shyly proffered the delicacy. His face broke out in the first sincerely happy smile since taking up refuge in the Hive. Bonnie gaped at him in confusion.

"Peter, I didn't notice you come in. How long have you been here?"

"For a while. I get around in my own quiet way. I wanted to surprise you anyway. I fear I may have appeared rude when you returned my glasses." Peter's pallid face reddened. "I watched you play with the elephants. You have such a way with them."

The longing in his voice gave Bonnie an idea. She sat on the rocks and spread out her lunch.

"Maybe after lunch I can introduce you to Tobi and the babies. You already know Chance." Relaxing, Peter cut into the crusty green bread to reveal the succulent red protein interior.

"Okay. I think that would just be fine." He nodded his head, a note of excitement in his voice. "Yes, that would be just fine."

And thus began a warm friendship between the embittered, awkward ex-attorney and the darling of the Hive, friend to all, and impassioned lover of the creatures. Through Bonnie's infectious enthusiasm, Peter's armor began to crack. It was a slow process which continued as they made a habit of meeting for lunch and joining Tobi and her herd to play in the water.

Peter's big breakthrough moment came when Tobi carefully ran her trunk over his face, emanating low rumbles as she offered her lowered foreleg as a stool, inviting him up her back to perch with Bonnie. After that momentous day Bonnie would often arrive at lunchtime to discover Peter already there with the keepers, chasing the babies and splashing water as they mock-charged his gleeful figure.

A few days later Bonnie had a surprise for Peter. Her big brother attachment had worn off and developed into an affectionate buddy relationship similar to the one she shared with Dezi. They were walking past the cat and bear swimming cavern where chuffing, splashing and hissing snarls emanated to the corridor. Bonnie's eyes lit up as she coaxed him.

"Come on, Peter. It's safe. The mom has an implant and can't hurt us. She's used to me now anyway. Abby said it's okay, and Netty didn't see any harm. Come on, you won't *believe* it." She grabbed his arm and pulled him toward the opening.

"Now, just stay to the edge of the wall." She propelled him in so fast that his protests fell unheard, swallowed in the sounds of the felines and ursine at play. Peter wrinkled his nose at the pungent odors.

"Don't worry, you'll get used to it." They rounded a bend and came upon a low wooden structure pushed back into the rocks away from the tumult of the play area. They could see movement in the shadows. Bonnie ducked her head slowly into the shelter and reached in to extract one of the first four baby white lions that had been born in the Hive. Peter anxiously scanned the area for the mother lion.

"I tell you Peter, it's okay. Here, you take him. The mom's just out for a break. She needs it now and then. These hungry babies can't get enough and paw at her all day." She unceremoniously dropped the small cub in his lap and pulled out another one while Peter held his arms in the air, afraid to touch.

"I don't, I mean, what if . . . ah . . ." Suddenly the cub let out a short squeal.

"He needs to feel more secure. Put your hands on him so he doesn't feel alone." Slowly, Peter lowered his arms to place his hands on the warm soft body. It started to purr as he gently patted it, becoming confident enough to cradle it in his arms. As he turned the cub to look at its wizened furry face, it reached out to cuff him softly and Peter fell in love.

"Oh my, this is amazing. He's so *little*. What's the little guy's name?" He lowered his head to rub his face on the fur of the cub, planting a kiss on its forehead. Bonnie could hear the enchantment in Peter's voice.

"We haven't named them yet. Why don't you think about names and come around before breakfast? Abby or Ginger Mae are usually here by then." At the mention of Ginger Mae, Peter's body tightened visibly, his face darkening with a scowl.

Bonnie rushed to explain. "Don't worry. She's just here to do the daily census. If she sees you, she'll leave us alone. Don't you think it's time you got over her, Peter?"

He startled, the cub squeaking again. "What makes you think I'm not over her, Bonnie? 'Cause *I am*." His tone of voice left no doubt. "I just don't *appreciate* being played for a fool."

"Shh, it's okay," she soothed him. "I'm happy to hear that. Sorry I mentioned her name. What do I know? I'm just a kid that hangs with animals, anyway." Placated, Peter went back to admiring his cub, beaming at his tender newfound love. The only thing Bonnie remained to be convinced of was that no insurmountable damage remained over his relationship with Ginger Mae.

Later that evening as the survivors filtered into Netty's vintage kitchen for dinner, they were all surprised to see the four Elders with their minions, Baby and Echo, standing expectantly to attention. Conversations ceased as the survivors muttered their surprise and curiosity. After greeting Barney and the posse of assorted dogs ensconced on the comfort of Netty's hand-braided rugs in front of the huge fireplace, individuals made their way to one of the long wooden tables that would serve as dinner and entertainment central for the rest of their evening.

As Captain Cobby and Karen took their seats, he called out to Abby, "Did someone die? You all look like you're going to a funeral."

Kenya screamed from her modified chair near the fireplace with Chance and the dogs. "You all are gonna see *me* kill someone real soon if you don't do something about this baby a mine. *I'll* give ya a funeral."

Johno knelt in front of her. "Shhh, Miss Kenya. You do not want to be talking like that. Crystal, can we bother you to pour some tea for Miss Kenya?" Crystal muttered under her breath as Salina passed her the copper teapot.

"Listen, chickey. Anytime you decide I have it cushy around here, you can take my place with this beach ball an all. I'll be happy ta pour you some tea now and then."

Crystal rolled her eyes as Kenya gave her a glare meant to fry bacon, if they had any. Ignoring the pregnant teen, Crystal poured her tea, giving Johno a shove. "Now you get your sweet butt over to the table. You don't need to be fussin' over this girl every night. Does he, Kenya?" She fixed Kenya with her own searing glare.

"I don't know why you gotta be so mean ta me, Crystal."

Crystal swiped Kenya's hair back off her neck. "Now Kenya, you hush now. Somethins up. If we can keep it down, maybe the beauties up there might have some news to tell us. This might be your chance to question Netty about your pregnancy since you're so sure she hiding something."

As Crystal scrambled back to her seat by Johno and the muttering fell silent, Jose stepped forward. Clearing his throat, he began. "I think it's safe to say that we're all happy to be here." Heads nodded as murmurs of gratitude floated around the huge kitchen. "And I'm sure it hasn't gone unnoticed that pretty much all of you are looking better than when you got here. Gloria, your diabetes is clearly gone. I bet you have never looked this great and felt this good in your whole life."

"You got that right, Jose," Gloria simpered as red-headed trucker Billy's arm wrapped possessively around her. "And Billy doesn't need to use his inhaler anymore."

Jose nodded his head in agreement. "And Peter, I notice you don't wear your glasses anymore. Are you seeing okay?"

Peter flushed to the roots of his nondescript hair, embarrassed by the attention. "I can see just fine."

Jose panned the crowd. "Ginger Mae, Abby says you sure look like your old self again. I'm so happy for you."

She nodded an acknowledgment, her mega-watt smile stretching from ear to ear as Dezi gave her a kiss on the cheek. Daisy jumped up and down like her mom was the guest of honor.

Jose turned to the fireplace and whistled. "Mimi, come here, girl."

The sweet skunk-like puppy mill mommy, one of Echo's favorites, trotted over to Jose, happy to be the center of attention. Jose scooped her up in his arms and turned her heartbreaking, agreeable face to the crowd.

"Has anyone noticed her cataracts are gone? She has no problem seeing now." Jose set Mimi on the ground with a hug sending her scampering back to the posse. Turning back to the crowd, he asked, "Does anyone recognize the miracles at work here?"

The voices in the crowd of hungry survivors shouted their jubilant agreement as Kane entered the kitchen and, with a wave to Scotty and Chloe, inched his way over to an anxious Kenya, who had not failed to notice the absence of Emma in the room.

Clyde stood up to address Jose as Salina tugged on his arm,

shaking her head with displeasure. He scanned the group of survivors at the table as if soliciting support. "You all know I'm a man of few words. So if ya don't mind, Jose, I wish you'd stop beating around the bush here. We're not stupid. We know there's something at work and it ain't the food. Not that I'm complaining about the improvements, it's just that I think we have a right to know what's happening to us."

"You tell 'em there, chickey. This girl done had enough." Kenya's indignation set the crowd whispering; infectious agitation whirling the room.

Billy stood up, giving Jose a nervous, respectful bow. "If you don't mind, Jose, I'm of a mind that you've known the truth for about six months now. So I'd like to hear the truth from those that have been hiding it." All eyes moved pointedly to Netty and Wil.

Wil shared a glance with the other three Elders before addressing the crowd. Lifting Baby from the floor by his side, he placed him on the counter. Stepping forward, he turned to Billy. "We have no ulterior motives in keeping the explanation from you. I realize it is now time for you all to understand what you are facing. I will be blunt."

Silence descended on the crowd, no one wanting to miss a syllable of the news they'd only gossiped about in dark corners of the Hive.

Staring with calmness into the collective faces of the survivors, Wil dropped the bomb. "The Earth will not be in a condition for any of you to resurface for the next one hundred years."

Shocked silence met his pronouncement. Ginger Mae grabbed on to Daisy, who sat holding young Kimir's hand. Kimir's tiny voice could be heard all the way to the front of the room. Out of the mouth of babes they say . . .

"We're all going to die here, without ever seeing the sun or the moon again."

The kitchen erupted with exclamations and invectives. A sob was heard from Kenya as Kane tried to comfort her. From the kitchen door, Emma quietly entered to take her seat next to Bonnie and Dezi.

Johno and his men sat, quiet and pensive, as Crystal added her quarrelsome voice to the bedlam.

Cobby stood, his hands held out in a supplicating gesture. "Please, please. We're all friends here. Can you give the man a chance? Let's hear him out."

The crowd slowly simmered down, turning their attention back to Wil at the front of the kitchen.

"The ground above is contaminated. You must recognize this. Many years have to pass before life can exist on the poisoned Earth. The Womb had planned to eliminate Homo sapiens safely while allowing the other species to flourish without the pain and assaults humans bring to their lives. This wondrous planet could then heal and regenerate from the multitude of wounds perpetrated by man. Now, the only life that is left is here with us. The Womb will eventually create new life forms and import a select few that will integrate with our wildlife and create a new world. You are all needed to help with the integration. Happily, you will all be able to find a new life with a new, peaceful purpose."

Karen's voice rang out. "Wil, how do you figure we'll be here in a hundred years? Won't we be all dead and buried? Except for you guys. You get to live forever."

Cobby reached over to comfort her as the bitterness rang from her voice, pumping up the crowd again.

"Please . . . can you all *please* settle down? *Let me finish.*" Wil's tail rose high in the air, his wings snapping like whips, his demeanor no longer calm. "Do I need to remind you that if it were not for Abby and the plans of the Womb, you would all be dead now *anyway*?" As Wil regained their attention, he spat out his words with no further regard for gentle niceties. "You will all live to see the day we resurface. Yes . . . you will all emerge the exact same physical age you were when you entered the Hive. The Womb has been ensuring your health since the first night you slept here, as well as the animals.

"As you sleep, microscopic armies of biosensitives enter through the pores of your skin to repair and replace any cells that have been damaged from free radicals, mutation, and existing disease. They correct or destroy any cells that have begun to divide improperly as a result. The age mechanism will never be allowed to turn on. That is, until you leave the Hive to resume living above ground."

The stunned silence deafened them all as fearful eyes cast around blankly in search of a way to absorb the ramifications of Wil's disclosures. Slowly, the women turned to Kenya, their expressions dawning with the horror of her obvious reality.

"No," she screamed, as the full brunt of Wil's words hit her. *"You can't do this to me."* Kenya's huge, beautiful eyes popped out of her sockets with incredulity. Her heaving breasts threatened to explode from her smock as she struggled to stand. Frantically, she searched the crowd for support.

"Johno, Salina . . . please . . . you can't let them do this to me. Kane, help me stand up." She continued to struggle to her feet as Kane tried to assist. Her eyes searched the crowd.

"Scotty, help me. You can talk to them. Make them stop. I need this baby *out* now. *I can't be pregnant for a hundred years."* Her face screwed up in tears and shock as her fellow survivors looked down, afraid to meet her eyes. No one wanted to stop the process, squeamish as it sounded. They wanted to live and continue to enjoy their miraculous heath. Kenya moaned and collapsed back into her chair, Kane as useless as most men when it came to pregnant females.

Netty approached with a mug of yellow liquid. "Take this, it will help."

Kenya flailed out knocking the mug from Netty's hands. "No. I want this baby out, *right now.* You can do it. I know you can. Talk to your Mr. Womb. Tell him . . . tell him I *promise* to be good." Her voice reduced to a whine between her sobs.

Johno hurried over to the distraught teen. She threw herself into his arms. "There, there, Miss Kenya." He turned and nodded to Netty, asking with his eyes for another mug of her medicine.

"We will all be here to help you. It's okay." He rocked her gently. "Yes, it's all okay. Everyone will help. You are not alone here, right Kane?" Johno stared at Kane who stood dumbfounded. *"Kane?"*

Johno's voice startled him out of his paralysis. Kneeling he gripped her hand. "Babe, you know I'm here for you. And the baby. We'll get through this together. It's just going to take a little longer, that's all."

A fresh bout of wailing erupted as Johno and Kane cringed. Johno shook his head at Kane, rolling his eyes as Kane's mistake registered on his face.

Netty appeared with a fresh mug of the yellow liquid, handing it to Kane. "Here, drink this. You'll feel much better."

Kenya eyed it suspiciously. "What is it? I don't want it to hurt my baby."

Netty answered in calm low tones, her voice as soothing as could be under the difficult circumstances. "It is a natural remedy from Oolaha. We have been preparing for this moment so we grew some of it from seed provided by the Womb."

Kenya took a cautious sip. "It tastes like plain water. Why doesn't the Womb just let me have my baby if he can do so much?" Her bitterness resonated around the kitchen.

"Drink up, my dear." Netty watched as Kenya finished the contents of the mug.

Suddenly, the walls of the kitchen started to undulate; streaks of color and light flashed with the gyrations. Netty and Wil froze. Auras from Baby and Echo slammed into the Elders, including Scotty.

"Brothers, Sisters, we have danger. *We must go.*" They took to the air in a wink, their wings invisible with the quickening of their flutters. Without a word, Netty and Wil drew their wings to their bodies, covering themselves from head to toe and just disappeared without a word.

One last aura, a plea from Echo. "Protect My Barney, Brother Scotty. He must not follow."

Scotty shouted into the air. "Where are you going, Echo?"

The aura faded as Scotty heard the words. "The big rock. Your big rock."

Chapter 7

All of the men in Netty's kitchen scrambled towards the door, Cobby and Clyde pausing in front of the women. Turning to confront Karen and Salina, they hugged them both. Clyde removed Salina's arms from around his neck, wrapping her hands in his enormous fists.

"You have to stay here and look after Kenya. I don't want you in danger. There's no telling what this is about." He kissed her hard as her wide frightened eyes spoke for her.

"Everyone, please wait." Captain Cobby stood on a chair. "The women must remain here. We don't know what to expect. Only the men should come. We don't even know where to go yet."

Scotty spoke up as Abby prepared to object. "Chloe, please make sure Barney stays with you. Keep all the dogs here. Abby, please keep an eye on everyone."

He lifted Mimi up to place her in Chloe's arms where she nestled down next to Teddy. He scanned the room quickly, spotting the pair of pit bulls. "I know where to go, Cobby. Let's take King and Queenie with us." The majestic pit bulls rose upon hearing their names, the fur on their backs standing up like bristles.

Ginger Mae drew Daisy and Kimir to the fireplace near Kenya, who searched frantically for a hand to grasp for reassurance.

"Abby, please hold down the fort for us here. We need you with the women in case danger gets this far."

Johno and his keepers stood anxiously waiting at the door, ready to spring into action. Scotty headed toward them, giving a shout. "*Let's go*. I know where they went. Echo is directing me." As they rushed out the door, Scotty spied Caesar, standing tensed, yet clearly not ready to join the rush of men. *Hmm, that's odd. He's not coming with me?*

Slipping over to the big cat's side, Scotty gave him a hug. "That's okay, boy. You stay here. Don't let anyone or anything into the kitchen until we get back. Keep your eye on Chloe and the women."

Caesar gave a deafening roar, something Scotty had never witnessed before. Reassured, he ran down the corridor toward the waiting men, Peter bringing up the rear.

The frightened men followed Scotty down the corridors, the membrane covered walls still exhibiting the contortions of light and color that had set Netty and Wil off with Echo and Baby. No one had visited the original cavern that led to the corridor by the entrance since they'd entered the Hive over six months ago.

Cobby caught up to him. "Do you think someone is trying to break in?"

"No, I only found the entrance to the Hive by accident when I was a kid. So did Jose when he followed Barney into the woods one day. And Netty never would have found it if Baby hadn't called her to the Hive so long ago. That's a remarkably low incidence of discovery over the one-hundred-year time span it's been here. It must be something else."

It had never occurred to them that someone could get in. Scotty now wondered if the problem was just near his childhood refuge. His granite rock was where this whole adventure had begun.

As they traversed the expanse of the cavern where they had huddled on their frightful inaugural night, Scotty realized they all were experiencing similar emotions. The demons that deviled them that night were back: Fear of the unknown.

Entering the corridor that led to the entrance of the Hive, they stopped to listen and catch their breath. The unexpected silence served only to ratchet up the suspense. Walking as quickly and quietly as they could, the group rounded the bend to a formidable scene.

Netty and Wil stood stoically and calmly at attention, their wings spread wide as Baby and Echo continued to flutter in the air behind them. The entrance of the Hive appeared to be nothing more than the translucent membrane: thin and stretched as the outlines of two humans were revealed in the organic glop. Slowly, the membrane stretched and began to tear as the two human forms put more pressure on the flexible wall.

Suddenly, the two figures fell through, followed by a foaming red fox, emaciated and rabid, blood leaking from every orifice. The two human figures were in no better condition: walking skeletons with unrecognizable features and bloody trails from various body locations. One appeared to be minus an ear and in the throes of a severe infection, swollen and leaking a viscous fluid.

Cobby and Clyde stepped up to the two figures as they attempted to dodge the whirling fox.

"Wil, get over here. These people are dying. Give us a hand."

They craned their necks wildly as they witnessed all of the attention directed at the dying fox. Baby and Echo landed and stood with their long bulbous tails high in the air. The smell of sulfur permeated the air as pressure was directed at the little fox. In less than five seconds, the fox fell on its side twitching, seemingly in the throes of death. As three quick heartbeats passed, the men watched as the fox shook and righted herself. She stood with legs straight under her, head flicking as she pawed at the drying blood and saliva on her muzzle. The miracle canine yipped, then trotted over to Echo to receive a pat on her head, depositing herself at Netty's feet as if to inspect the rest of the crowd.

"Over here . . . *now*. Can we have some help with these two? I don't think they're going to make it."

Clyde desperately tried to get the attention of the Elder, his voice indignant and incredulous as they helped the two people to the ground before they collapsed. Scotty watched as the smaller of the forms opened its eyes. Clyde pierced him with a withering look.

"For Pete's sake, Scotty, *can you do something?* They're on their last legs. *Heal them.*" Johno and his men clustered around the dying twosome.

"Kerp . . . ca . . . Clyde." The voice was a cracked whisper but everyone close by clearly heard the whisper call Clyde's name. "Clyde . . . hake . . . we . . . we made it." The figure, now identified as that of a woman, reached out with a trembling skeletal hand. "My love . . . ca . . . am I dreaming?" Her words came in faint, choked whispers.

"*Holy shit. Help, I need help!*" Clyde cupped the woman's head in his arms, tears flowing from his disbelieving eyes.

"Baby, you made it. Oh my baby. Lorna, Lorna." He covered her face with kisses. "*Help . . .* for the love of God. *This is my wife!*"

Netty approached, calmly assessing the condition of the two figures. She signaled to Johno and his men.

"Carry them to the sleeping quarters. We will attend to them there."

"No. You will *goddamn* cure my wife now. *Right here.*"

The keepers moved in to lift the man.

"No, Wil . . . Netty. *Come on, Scotty . . .* this is my *wife.*" He sobered momentarily to scream. "*Where are my grandbabies?* Jen and Suzy, where are they?"

He let go of his wife's head as she closed her eyes as if dead. Rising, Clyde grabbed Scotty, lifting him up off his feet, his wings crushed in Clyde's strong grip. Before he could blink, Echo and Baby flanked him, their crystal antlers swirling with red and black color.

"Put me down, Clyde. It's okay, Echo. Let me handle this."

"*Enough.*" Wil appeared alongside Echo and Baby. "Dezi, Billy, Peter . . . *Peter,* can you please get over here?" Peter jumped, obviously surprised to be asked to help as he lurked in the background, trying to fade into the cavern walls.

Clyde stood alone and morose as they carted his wife away to the sleeping quarters. His dejected shoulders shook with the tears he shed, making Scotty unsure what to say to the man who had been giving Salina—his Mama Diaz—his love and support.

"Why . . . why, Scotty? Aren't we worth as much as the stupid animals?" Clyde's voice gagged with bitterness.

"Come on, Clyde. You know I can't heal her. None of us can. Let's just get to the sleeping quarters and see what Netty has to say." Scotty shook out his wings, discovering several of his flanges twisted and broken from the force of Clyde's attack.

"Don't worry; I'm sure your pet freak will fix them for you." Clyde spat in Scotty's direction, causing King and Queenie to rise and pad over to Clyde, their growls forcing him to back down and head for the sleeping quarters as Scotty's wings healed themselves in a matter of minutes.

Turning to the entrance of the Hive, Scotty inspected the opening that had closed behind the fox, Clyde's wife, and her companion. The wall looked solid with the membrane firmly back in place, undulating now over the solid rock.

Calling to the royal pit bulls, they hurried to catch up with the crowd on its way to the sleeping chambers.

As Scotty re-entered the first cavern, he found Echo fluttering heavily in the air. Echo's aura reached for him. "I sense the heartbeat of another, Brother Scotty."

"Another what, Echo?"

"Another dying human and the creature that is near her."

"Take us there now, Echo."

Echo flew over Scotty's head to journey back to the opening of the Hive with Scotty, the pit bulls bringing up the rear. They watched as Echo landed and stuck her hand into the wall, the membrane closing on her tiny leather arm up to her elbow. Before Scotty's eyes, the cave wall parted and let in the gloom of the dangerous surface into the cavern.

"We must hurry. There is danger in the air." Echo wobbled out followed by Scotty and the dogs. Rounding the huge granite rock, they were greeted by an empty pathway. Scotty surveyed the trees in the forest, no longer familiar and comforting but with the limbs denuded, gray and mourning. Searching for a spot of green became futile. The wind chilled and left them with a coating of dull grit.

"The heartbeat is down the pathway. We must hurry." Echo took to the air as they rushed down the pathway to come upon a contraption piled high with rags. Another emaciated fox, not as far gone as the other one, sniffed suspiciously at the rags, desperate for a morsel to eat. As they approached, the fox growled, unwilling to relinquish or share the jackpot that had appeared in its territory. Scotty could see an arm outthrust from the rags that the fox had been worrying meat from, the bone now exposed and gnawed on.

Echo landed and faced the fox: a male, perhaps the mate of the one in the Hive. Echo's crystal antlers spilt and a red projectile sallied forth to land on the ear of the fox, quickly disappearing inside as the fox gave a quiet yelp accompanied by a whine, then promptly turned and marched toward to the Hive.

Scotty knelt on the hard, cold ground, clearing away the rags to reveal the creature that was once called a teenager, now unrecognizable.

"She's still alive. Let's get her to the sleeping quarters with the others. Maybe this is one of Clyde's granddaughters he was screaming about." Establishing the likelihood it was a she, Scotty picked up the lump of bones in his arms and rushed back to the Hive, stealing a furtive glance at the unrecognizable sky.

Scotty and Echo arrived in time to witness the reunion of the mated foxes. Baby surreptitiously directed his tail and its healing powers on the sick fox, completing its recovery as Clyde sobbed in the corner, watching Netty and Johno make his wife comfortable.

"Hey, everyone. I found someone else."

Clyde rushed to Scotty's side to help with the pitiful bundle, her arm with the exposed bone extended for all to see. "Oh, my Lord. Jennifer?"

They eased her over to a stone dais and made her as comfortable as possible. Clyde cupped her head to stroke her unrecognizable face, quickly pulling back. As her filthy, shedding hair came away in his hands, he held his fingers up in horror.

"My sweet baby. What has become of you?"

Scotty cringed as Clyde turned to him, wild eyes filled with hate and insanity. "Where is she? Where's Suzy? My baby . . . *where is she, Scotty?*"

"Calm down, Clyde. No one else was there. This is all I saw. Now let's get them some care." Scotty turned to the bones on the dais as Billy returned with wet cloths and water. Clyde calmed down with the effort of cleaning Jennifer's body and Scotty's attempt to dribble water into her cracked and blistered lips, swollen beyond all recognition.

Suddenly, Netty and Wil withdrew from around the other two figures, motioning for everyone else to stand back. Scotty dragged Clyde away from his granddaughter, her shedding hair still gripped in his hand, his face drained of color.

From the walls emerged the tendrils of the night, never before witnessed by humans. They inched over the cool, hard floors and up the three daises to sink into the minute pores of the newly washed figures. All movement stopped as the figures appeared to be sleeping.

"What the fuck are you doing?" Clyde broke free of Scotty's restraining arms to approach the fragile tendrils, stomping on them and ripping them from his wife's body.

"Stop, you will kill her!" Wil and Netty converged on Clyde, grabbing at his arms. *"Johno, Scotty,* help here," Wil shouted. They pulled a wild and ineffectual Clyde away from the dais, his breath heaving, his face now raging with blood. Netty stepped up to face him, her dazzling eyes forcing him to look away.

"No, don't you dare look away." She gripped his chin, forcing him to confront the luminous glare of her anger.

"How dare you question our methods with violence? So much like a human." The strength of her bitterness and condemnation sobered him. She turned, pointing to the remaining tendrils at work on his wife. "They are healing her. You may have done damage. If your wife lives, it will not be because of you. Now take him out of here."

Clyde threw her an emotional plea as they escorted him out. "Save her, Netty . . . please. My grandbaby . . . Lorna . . . ." His sobs could be heard down the corridor echoing loudly as the men returned to Netty's kitchen to face the blank stares of the women.

Clyde jerked his arms from the grip of the men who held him, flopping down on a chair to lay his face in his arms. Salina hurried to his side, where she was met by Scotty who pulled her away, whispering in her ear. All eyes rested on her face as she registered her shock. Quickly, the word of the new survivors circulated the room. All were sad for Salina, but the possibility of increasing their numbers overwhelmed the personal considerations of Clyde and Salina.

"New people . . . now that is music to my ears. They were topside. They'll have news." Crystal clapped her hands with joy, while giving Salina an embarrassed and sympathetic glance.

"If they live." Johno's somber voice cut through the speculation.

Clyde's head popped up; his voice emphatic, belying the tears. *They will live*. They got this far. Don't talk like that, Johno. They *will* live."

Johno nodded his sage head. "Yes, my friend. We will pray to the Womb that they live."

Days passed as the original survivors waited impatiently for word of recovery for Clyde's wife Lorna, his granddaughter and their male companion.

The atmosphere at dinner was glum. Sidelong glances at Salina and Clyde failed to elicit a sign that their relationship would weather this unimaginable roadblock. Since they were not interacting themselves, everyone refrained from bringing up the subject. Even Kenya felt the charged atmosphere, dampening her nightly pregnancy complaints.

Then a sudden turn of events. Late one night, as the subdued survivors enjoyed the day's confections from the ever-changing menu of Salina's desserts, and Wil and Netty relaxed at their table enjoying a cup of tea, Baby waddled into the kitchen, sending auras to the Elders. Scotty felt the excitement of Baby's aura as he rushed them with his announcement.

"Brothers and Sisters . . . there is change. Come quickly."

Wil jumped up, calling to Clyde to join them.

Clyde shot up like spring and raced to the kitchen entrance without a word. Scotty turned to see the pain on Salina's face. Rising from his seat, he went to her side where he was joined by Bonnie and Emma. They wrapped their arms around her.

"Don't worry, Mama. We're all here for you."

"No matter what happens, Mama, we're here," echoed Emma and

Scotty. Salina bent to kiss all three.

"I have everything that's important to me right here." She glanced over to Abby and Jose to be met with their smiles of encouragement.

But some things never change. Scotty observed Kenya watching them from the corner of her eye as Kane hovered nearby. Reaching out for his hand, she hollered over to Emma. "Can you please bring me a cup of tea, Emma? I'm feeling a bit uncomfortable."

Emma glanced up from the huddle around Salina. "Can't Kane get it for you?"

Kenya's smug grin feigned innocence. "Oh, he needs to be here with me, don't you Kane?" A burgundy flush crawled up Kane's face as he kept his eyes averted from Emma.

Kenya arched a brow. "You don't mind now do ya, chickey?"

Emma moved to Netty's stove, ignoring the question, her face set, trying not to show the humiliation as she poured Kenya her tea. Kane averted his eyes as Kenya watched every move she made.

"Thanks, chickey. I think I'll just take this tea to my bedroom. Kane, you coming?" As Kane wrapped his arm around Kenya to assist her rise from her chair, Scotty could not fail to notice the pain in Emma's eyes and the smirk of triumph on Kenya's beautiful lips. Yeah, even in the veil of chaos, some things never changed.

"Mama, I think I'll bring some soup down to Clyde and Wil. They may need some more nourishment for the new people by now." Emma made herself busy at the fireplace warming the soup.

Salina cast her eyes at her eldest daughter. "Why don't you let Abby go with you?" Salina motioned for Abby to join them.

Bonnie hopped up quickly, her words bubbling out. "I want to go too, Mama. I can help."

Abby placed her hand on Salina's shoulder. "Don't worry. I'll look after them." Abby tousled Bonnie's hair. "Come on, pretty girl. Let's go see if we can help."

Chapter 8

A few minutes before Wil and Clyde reached the sleeping quarters, Seth sat up, dumbfounded to find himself in what appeared to be a cave and lying on slabs of rock that felt like velvety feathers.

He spotted movement from the corner of his eye, spinning quickly enough to catch a glimpse of the tendrils as they receded back into the membrane of the wall. *What the fuck?*

Seth scooted back up on the dais, drawing up his feet. The quickness of his response amazed him. He held out his arms to inspect them, reaching up to his ear as he realized he no longer felt pain. His wound felt closed for the first time since the ear had been removed by Doc Benjamin's man's machete. He could actually feel a nub of skin where his wound used to be.

Seth remembered the dead end he and Lorna had found as the sick fox attacked. Lorna had been on her last legs and they'd left the sled with Jennifer down the trail. Looking around, he could see their bodies on another rock. Squinting closer, he noticed webbing of some sort plugged into their bodies in various locations. *Are they dead? Why do I feel so much better?* He remembered nothing from the point at which the fox launched its attack. A gleam of cunning sparked his eyes. They must have been saved by someone. *I'm saved.*

He licked his lips compulsively as his attention rested on the other two forms on the stones. If he was alive after residing on the verge of death, there was a better than even chance that the other two would also live. Could he stand those odds? *Not by a long shot. The first thing the old bitch will do is start flapping her mouth.*

He slid to the edge of the rock, still amazed by the contradiction in texture. Tenderly, he stepped on the floor and eased his weight to a standing position. He scanned the room to search for cameras or an alarm. Satisfying himself they were alone, he quietly inched over to the stone that held Lorna. He took one look at her and realized she looked the same as she did the day they met the fox. *How long have we been here?* For some reason, she wasn't getting the health benefits that he'd had from their hosts. Easing away from the strange webbing that appeared to be connected to her, he wrinkled his nose. For sure, he couldn't have her recovering and blabbing her fat mouth.

Sayonara, Lorna. I think I'll just have to hasten you along to the big daddy in the sky. He jerked his fingers away from her nostrils as he was startled by the approach of a strange sight.

"What the fuck?" Stunned, he inched back to his stone to crouch at its side as a golden man with shining eyes and huge wings approached. He was followed by a winged creature easy enough to swat as it fluttered like a golden furry overgrown gnat in the air above the man's head.

A tall, lean man in his late fifties rushed over to Lorna. Seth's eyes stayed on the glorious winged ones, unable to formulate a thought as vertigo attacked him from the luminescent sheen emanating from their eyes.

A voice pierced his dizziness as he realized the man with Lorna was her husband. Time stood still as he inched his way over to her stone. He weakly extended his hand. "Hi. You must be Clyde."

Clyde turned from Lorna to embrace Seth, blubbering and leaking tears all over the new smock they'd given Seth to wear.

"Easy there, guy. We made it. Everything's going to be fine now." Seth attempted to extricate himself from Clyde's embrace.

"I am Wil. And you are?" The winged man approached, holding his pet on his hip.

"My name's Seth. I've been traveling with Lorna and the kids for a long time now." He paused, mesmerized by Wil's eyes, unable to stop himself from looking away. Blinking rapidly, he turned back.

"So . . . er, Wil. Where the heck am I? And do you mind if I ask what . . . er . . . who you are?"

"I am an Elder. Perhaps you should sit down. We have a few questions as you probably do, too." As Seth returned to his stone bed, two more figures entered the room.

A female winged creature directed two pretty young girls to his side. One smiled shyly down at him.

"I'm Emma."

"Well heeeello, Emma." Seth grinned as he decided things were looking up. Taking the mug of soup from Emma, he grazed his fingers with hers, eliciting a rise of blood in her face. She met his eyes with her own and received a quick wink from Seth. Casting her eyes down, she scampered over to Clyde, who put his arm around her.

Seth settled in for a long inquisition, but he had a little cross-examination of his own in mind. Plastering a simple, blank expression across his clean-cut face, aware of flutters of anticipation in the pit of his stomach, and a shiver buzzing in his psychotic brain, he turned to face the possibilities.

Scotty and Chloe lounged near the fireplace watching Barney and Echo snuggle as they tried to fend off Chance's relentless attempt to insinuate herself between the two. Penny, the springer spaniel, tiredly fended off Teddy's advances to her ear. King and Queenie monitored all as Mimi scuttled from one person to the next, looking for affection. As the rest of the dogs dozed, conversation turned to the mundane routines of the Hive and the projects in which the survivors were involved.

"Tatit, swartit, lyii, donktit, chee." Daisy sat mumbling to herself as Ginger Mae started at the strange sounds.

"Are you okay, baby?" She swept her daughter's thin hair back from her pallid face.

Daisy grinned wide, the now six-year-old savant patient with her mother's curiosity. "I'm just learning, Mama. I need to know how to talk."

Ginger Mae frowned. "That sounded like you were choking, not talking. Are you playing with me, you little silly?" Daisy sighed then started to gab a mile a minute about the wonders of intergalactic syntax and the limitations of the human throat. Ginger Mae's eyes glazed over as Scotty slid by, giving Daisy a high five.

"How's it going, peewee? You seen Kimir around?"

Ginger Mae answered for her daughter. "He left with one of the keepers. Elias, I think. Since he just sits here and glowers at Kane and Emma, I suggested he spend some time thinking of someone else. Kimir wanted to go see Tobi of course, so off they went. Why?"

"Abby wants Kimir to work in the library with Daisy. He needs to get an education. He might as well start now. He needs some structure instead of running around here like a wild boy." Scotty laughed as he walked away. "He should be able to learn quite a bit in the next hundred years."

Scotty finished his tour over by Peter's table. Bonnie sat next to Peter, having returned from her trip with Netty to see the new survivors. They sat whispering up a storm about their plans for the lion cub that had stolen Peter's heart. Watching Peter's eyes light up and his expression so animated pleased him enormously. He was very fond of Peter and it hurt him to see the exile he'd imposed on himself. He didn't know what had brought him out of his shell, but he'd bet Bonnie's infectious joy for life had something to do with it. Jose's adopted sister, the chubby little girl they'd all grown up with in Mama Diaz's house was just a delight to be around.

As Scotty slid into a seat next to Bonnie and Peter, Bonnie's eyes bugged out. Turning to investigate what she was looking at, Scotty watched Clyde walk into the kitchen with his arm wrapped around the man who'd been rescued with Clyde's wife and granddaughter. The man limped and had a shit-eating grin on his face if Scotty ever saw one before. He was followed by Emma, Wil and Abby. Clyde helped him to a rocking chair and clapped him on the shoulder.

"This here, ladies and gentleman, is the savior of my wife and one of my grandbabies. Meet Seth."

Clyde glanced over to Netty. "Can we please have some of our best grub for this remarkable man? He's a hero." Netty hurried to set him a place, filling it up with fruit pie, crusty green protein bread and tea.

Seth glanced back toward the kitchen door and whined up to Clyde. "You're sure that tiger won't come in here?" His eyes searched the room. "Anyone have a gun . . . just in case?"

Scotty spoke quietly and firmly. "Caesar is no threat to anyone."

"Are you sure you can eat solid food, Seth? We do not want you to get sick on us." Netty smiled sweetly as she served him and returned to the fire. Scotty watched as the man's eyes feasted on Netty as she turned her back. *I bet he's never seen anything like us Elders before.* Seth's gaze rested on Chance and the dogs, then looked down at his pie.

"What kind of food you serving me? Sure looks good. What is it, pig or dog?" he asked with a knowing grin. His question was met with shocked silence.

Netty froze, her tone glacial. "We don't eat our loved ones here . . . *Seth* . . . We protect them." Surprise flickered in the man's eyes as Scotty rose to join Chloe at the fireplace again.

"How many of you, exactly, are winged ones?" He turned back to Netty. "No offense ma'am. I'm not one to turn away food after so long, no matter what's cooked in it."

"Excuse me, Seth. I find your comments more than a little offensive. As soon as you finish eating, I think we need to get a few things clear regarding the Hive." Scotty sat down again, picking up Echo and Barney to place them on his lap as Seth sputtered and choked on his tea.

"*Hive*? What the hell is that? What, you have some kind of commune going on here?"

Clyde tried to shush him, patting him on the arm. "Now, now, Seth. You just eat. The folks here are just sensitive about their animals, that's all. You'll understand after a while. You'll get used to it. Let me just tell these fine folks what you did for my family while you taste Salina and Netty's delicious grub." Seth shut up and devoted himself to eating, while Clyde waxed on about the heroics of Seth and the herculean efforts he'd made on behalf of Lorna and the grandchildren. Tears came back as he continued between sobs.

"This man deserves all the help we can give him . . . he even tried to fend off the villains that came in the night to kidnap my Suzy." Salina rushed to his side as he broke down. He held up his hand to her, warning her to come no closer.

"I can never repay the debt I owe Seth. Thanks be to the Womb for beginning to give him back his ear that was damaged when he heroically defended my family from the hordes that attacked them. It is to *this man* that I owe everything. And I promise I will spend the rest of my life making it up to him." He looked down at Seth stuffing his face with Netty's goodies. "If he'll allow me." Seth swallowed as Clyde enveloped him in a big bear hug again.

"Seth, I want you to bunk in with me so I can show you the ropes around here. Break you in, so to speak." Clyde stood tall with his hands on his hips as if Seth would be prostrate with gratefulness.

"Well now, big guy, why don't we keep things the way they are for now? I'm still feeling a bit weak. And I'm just not ready to turn my back on Lorna and Jen. They've been like my family for so long now." His eyes lids fell slowly then rose, fluttering with brave innocence. "I don't think I could bear to part from them until they can join me in good health."

Wil raised his voice to pipe in on the conversation. "I must say, I don't know when that might happen. Jennifer's recovery is going well, even though she has not awakened. But Lorna will be touch and go. There was some other damage." Wil looked at Clyde with his shining eyes.

Clyde reacted with defensiveness and outrage. "Well, if *some* here had as much respect for people as they do varmints, then my wife and granddaughter would be sitting right here with us." His voice rose, shrill and accusing. "And if *some* people hadn't been so secretive about the source of our good health, then maybe I would have understood when I saw the creepy fingers come out of the wall and attach to my wife. Maybe if *some* people *shared* their information, we'd all be a lot happier here."

Clyde stared back at Wil, clearly an example of testosterone at play. Scotty saw it as the men endured their pissing contest; and it didn't escape their new guest either. Wil's wings fluttered ominously.

Seth blinked, assessing the conversation. "So . . . Lorna's not doing as well as she should be? Hmmm . . . I'll just have to keep a closer eye on her. I wouldn't want to lose her now, would I? She's become like a mother to me." Seth beamed with concern and touching self-sacrifice. Scotty warmed with the thought of Clyde's family in such good hands. Everyone in the Hive had given up on them months ago. To get such good news and have new members of the Hive was a miracle.

Suddenly, there was a commotion at the kitchen door as their ears split with the shrieking trumpet of Tobi's surprise appearance. Little Kimir and Elias ducked under her neck as she tried to get her head in the doorway.

Seth dropped what he was doing and stood up on the table in fright.

Bonnie came running forward. She glanced at Seth. "That's not necessary. Tobi's just here looking for me. Peter . . . Dezi, let's get Chance and take Tobi back to the herd." She looked at Salina for approval. "Don't worry, Mama. Tobi knows it's almost time for bed and I haven't been down to say good night. She knows something's different and it scares her. She's just looking for reassurance so she's confident the herd isn't in danger."

Ginger Mae rose with Daisy to pet Tobi's big head. Even Chloe got up to pay her respects. Bonnie slipped her a green, crunchy treat and backed her out the door to go back to the herd.

Seth eased himself down off the table. He steadied himself against Clyde. "Well, I see you have some very big pets." Seth plastered a huge infectious smile on his face, flashing it to all who were left in the room. "I can see I have a lot to learn from all of you good people. I look forward to becoming part of your family, just as I have with my sweet Jen and Lorna. Clyde . . . shall we?" He gripped Clyde's arm to be guided back to the sleeping quarters. "Good night, all my wonderful new friends. I'm sure we're all going to get along just fine."

Chapter 9

Seth found it difficult to find time alone with Lorna. When he lay down to sleep, he couldn't wake back up until morning, finding himself stronger and stronger each day. His limp was gone and his ear clearly reformed. His scabs healed and even his hair was growing back in. He knew he looked better by the reaction of Emma, who brought water to bathe Jen and Lorna every day. He never knew when she would show up because she had to fit it in between her chores in the kitchen and her turn for the delivery of lunches.

Clyde had become quite the pain in the ass with his constant hovering over his family and his determined efforts to integrate Seth into the community. He guessed he'd met everyone several times by now. He noticed the Elders hadn't yet warmed up to his charms, but they were probably naturally suspicious. And the lady from the kitchen . . . Salina. Clyde seemed to avoid her. *Wonder why?* But Seth knew if he was patient, the moment would come. He just had to hope it was soon. He couldn't have them actually recovering. Lorna wasn't a problem since her healing was so slow. If he was lucky, she'd die on her own anyway.

It was Jennifer he was worried about. Two deaths might just look suspicious. Maybe he could find some way to control her. It shouldn't be too hard. She was just a snot-nosed kid after all. He'd show her sassy ass a thing or two when she woke up.

Emma entered the room as he lounged on his stone dais. Her smile brightened as she realized he was awake. "Hi, Seth. How do you feel this morning?"

Seth picked at his developing ear lobe and grinned. "I feel a lot better now that you're here, Emma."

She flushed a pretty pomegranate shade. "I'm just stopping by to give you fresh water. I'll be back later."

Seth watched every move she made, his eyes feasting on her young vitality. "Bet you have a boyfriend here don't you, Emma?"

Seth smirked. Emma turned to face him, her earthen jug now emptied into their water bowls. She lowered her eyes to the ground, making circles on the floor with her toe as she watched him from under her eyelids. "I might."

Seth knew he had her. "If I was a young guy again, I'd sure give him a run for his money."

Emma raised her face up in astonishment. "You're not old, Seth. What are you, thirty five-ish?" Emma's voice rang with coyness. "Some girls like an older man." She innocently licked her lips, inflaming Seth who wanted to get his hands on her so bad he didn't know if he could stop himself. The demons that ruled him begged for release.

"Why don't you come on over here, Emma? I could sure use a back rub." His innocence blared right at her as he worked to keep his heaving breath under control. He eyed the lush figure outlined in her smock as she bent down to let go of her water jug.

Suddenly from around the corner, Clyde and Netty—the golden babe with the wings—entered. Waving to Seth, Clyde escorted a frowning Netty to Lorna's side. Netty appraised her condition, lifting her arms from side to side with no response.

"I do not know, Clyde. She still looks serious. She is in a coma, the best state for her to heal. But you did great damage to her potential recovery. We talked about the process before."

"But you didn't tell me about the monstrous *creepy things* that burrowed into her. A heads-up might have saved her. You can't let her die, Netty. This is my *wife!*" Working up a steam of resentment, Clyde wiped away the sweat from his florid brow with the sleeve of his tunic. He moved over to Jennifer's stone dais. Netty followed, placing her hands on the teen's temples.

"Now Jennifer appears fully recovered." She lifted an arm, turning it over to search for unhealed scars. "She looks fine, Clyde. I just don't understand why she still sleeps." They both turned to Seth. Netty raised her golden eyebrows, mesmerizing Seth with the luminous and hypnotic quality of her eyes.

"It has been one full week now, has it not, Seth, since you

awoke?"

Seth gave her his most beguiling smile. "Yes, Netty. It has. Why?"

"Well, according to Clyde's reports of your heroic deeds, you spent more time in the open, exposed to all the radiation and microbe soup in the air. Yet you healed one week before Jennifer."

Seth didn't know where Netty was going with this line of questioning as the facts were perfectly correct. Even though many of his excursions had been to locate water and food, he always fully assuaged his needs first so he could avoid the need to put up with Lorna's bitching about sharing.

"She is younger and presumably healthy. She should have healed *before* you, Seth."

Emma worked her way over to Jennifer. Netty glanced her way, pointedly saying, "Emma, I think you are needed in the kitchen." Netty turned to follow behind Emma, a vision of perplexity. "We will keep an eye on her and hope, Clyde. That is all we can do as the Womb finishes any repairs she may need."

Grumbling, Clyde left Jennifer's side to return to his wife, offering explanations to Seth as he patted her head that was beginning to show signs of hair regrowth. "If they wanted to, they *could* heal her." His bitterness clearly reflected his worry and fright for his family.

Seth motioned to Lorna. "Looks like they *are* healing her, Clyde. At least they're trying. I don't want to scare you, big guy, but Lorna was almost gone when we got here. Maybe too much damage was done. Maybe she has too much poison in her. You should prepare yourself." Seth slid off his dais and wrapped his arms around Clyde's wide shoulders. "She looks to me like she's not going to make it." His voice dripped with compassion and concern. He sniffed, causing Clyde to glance up. He sniffed again as Clyde held him tightly.

"I just don't know what I'm going to do if we lose her. She's my family now. I haven't had much of a family in my life. My parents died at an early age. I was just a kid. Eleven years old."

"Gosh, Seth. I'm so sorry."

"I know you are, Clyde." He patted Clyde's hand in sympathy. "They died in a bad house fire, so long ago I barely remember. I just can't go through losing Lorna, now that I've found her. But don't worry, Clyde," he said as the big man's eyes started to flash with overwhelming emotion. "I'm here to look after her. I'll do everything she needs. Just leave it to me. You know you can count on *me*, right?"

"I sure do, my boy. I sure do."

Seth held up his hand with all the drama he could muster, poising it near his face.

"What? What is it, my boy?" Seth's fingers squeezed his nostrils, a loud sob escaping his trembling lips. He choked back another sob, clutching tightly to Clyde.

"It's just the nightmares. Suzy . . ."

As the two female survivors of the Armageddon and their own personal hell named Seth lay wholly in their comas, the two grown men cried and consoled one another deep underground in comfort and safety as the last of the lingering sparks of life above ground slid into the quiet release of death. Before long, their desiccated bones would reduce to powder; all moisture leached away; the calcium breaking down to sift lightly into the cold ambivalent wind. Ashes to ashes . . . dust to dust.

Emma hurried for her assignation with Kane, disobeying Netty once again. Her excitement was palpable as she made her way to the deep cleft near the bathing caves that worked so well when hiding the activities of two hot-blooded young lovers. Today was the day she planned to force Kane to declare his loyalty to her. She no longer wished to be the girl in the shadows, a joke. Kenya's passive aggressive remarks indicated to Emma that she suspected the worst anyway. So she would hardly be blindsided. Maybe a shock to her system would be a good thing, bringing on the delivery of the baby and putting them all out of their misery with her constant bellyaching.

A hand reached out to grab her arm and pull her into the cleft. She laughed as Kane crashed his lips down on hers.

"Easy, baby. Let me catch my breath." Her arms snaked around his neck as he ran his hands up over her back and down to her butt where he squeezed hard.

"I want this, *now*. Just feel me." Kane slammed his body up against hers, showing his erection in all its youthful glory.

"Ew, ha, ha, ha. I like." Emma ran her tongue down Kane's well-developed chest as he tossed his smock aside, arriving just where she knew she would force him to groan. Emma tipped her head to see his tormented expression. "You like this, baby?"

Kane's eyes glazed as she plied her tongue and fingers to their best advantage. "Goddamn, Emma. You know you're killing me." He pulled her roughly to her feet and ripped off her smock. She stood proudly while he admired her sleek, curvy figure. He turned her around and placed his erection along her backside. Emma squirmed, wanting to see his face to judge her control.

Kane bit down on her neck. "Come on, babe, let me."

She twisted around to face him as he tried to convince her. "Do you love me, Kane?" Her voice was a low whisper as her cool fingers caressed his erection that throbbed hungrily against her skin, seeking her moist warmth.

"What are you talking about, Emma? You know I love what we have."

He lifted her up to his waist and sank his erection inside as she wrapped her legs around his waist and moaned. "Oh . . . God, yes, Kane."

Kane's face was a tight mask of pleasure as they both breathlessly forgot all of their responsibilities and grabbed for the exquisite pleasure their young bodies craved.

After they dressed quickly, Emma asked, a plaintive note in her voice, "Kane, do you think you could meet me after dinner tonight? We can sneak down to the bathing caves." She ran her fingers over his chest suggestively.

Kane put on his cotton smock hurriedly, all attention on getting back to work before he was missed. He pushed her aside as he tried to locate a shoe. "Come on, Emma, you know I gotta go." He shot her a quick grin. "Besides, you know I need to be with Kenya tonight. Why ask such a silly question?"

Emma took a deep breath. "I wanted to talk to you about something special."

Kane raked his long wavy blond locks back with his fingers. "Babe, you know that's impossible. Besides, Scotty has something planned for tonight after dinner, a surprise for Echo. I promised Kenya and I would stick around for it." He kissed her quickly on the forehead.

"But—"

"Gotta go." And Kane was gone, leaving Emma dejected and mad at herself for losing control and not confronting Kane while she held the advantage. *Damn. I'm just too weak around that guy.* Promising herself the next time would be different, she hurried back to Netty's kitchen to help with the chores.

That night seemed to be the same as any other night. Kenya set everyone's nerves on edge before they had a chance to enjoy their sumptuous dinner, forcing Johno to step in as usual, which prompted Crystal to add to the melee, setting off Chance and the dogs.

Echo perched as always near the fireplace, one arm stuck into the gelatinous wall for sustenance of her own kind. The crystal of her horns reflected prisms of light around the room, competing with the golden sparkle of her effervescent eyes. From time to time, a survivor would glance her way as they sensed the stroke of an aura in their mind, recognizing the tentative forays the minion made as she tested for other minds she deemed a possible fond connection. The other diners waited patiently for things to settle down and begin dinner.

Emma poured tea as everyone socialized. She rolled her eyes at Bonnie holding court with her buddies, Dezi and Peter, obviously discussing the best way to clean elephant poop off their shoes. Gloria and Billy played kissy face at the table, reminding Emma to keep her eye on Kane who fawned at Kenya's feet. *For Heaven's sakes!* She quickly moved her line of sight away from the keepers' table as she caught Elias' intent stare. She glanced at the kitchen doorway to see Netty and Wil enter with Baby, late as usual. Other eyes followed them as they busied themselves, Baby toddling off to join Echo at the wall.

Soon everyone settled down to eat, Salina's anxious and solemn demeanor unnoticed by most in favor of the new confection she handed out for sampling.

"I know this doesn't look as appetizing as it tastes, but trust me, you'll love it. It is just the latest new seed the kids will be growing. A gift from the Womb, I take it, Netty?"

Everyone listened as Netty stepped up to reassure them about the grey fibrous lump with streaks of black matter that popped as you bit down. "This will be an important source of food for many of the herbivores that will populate this planet. That includes you. There will be no more human carnivores." Netty's gentle announcement caused a rustle among the survivors.

"You mean to say we'll never taste a nice juicy cheeseburger again? Or a thick T-bone steak?" Seth sat up straight, hands on hips, his incredulous face a reflection of many of the men in the crowd.

Ginger Mae shouted out, "What . . . you'd have us eat some of the animals in our care, Seth?"

"Well, why not? They're breeding. And that's what they're supposed to be for."

A hush descended quickly on the crowd as Scotty got up from his chair so fast it tipped back, crashing to the floor. His tail escaped from around his waist to snap frenetically in the air. He loomed over Seth, forcing him to lean away.

"Just to make things perfectly clear, *Seth.* These creatures are not here for our personal *use.* Their lives are their *own,* just as your life is. They feel pain and love just like we do. They were *never* here for us to eat." Scotty slammed his fist into the palm of his hand. "We have *plenty* to eat. Our digestive systems were never made for a diet of animal protein and fats anyway. If there's not enough food to feed humans, it's because there are too many of us. The planet was not meant to be overwhelmed with humans or *any* species without it causing problems. The only food chain you need to concern yourself with is the one that puts us on the bottom. We are here to care for the animals until the planet is whole again. They will learn to care for themselves once we resurface. But let me assure you: This is our last chance. There will be a revised list of the Ten Commandments. And the first one will be: *Thou shall not kill any creature for thine own pleasure.* If that's a problem for you I'll be happy to give you a one-way escort back to the rock where we found you."

Clyde's and Seth's eyes bugged out. "Now, Scotty, there's no need to get aggressive. Seth understands, don't you buddy?" As Seth glared at Scotty, Clyde gave him a kick. "Scotty's just a kid; he didn't mean nothing by it."

With that remark, Wil rose, stretching his wings as wide as the room would allow. "Allow me to assure you that everything said by this young Elder is the law. I thought we were past this. Does anyone here need a further explanation about the purpose of the Hive and the lives that are harbored here?"

Wil's luminous eyes bore into the faces of everyone there, lingering on Seth. "You are welcome here, Seth, but only under the terms of the Womb. You will not like the outcome if you choose to test us."

The tension broke as Seth flashed a big grin and held his hand out to Scotty, who turned away a split second before. Seth brushed off the awkwardness. "Hey, hey. We're all family here. All's good." He picked up the plate Salina set in front of him to spoon up the new dish. "Ummm, my compliments to the chef."

As he sat down and everyone resumed eating, Emma observed a spark of resentment quickly extinguished in Seth's handsome face. *Oh, hmmm, maybe we have a rebel on our hands. What a neat guy.* She glanced once more in Kane's direction to see if he was looking her way. Assured, she picked up her plate and paraded over to plop herself next to Seth, letting Kane get an eyeful as she slid her hand down Seth's arm before she sat.

Out of the corner of her eye, she barely noticed the scowl on Elias' face as he stomped away from the keepers' table to leave. With a toss of her hair, she reached over to Seth to dip her spoon into his plate, raising her utensil slowly to her mouth where she swallowed and licked her lips as Kane and a beaming Seth both watched. Kane shook his head and turned his attention back to Kenya, leaving Emma to congratulate herself on her small victory. *Maybe I'm on to something*, she thought as she resumed her flirtation with Seth.

Dinner progressed uneventfully. Emma soon excused herself to collect the dirty dishes from the diners. As the plates were cleared and more tea offered around, Scotty stood. "As some of you know, today is my twentieth birthday. I'm going to celebrate it a bit differently this year. I knew since we've all had birthdays, Salina would make my favorite dishes. But for today I've asked her to try to make me a *cake*. This is a special cake. Like one I once had, so long ago."

Scotty turned to Salina as she uncovered a big round chocolate birthday cake from its hiding place to deposit it in front of Scotty. Scotty reached out his hand toward Echo, who had wiggled her way down from the wall. They just stared at each other as Scotty laughed. "Yes, Echo . . . *cake*." Turning to the crowd, he added, "This is for Echo. I wanted to share my cake and my day with her, as I did so unknowingly when I was eight years old. Echo was just a little boy's version of a wood fairy friend before I fell off that granite rock and was injured." He glanced with pride at Echo. "Remember that, girl?" Scotty turned back to the survivors to continue his story. "I would have died if she hadn't healed me."

Clyde quickly shouted out, his words slobbering with indignation. "Hey, I thought they weren't allowed to heal people. Why were you healed? What's so special about you?"

Netty raised her hand to calm him. "One of the exceptions is when a minion or Elder has caused the injury themselves."

Scotty explained further, "I brought a piece of my birthday cake to make friends with her. Unfortunately, I fell asleep on the rock in the warm sun while I waited for her to appear. When I awoke, she startled me, causing me to fall to the sharp rocks below where I was knocked unconscious with a head wound. When I came around, she was gone. I was healed and the cake was gone. Unbeknown to me, she'd taken the cake back into the Hive to remember me by. Poor girl, she was so lonely."

Scotty held out his arms as Echo tugged on his smock. He swooped down and raised her high in the air.

"Yes, girl. This cake is for you. It's a celebration for you and me." He paused as if listening. "To celebrate the day you saved my life. You're the guest of honor tonight." The crowd broke out in a show of applause as Echo preened in Scotty's arms, clapping her hands together in delight.

Voices from the crowd shouted their best wishes for the strange little creature they had come to love and respect.

"What'd she say?" A question from the crowd.

Scotty gave a snort and rubbed his temple. "She says, *CAKE!*"

As the cake was distributed, Emma watched with envy. Echo touched Scotty's face with her finger. They stared into one other's mesmerizing eyes and spoke their special language. Then he tossed the creature in the air again to catch her and hold her tight. Echo turned to wave a leather hand to the crowd then threw her arms back around Scotty's neck. Lucky Scotty had everything *she* wanted: a girlfriend to share his love with, a buddy like none other in Echo. And Scotty was special: an Elder. Emma was beginning to understand what they meant when some said he was "The One."

She smiled inwardly at the memory of the skinny, young boy back on Lily Pond Road. When they'd all first come to live together, he'd been quite a sight with his impetigo scars and his crossed eyes. No one wanted to play with him in school, but he was still like a brother to her. *I don't know why he couldn't have fallen for me.* She glanced over at Abby and Jose, remembering how they'd all grown up in the same household. Sighing at her feelings of loneliness, she returned to the kitchen sink to help Karen and Crystal with the dishes.

*

Later that evening, as they all prepared for bed, Scotty waited for Chloe and Barney, and Echo took the opportunity to sneak onto his dais, curling up together at the end of the stone bed. Scotty smiled down on Echo as he felt the familiar aura gently stroking his mind.

"I am the guest of honor, is that not correct, Brother Scotty?"

Scotty nodded wondering where this was going.

"Have you ever been the guest of honor?"

Scotty nodded yes, thinking of the delight he'd had with the birthdays Abby and his mother had given him.

"Has My Barney ever been the guest of honor?"

Scotty laughed. "No, I don't think so."

"Does that mean My Barney has no honor now?" Echo's aura swirled.

Oh, boy. Scotty grimaced. He snapped his fingers, calling Barney to his side. Barney stood up and stepped toward Scotty then glanced back to Echo. Taking a few steps toward Scotty, he whined.

"Come on, Barney. It's okay." He reached out to sweep the white dog into his arms, holding him close. Barney gave his face a sloppy kiss with his rough tongue then craned his neck to turn back to Echo. Relenting, Scotty released him so he could run back to Echo and cuddle up next to his best buddy who promptly curled his lion-like tail around the sensitive dog for comfort.

"Echo, Barney *always* has honor. He is a fine, loving dog and an important part of our family."

The aura shifted in his mind. "Is Barney a guest?"

"No, silly. Neither of you are guests. You are family. Guest of honor is an expression that's used when it's your special day. When everyone is extra good to you."

"A family member can have a special day? What do they get that is special?" Echo's innocent aura quickened.

"Alright, Echo. Spit it out. What are you getting at?"

Echo stood and clasped her leather hands together. "I want my special wish. I want what I wanted when you were eight years old. I want what I always wanted."

Scotty rocked back on the dais, feeling the desperation of Echo's aura. Concerned, he carefully measured his words. "Echo, I love you. I would do anything for you. You *know* you can tell me anything."

Echo's aura brightened. "*Anything?*"

"Yes, silly. Of course." No sooner had his lips stopped moving than Echo and Barney bounced their way up to him, throwing themselves against his chest, then making a great fuss looking for a spot on the dais that brought them snuggly up against him, just like it used to be.

"What are you doing, girl?" Scotty watched the twosome; joy in his heart and over-spilling with love.

Chloe chose this moment to enter the room. "Oh, *no*. Hey, you two. Get down."

Echo's aura rotated wildly in Scotty's mind sending shoots out to Chloe, her fur raised and glistening as the mysterious light in the Hive dimmed, signaling the beginning of the survivors' healing sleep.

"I am family guest of honor. It is *my* time, Sister Chloe. You can go sleep somewhere else. I choose to sleep with my Brother tonight to commemorate. It is what I wanted to do when he was eight, and what Barney and I did when we all lived together, before *you*. You have made Brother Scotty not want us the same. Tonight he will want us the same. *Go away*." With that, Echo and Barney turned their backs to Chloe and shut their eyes, leaving Scotty and his astonished girlfriend with their mouths hanging open.

Chloe gave Scotty her evil eye, jettisoning her thumb in the air toward the doorway. Mouthing the words and pressing his hands together to beg, he conveyed a silent message to her.

She stood with her hands on her hips. "*No*. Absolutely not."

Again he mouthed the words *please, just for tonight*. Sighing, she relented. "This is for you, birthday boy." Coming close to the bed, she leaned in for a kiss from Scotty, her lips cool and tight with annoyance. Barney turned to give her a quick tongue flick as Echo turned to watch her every move. Scotty mouthed, *thank you* and kissed her back, knowing there'd be hell to pay in the morning.

After Chloe left the darkening cavern to locate another dais, Scotty rolled over to relax, his day full and draining. His mind closed down, his gentle journey into slumber well underway.

Echo's aura pricked at his unconscious mind. "I will be patient, Brother Scotty. She will not live forever."

Seth had a plan. Observing Clyde from under his eyelids, he pretended to sleep. He watched as the man tenderly stroked his granddaughter's face, holding fast to her hand.

"Good night, baby girl. Please come back to me." He turned to Lorna, to kiss her goodnight. "My wonderful love. I knew you wouldn't fail to get here. I'm so sorry I doubted. Never again. Promise." He straightened his tall body up to glance at Seth and whisper a goodbye.

"Goodnight, my special friend. You'll never understand the extent of my debt to you. I praise the Lord for bringing you to our door." And with that, as the light settled seductively into dusk, he took his leave.

Shhheesh . . . Thank the Devil the dumbass is gone. Springing up quickly before he could be tempted to sleep, he approached Lorna. *Soon, you old miserable bitch, soon.* He reached out to squeeze Lorna's pale scab-covered cheeks painfully between his fingers. She made no movement. *You're lucky or I'd have to do it now.*

He watched her pitiful chest rise and fall with each breath she took. Her breath sounds were smooth and hitch free. An improvement. He backed away from the abhorrent viscous webs that fed her. His time was drawing close. He calculated he had maybe a week or two before her health improved enough to be apparent to the others. A sudden death at that point would be too risky. *Soon*, he thought as he directed malignant thoughts to the vulnerable Lorna.

That would leave the delectable Jennifer to worry about. Pondering the likelihood of controlling the pre-teen through intimidation, he acknowledged the probability she would blab all to her grandfather. He had no way of knowing how much she would actually remember. The possibility existed that she'd recall nothing.

Slapping the palm of his hand rhythmically into the side of his thigh, he cast about for a plan. *Hmm . . . Clyde. Yes. He's the answer. If Clyde wasn't here, she'd have no one to confide in.* She'd be easy to control if he were the only familiar sight in this nightmare. Slowly, the makings of a plan emerged in his reptilian brain.

He must search the Hive for the perfect location. As of yet, the topography shown to him would not lend itself to his plan. He crept to the doorway, casting a last glance at the two women. As far as he knew, no one ever mentioned checking on the women in the night. He listened carefully to the silence in the cavern hallway. To his surprise, he detected movement. Quiet and steady.

Peering around the cavern wall, careful not to touch it, he froze as Tobi and her herd swept by, swift and silent. *What the hell are they up to?* Letting them pass, he eased his frame silently around the wall and into the corridor, just catching a glimpse of the hind end of the herd. Letting them run far enough ahead so he could avoid detection but not lose sight of them, he decided to follow.

An hour later, he considered giving up as the herd continued their march. The rare pile of drying dung indicated their journey was a familiar one. *It can't be for water* he realized, remembering how he tried to evade the almost mature piglets and their antics with the herd at the elephant baths.

Every time he saw the pigs he was reminded of greasy pork and bacon. Who knew the animals were off limits for eating? *Stupid ass rules if you ask me.* His face burned with the memory of the snot-nosed punk Scotty lecturing him at dinner. If he didn't have those wings and scary eyes and that damn tiger and the creepy little yellow monstrosity dogging him everywhere, he'd take care of Scotty the best way he knew. Nothing like a few broken bones and missing fingers to clean up a smart mouth.

Seth continued his furtive trek behind Tobi and the herd; the silence in the cavern corridors oppressive and the vaguely organic tang in the air contributing to his unease. After almost two hours and numerous warring decisions to turn back or go on, Seth came to a large boulder. Dead end. No herd.

Creeping cautiously behind the boulder, he came upon an opening large enough for Tobi. Peering into the dimly lit unknown beyond the boulder, he surmised the herd had gone in and disappeared. Approaching the opening with great trepidation , his eyes adjusted to the dusk.

Creeping in slowly, a split trail revealed itself. Choosing the one to the right, he felt the trail rise. Before long he had reached the zenith.

"Holy shit!" Seth's eyes bugged out as he took in the grandeur before him. The trail fell off a cliff with the ceiling continuing to rise. The cathedral must have been another twenty stories high with the far wall at least two football fields long.

Peering over the edge, he was struck with a case of vertigo. The drop to the floor was unfathomable. Enormous boulders and stalagmites appeared as child's toys. Seth noticed that the wall and distant floor shimmered with a faint golden material not easily detected in the low light. As he concentrated on it, he thought he sensed movement. Dismissing the effect as a trick of the poor lighting, he moved back from the edge and sat down on the hard rock ground.

Slowly, he panned the cavern, scouting for a trace of Tobi and her herd. From his position on the floor, he almost missed the evidence of the trail that had gone to the left as it rose higher in the cavern, looking down at him. *Hmm, that must be where they went.* Focusing back on his immediate surroundings, he had an epiphany. The cavern would play beautifully into his plan for Clyde. *Just can't keep me down.* He giggled manically; a familiar, telltale warmth suffusing his loins. Rising, he stuffed his hands in his tunic pockets, stole a last satisfied gander at his new discovery, and began the long walk back to his sleeping room, a tuneless hum on his lips and a gleam of insanity in his eyes.

Preoccupied with his exciting plans, Seth failed to notice the huge, ghostly gray shadow that flitted quickly down the trail, a wise unblinking eye keeping him within sight.

Chapter 10

Emma sat morosely at the edge of the warm pool in the bathing cave. Tendrils of fog floated on the surface, rising with the warm air, failing to obscure the sight of Chloe, Scotty, Kane and Kenya as they entered the water. In the other direction some of the keepers, Johno and Crystal, Cobby and Karen and Billy and Gloria washed up and socialized in the volcanic water, serving to make her even more miserable, hating the happy couples.

Caesar, the imposing tiger, paced near the water's edge, Echo riding his back as if she sat on a personal chariot. Barney romped at Caesar's huge feet. It was clear Caesar wanted to join the fun in the pool, but he wasn't allowed. Everyone had decided his massive size could inadvertently hurt someone during the horseplay. So he paced at the water's edge, laser eyes following Scotty's every move as he frolicked with Chloe.

Barely a week had passed since Scotty's birthday and Emma's aborted attempt to speak to Kane about their relationship. Trying to combine her ultimatum with a chance to show Kane how much she loved him would always fail. She couldn't help it. She just lost track of her senses when she was alone with him.

Thinking of him inside her made her dizzy with longing and resentment. She speared Kenya with a withering look. Not much good that would do with the foursome bathing, their backs to her.

She couldn't help but compare herself to Kenya, who was only a year or so younger. She watched as Kane helped her to steady herself as she stood in the knee-deep water, her long perfect legs and her slender frame belying the fact that she was almost fifteen months pregnant. She gritted her teeth as Kane casually wrapped his arm around her shoulders and suddenly lifted her off her feet amid her shrieks of laughter, setting her down again, cradling her on his lap, and allowing the water to support her weight. Her lush walnut hair floated down her back, spreading wide in the water and showcasing her natural curls.

"Don't you dare drop me, chickey boy," Kenya squealed. Emma cringed as Kenya tipped her still-sculptured caramel face and mouthwatering lips to receive a smooch from—*My man, goddamn it. My man!*

It didn't help matters for Emma that Chloe was giving her the cold shoulder. That's what she got for sticking up for Scotty.

Chloe had been bitching for days about the inconvenience of having Echo and Barney around when they slept. All of the other dogs, including Chloe's own Teddy, along with Chance, the pig that everyone spoiled, had been firmly relegated to Netty's kitchen to sleep in an assortment of beds near the fireplace. The dogs didn't object. They enjoyed being together with the pitties, King and Queenie. God knew Teddy followed wherever Penny the springer went. He liked to keep his tiny, beady eyes on those ears of hers, guarding them jealously from imagined rivals.

When it had been Emma's turn to deliver lunch to the growing fields, she'd walked in on a heated Chloe whining to Scotty as he tried to play with Echo and Barney on his break. *I don't know what he sees in her.* Sticking up for her almost-brother, she pointedly remarked, "For Pete's sake, can you please just get off his back with this?"

Scotty shot her a wink while they waited for the bomb to drop. Chloe opened her mouth to speak then promptly turned away, walking down to the row of plants she'd been weeding . . . with the help of Baby, no less. And she hadn't spoken to her since. Emma sighed, wondering if things could get any worse.

Suddenly, a running figure splashed by her with a frightful shallow dive into the deeper water. A cunning smile curved her lips as she realized it was Seth. And he sure looked good. Netty's stellar meals had put important weight back on his weakened frame. His hair had come in completely dark brown, thick and curly, making his blue eyes pop, transforming a somewhat mild presence into a seductive charmer when he smiled that big wide smile.

Hmm, too bad that missing tooth on the side hasn't come back in.

She recalled Lorna's teeth were *mostly* missing so Seth was ahead of the game. Maybe when he was healed completely it would come back just like his ear had. Time would tell.

"Emma . . . hey, Emma." Seth's voice floated over the water causing the foursome to glance her way.

Spying Kane watching her, she stood and removed her robe to expose the tiny triangles of cloth she tried to call a bathing suit, revealing her firm, lush curves.

Taking off at a seductive lunge, she forged into the water and paddled out to meet Seth. Breathing heavily when she arrived, her chest heaved.

"Here, let me help while you catch your breath." Seth held out his arms. She glanced behind, trying to make out the outlines of the foursome in the wisps of mist. Hoping Kane could see, she glided slowly toward Seth's outstretched arms.

He pulled her close, easing them further from shore until they were obscured from sight by a stalagmite. Shadows danced like lovers, casting an intimate beauty enhanced by the glimmer of the many iridescent mineral and rough jeweled stones embedded in the age-old fossilized rock.

"Wow, this is beautiful back here." She felt dizzy from the effects of the minerals, holding tighter to Seth and boldly wrapping her legs around his waist to steady herself. Turning to him, she met his blue eyes which stared deeply into hers as if he were reading her soul.

"You deserve all of this. You're even more gorgeous than this natural beauty."

Seth's thumb began to stroke her back as he slipped his arms around to support her. She gave him her sweetest smile. His right hand moved slowly down her back pressing her into him where she could feel his erection.

Ignoring Seth's soft groan, she distractedly craned her neck to see if Kane was watching. She could feel Seth's hand crawl toward her breast as she realized there was no way Kane could possibly see her. She must direct Seth closer to shore and out of some of this damn mist.

Unwrapping her legs from around his waist, she felt him catch her foot.

"Where you going, Emma?"

She threw him a tight smile as she squinted through the mist.

"Let's move to a better spot, Seth."

His face fell, all expression gone. His voice raised an octave, demanding her attention. She searched his face trying to figure out what was wrong.

"I like this spot."

"Yeah, well, I can't see the shoreline and we shouldn't be out this far."

"I like this spot." At his monotone repetition, she felt an eerie warning in her stomach. Like a small evil snake waking and uncurling. She hadn't felt that way since the night they'd run to the woods from their old house on Lily Pond Road. The very night they'd entered the Hive, the second bomb yapping at their heels.

"Eh, Seth, I'm going to head back now and join my friends."

She felt him place her foot between his legs, wedging it in tight. His finger began to move back to her breast as he remarked, "They aren't your friends, Emma. You don't have any friends. Just me. You have me. I'm all you need . . . let me show you."

She felt paralyzed as his lips landed on her neck, sucking and licking as they traveled down to the breast his hand had managed to liberate.

She felt a sobering shock course through her body as his lips found the taut nipple on her breast. *Taut from fear.*

With all her might, she shoved him away from her, accomplishing nothing as her foot remained trapped between his legs. Pulling back the flat of her hand she shot it forward, landing on his nose as she screamed, *"What the hell do you think you're doing?"* Her face drained of color as she watched the blood stream from his nose, while Seth acted as if nothing had happened.

"I know you want this, Emma. I've known for a long time." He pulled her roughly back against his erection. "Feel how I want you? This is what you want, don't you?"

Emma went limp with shock as he ground his erection into her pelvis, his fingers busy trying to remove her bathing suit.

"I'm going to give it to you like a man does." His lips crushed down on hers, his fingers grabbing her wisp of a suit. "Not like that boy you taunt. Have you fucked him yet?" His lips bore down again, robbing her of all breath or thought. "Have you? Have you fucked him?"

Gasping for air, she realized Seth was going to rape her. He pursed his lips and whispered in her ear. "You can't fool me, babe. You want it as much as I do." He pawed at her exposed breast, holding her locked between his legs, blood leaking over her chest as she felt her bathing suit give. His hand trapped her arms behind her back, thrusting her breast at him. Inflamed, he licked her ear as he fumbled with his other hand under the water to free his bulging erection.

"Tell me you *want* it, Emma. *Tell me now!*" He groaned pitifully as his erection pressed into her. With all her strength, she screamed, freeing a hand that swung around in a fist to land again on his injured nose. She heard a crunch. Seth recoiled in pain, holding his nose and releasing her.

She could hear scattered voices from the shore. Scotty called her name.

"Well, my little *bitch*. You're going to be damn sorry you did that. I'm going to have to teach you a lesson now." His hand shot out like a whip, catching her by the hair. He slapped her hard across the face, stars and pain unable to block the sound of Scotty's voice getting closer. As she blinked, Seth drew her near, his voice calm again, a frightening contrast to his depraved pronouncement.

"You better keep your trap shut, little girl. I might just have to tell your mommy what a tramp you are. Then I'm going to come find you and slice off those little titties you're so proud of. Hear me?"

She could feel the blood drain from her face as she watched the sickness surface in the blue eyes she had found so attractive. Then he sank quietly under the water, disappearing as Scotty's voice and splashing warned her of his approach.

Panic had a reverse effect on her. She calmed. Gathering her wits, she knew she could never face anyone again if they discovered what had happened. She splashed at the blood on her chest, washing it away. Grasping her suit that dangled from one leg, she hurriedly struggled to get her other foot inside, the water a hindrance. *Oh, my God, oh my God. Did he really say that?* Her heart tripped faster as she wondered at the ramifications of a nutjob loose in the Hive. All her plans with Kane would go up in smoke. *Will anyone believe me? Will they feel sorry for me? Will they blame me?* Her head began to spin with the possible fallout. She remembered the talk her mama had with her months ago after the Elias incident.

"No," she moaned. She couldn't bring this shame and disappointment down on her mama. Not when she was just learning to deal with her own disappointment over Clyde and his wife. She let out a sob as she felt the swelling on the side of her face where Seth had clocked her.

"Emma, can you please answer me?" Scotty shouted.

She finished fumbling with her suit, took a deep breath as she stifled a sob and called out numbly, "Here, Scotty. I'm over here." The splashing got closer as Scotty came into focus, his wings dripping wet and weighing him down.

"For gosh sakes, Emma. Didn't you hear me? What's wrong?" He swam over to her, concern on his familiar and dear face. She threw herself into his big arms, the sudden comfort bringing on uncontrollable shakes.

"Hey, hey there. What's wrong, Emma?" He looked around the water. "Where's Seth?"

Emma scrunched her eyes tight, still clinging to Scotty and forcing her tremors to abate with prayers. *Oh Lord, I promise to be a good girl. I can do it. I'll leave Kane alone and stay away from sex until I'm twenty one. Please, please . . . I promise.*

Scotty held her in the water, silently waiting for her to calm down and speak. Emma opened her eyes.

"Ahem . . . a . . . Seth . . . yes. Well, he's not here," she said as brightly as she could to mask the tears that threatened to undo her.

"What do you mean, he's not here? We saw you swim out here after him." He touched the side of her face. She winced, unable to cover her reaction to the pain.

"Did you hurt yourself?"

"Yes, yes. Eh, I tried to climb the stalagmite. I know . . . stupid, huh?"

Scotty studied her face, touching the tender skin as she flinched. "But it's not scraped. Just a bad bruise. I can't imagine how you managed to do this." He shook his head. "When are you going to start taking things seriously?" He took her arm as he guided her towards the shore. "You need to get a cold compress on that. You're going to look like hell for a few days."

Emma gritted her teeth and remained silent, fighting the urge to bare all. Seth's unbelievable words rang in her ears. As she exited the water, Kane and Kenya drew near with Chloe. *I can't face them right now.* Bending down to pick up her things, she reeled from the rush of blood to her head, feeling a massive headache coming on.

"Scotty, I just want to go lie down for a while." She backed away, calling over her shoulder, "Tell Mama for me?" Holding in her trembling, she hurried to the privacy of the room she shared with Bonnie, whom she was positive would be flitting around Tobi and Chance somewhere.

Curling up on her stone dais, she lay there with her head spinning and throbbing with pain. All she could think about was how lonely she was, with no one to confide in. Vowing to reform her ways and spend more time with Bonnie, her mama and the animals, her consciousness deserted her, finally called by the siren of slumber.

Ginger Mae entered Netty's kitchen, clipboard in hand, finding it quiet with only a few survivors still in attendance after breakfast. She glanced over to the fireplace where Emma sat on the floor slowly stroking the elegant coat of Queenie the pit bull, her face stoic and drawn as her flat eyes focused on a spot in front of her lap. *Now what's got that child in such a mood?*

Reaching behind her back, she pulled her now shoulder-length russet hair securely to the top of her head. Only a few more months to go and she could shear the rest of the blond tips right off, although why she bothered to put her hair up was beyond her. She wondered how long it would take before Tobi or one of the other elephants tugged it down with their playful trunks. Or the camels. They loved to sneak up behind her and chew on her hair. She couldn't be sure if it was play, boredom, or just a fascination with her hair; their big eyes and ebony lips always reflecting a fixed expression of contentment.

Sweeping her eyes around the comfortable room, she spotted Gloria with a colorful rag rug on her lap doing a repair, as Billy and Tucker discussed the morning distribution of food to the creatures of the Hive.

Nodding to a busy but quiet Salina, she guessed the worried, sick expression on her dour face had something to do with either Emma or Clyde. *Poor Salina. Can't she ever catch a break?*

Hurrying over to a table in the back of the room where Abby and Netty awaited their meeting with her, she wondered what could be up. Maybe a change in her duties? She prayed it wasn't that. Her days were full of joy and laughter as she continued to develop an abiding love for the creatures she counted daily. She honestly felt she could survive anything as long as she could share their company.

As her love for the creatures deepened, she began to understand why the Womb was fed up with the human race. The guileless innocence of her counted creatures never failed to charm and astonish her. She cringed with the memory of the many that had been abused, eaten and discarded like rubbish by the very people who should have known better. *Man preaches humanity while practicing the inhumane.*

As she approached the table of the glowing Elder women, she studied the elderly primate that was sitting cuddled in Abby's lap. The white-faced monkey now wore diapers fashioned from cloth supplied by Netty. The monkeys had the freedom to roam as they pleased and spent most of their time in the growing fields. But this female had become attached to the attention and affection she desperately hungered for and rarely received, having spent most of her entire life in a small iron cage. She could usually be found near an Elder, begging for affection, Jose being her favorite.

"Thanks for coming, Ginger Mae." Abby smiled as she pulled out a chair. Ginger Mae's finger rose to rub at her temples, feeling the sporadic aura she sometimes felt, heralding the presence of Baby or Echo. Peering behind Netty's skirts, she located a lurking Baby whose larger frame and more solemn demeanor made him easier to distinguish than Echo.

"Hello, Baby. Are you trying to talk to me?" Ginger Mae squatted down to Baby's level, only to have the enigmatic creature turn his head away in indifference.

"Humm." She rose from the floor, miffed and curious about the rejection. Maybe Baby was jealous of the attention Echo had received over a week ago during Scotty's birthday.

"Don't be concerned, Ginger Mae. If Baby didn't like you he would never cast his aura to you. He just isn't ready to engage fully yet."

Ginger Mae sat in the proffered chair. Netty and Abby exchanged unreadable glances.

"What's this all about, ladies?" She remained perplexed as she tried to interpret their expressions. Netty took the lead with a subtle nod from Abby. Reaching out to Ginger Mae, she covered her hand with her own and leaned in, her voice soft and oddly beseeching.

"My dear, I hope you understand how fond of Daisy we all are. She is an exceptional child and it has been a pleasure to work with her."

Ginger Mae felt the first stirrings of alarm. "Daisy? What do you *mean* work with her? She's just fooling around in the library. What's this about, Netty?" Her head bobbed from Netty to Abby, unnerved by their silence. "Do you mind telling me exactly what's going on here? She is *my* child after all." The resentment she thought had long gone regarding Daisy's attachment to Abby, resurfaced now.

Abby spoke up. "Yes, of course she is. That's why we're here. We need your consent."

Slowly, as the feeling in the pit of her stomach accelerated, she responded firmly, "My consent for *what*?"

Abby looked down at the table, not meeting Ginger Mae's eyes.

"Okay, just what the heck is going on here?" Ginger Mae felt a spasm of fear. Sending her chair careening backward, she stood abruptly and turned to leave. Catching her arm, Netty forced her back gently into her righted chair.

"Okay . . . I'm going to give it to you straight. Daisy is fine, by the way." Taking a deep breath she began. "We became aware of Daisy and her special *capabilities* when you visited Peter's home in Sarasota."

"You were there?" Ginger Mae frowned.

"No, actually we were able to *see* you through Abby. Anything she viewed, touched, smelled or felt was transmitted to us. We had the capability to interpret the data in such a manner that we actually saw *into* Daisy. You remember Abby's implants?"

Ginger Mae nodded her agreement.

Continuing, Netty dipped her head in time with her speech, a smile of deep pleasure possessing her features. "The Womb had never encountered a child such as Daisy. Her mind is . . ." Netty swept her arm, her gesture wide and encompassing. "Remarkable."

Ginger Mae relaxed, but stayed on her guard, speaking defensively. "We all know that. She reads well beyond her years. Beyond my years."

Abby chimed in very softly, "Beyond all of our years."

Ginger Mae felt the fear return with the look of awe on Abby's face.

Netty reached out again. "My dear, Daisy has not been 'fooling around' as you put it. She has been studying."

"Well, yeah, I assumed she was doing some studying around all those books. She loves books."

"She has been studying more than books. Or should I say books written by man." Netty ignored the puzzlement on Ginger Mae's face and continued. "She has been studying the language of different cultures."

Ginger Mae's confusion turned to annoyance. "What's the big deal? Yeah, she's an extraordinarily bright child. I think it's nice she's learning other languages. She can practice her Spanish right here with the Diaz clan."

Netty and Abby exchanged pregnant glances. Trying again, Netty changed the subject. "What kind of future do you think your daughter has, Ginger Mae? Let me give you a glimpse into her future as you now know the facts.

"Eventually, you will all leave the Hive. You will be forced to start your lives on unfamiliar territory with new and unfamiliar creatures. You will all be required to scrabble for shelter, locate water, and find food. You will need to farm just as we do here. My seeds will be of a great help to you, of course, but there will be no doctors, no drug stores, no automobiles, and no electricity for quite some time. It may be years until you figure it out. And what of a mate for your daughter? Her choices are limited, not that she won't *have* choices. But will she be fulfilled with them? Where will she find an equal? A mind is a great thing to waste. Is that not an expression in our formerly civilized world? Yes, formerly. How long do you think you can rely on the benevolent nature of your fellow survivors? There will be conflicts. There will be an absence of law." She paused for breath. "Is that what you plan to bring this extraordinary and fragile child into?"

Ginger Mae listened, overwhelmed by the canvas Netty painted. She responded slowly, "I'm well aware of the difficulties we may encounter. But what choice will we have? I'm just happy enough we're all still alive."

Netty resumed, nodding her head. "Has it occurred to you that the life you may encounter will come from other planets?"

Silence.

"Well, why in the world would that be?"

Netty's glowing eyes turned frigid. "Well, what do you expect to happen to this planet after the poisons of man are gone? Will the Womb just turn it back over to man? The Womb made plans for this Earth long before you survivors came into the picture. You will not recognize your planet in a century. Someone will be needed to communicate with other life. We will have no more conflict. We must guarantee that you survivors will adapt peacefully . . . through communication. Or the planet can do without you."

Ginger Mae felt a stirring of emotions. *Is that a threat?* "Well, that's all very interesting. So we'll *learn* to do all those things and adapt."

"No, Ginger Mae, you don't understand. Daisy is learning to *understand.* She is learning to communicate beyond what you know and are . . ." Netty paused, searching for a word, ". . .*comfortable* with."

"Okay . . . I still don't know what you're asking of me. Or of Daisy." Ginger Mae squirmed, uncomfortable with the conversation. Changing direction, Netty and Abby passed a signal between themselves, rising together. They each took a hand, prompting Ginger Mae to rise. She felt a tug at her hem. Glancing down, she discovered Baby holding his hands out to be lifted up. Holding his hands out to *her.* Disengaging from Netty and Abby, she raised him up to sit on her hip. Netty suppressed a smile.

"Come with us, Ginger Mae. Let us show you something." The three women left the kitchen after Abby handed off the elderly monkey to Emma, who was still holed up moodily with Queenie at the fireplace.

Out in the corridor, Ginger Mae asked, "Where are we going?"

They answered together.

"To the library."

Ginger Mae had been very curious about the library for a long time. Many of the survivors had worked there, taking their turn at cleaning up what had been reported as a shambles. The dirty, messy part had stopped just a few months ago as she noticed Daisy no longer returned for dinner covered in filth. *How and why in the world would anyone put a library down here?* Ginger Mae kept her mouth shut.

As if reading her mind, Netty said, "This library was brought here by the Womb. It was accomplished at the last minute after becoming aware of the number of people Abby planned to bring here." She turned to smile at Ginger Mae. "How can you begin a new foundation for a fledgling community without books? They were my most treasured possessions when I was a child. I remember my mama . . ." Sighing, Netty shook her head, forcing herself out of her reverie.

They walked for about forty minutes, the monotonous corridor walls the same as the rest of the Hive, vaguely organic with sinuous membranes everywhere. As they cleared a sharp bend, Ginger Mae noted the sudden absence of membranes, the corridor widening and spreading out. From the far side of the expanding space, she could see dark wood paneling.

As they crossed the wide, open room, the three women found themselves dwarfed by a magnificent rosewood Renaissance revival banquette polished to a deep luster. Abby ran her hands over the top of the gargantuan and valuable piece of furniture, her face prideful, stroking her finger over the round red, white and blue seal that hung down the front.

"We worked so hard repairing this. But it was an absolute imperative." She turned back to the other two women, her eyes shining brighter. "You can see that, can't you Ginger Mae? It's the only treasure we have left intact from our old past."

Ginger Mae approached the magnificent library piece. Bending down, she squatted with Baby in her lap. Her hand caressed the seal reverently. Her eyes filled with unshed tears. "But how did it get here? I mean you can't just . . ."

Abby spoke with pride as she announced the simple truth. "Yes, the Womb *can*. If it can be reached anywhere on this planet from underground, the Womb can obtain it." She quickly sobered. "But no more. Everything is dust. Ruined." She shook her head as if to erase memories. "Come, let's go in and find Daisy."

As they passed the relic from their past, Ginger Mae gave one more sad, fleeting glance to the once proud seal of The United States of America, Library of Congress.

*

It took the three women an hour to find Daisy. Abby's apprehension grew as they passed through the racks and racks of no-longer dusty or dirty books from the Library of Congress. The air filled with the flat fragrance of old paper. She studied Ginger Mae, weighing her reaction, as they strolled around the stacks they had worked so hard to organize. The job had been monotonous and not difficult; if you discounted the enormity of the task.

Abby recalled the time she had first absorbed the shock after laying eyes on the mess: books and boulders everywhere. She had never been able to get a straight answer out of Netty or Wil about how the contents of the library had arrived here. But she knew it had something to do with the massive hole in the back of the library.

Jose had taken a few minutes to investigate it when it had been discovered by one of the truckers who had helped with the initial debris removal. Tucker had come to them covered in fine ash and dirt. They'd just been sorting the important fictional classics from the eclectic mix of zombie/vampire/sci-fi/romance that everybody and their mother's dog had decided to pen at the beginning of the e-book revolution in 2005. Unfortunately, any electronically published books were lost to history unless the authors had taken the time and huge amounts of money to create what had been known as paperbacks. Eventually, with the advances in electronic devices for reading, over the decades the little gems called paperbacks had ceased to exist. Abby had praised the Lord rather ruefully as she'd eyeballed the enormity of the mound of books left to sort. Conversely, they may not be important now but, over time, the survivors might be grateful to have access to such satisfying entertainment.

"You two want to take a look at something?" Tucker had been breathing heavily and rivulets of sweat had left clear tracks down his flushed face and scrawny neck. Following him to the back of the cavern, they had stared, stupefied, at an enormous hole.

"After clearing enough books and debris to make it back here, this is what I found."

The hole had been as wide as one of the Mack trucks that had delivered them to Lily Pond Road. Rocks and books had lain strewn everywhere as if left behind as an afterthought. They'd approached the opening; a faint hint of sulfur in the air. Abby had wrinkled her nose as she'd touched the hard, almost burnt wall of the hole.

"It looks like it was man-made."

"Why do you say that, Jose?"

"It's too regular. The walls have been compacted under some kind of extreme pressure." Jose had stood with Abby as they'd taken a step into the dark hole.

A curious feeling of fright had overcome Abby. "No, let's not go in there. It's obvious the library came in this way." She had scanned the debris behind them. "It looks almost like the books were pushed by some ungodly giant and just dumped here. I don't like the looks of this tunnel and we need to get back to work." Pulling on Jose's wing, she had nodded to Tucker and gone back to the job at hand. "If I see Wil, I'm going to ask him for an explanation. Why don't you come help us, Tucker? Let's stay away from here until we know what it is."

Abby never did get a chance to ask Wil about the massive hole, for Netty had sought her out the next day at breakfast as they'd prepared to head back to the library, changing everything.

"Would you mind working on a special project with me, my dear?"

Abby had glowed brighter. "I'd be honored, Netty."

Netty's satisfied expression had held an exciting note of wonder. "It's time we begin to teach you a few things. After all, once we are free from the Hive, you need to be ready."

Abby's nerves had quickened as she'd felt a fateful turn in her life was upon her with Netty's ambiguous words.

Surprisingly, Netty had led her back to the back of the library where they'd discovered the huge hole. She'd quaked with astonishment as Netty had indicated a spotless iron wall with a human-sized door offering a thick glass window into the hole. As Abby had approached the window, she'd detected a glow that had thrown off a pastel pink radiance behind the door.

"But . . . Netty, this can't be. This wasn't here yesterday. We . . ."

Netty's finger had risen to her lips, eyes glowing richly, and with a strange smile tinged with a faint hint of sadness.

"Shhh, I'm going to show you. This is *just* the beginning for you." With that, Netty had taken a large, dull key from around her neck, inserted it in the door and swung it open to be confronted with the visage of Baby waiting for them inside what was clearly no longer a tunnel.

That had been months ago, and progress on their project had been slow but fruitful. *Thanks to Daisy.* Now, without Ginger Mae's consent, they might be forced to accept that no further progress would be possible. Bringing her thoughts back to the present, Abby quickened after the other two women.

As they approached the back of the library with Ginger Mae, Baby slipped down off her hip, scuttling away. Ginger Mae asked, "So where's Daisy?"

Netty stopped, turning to face Daisy's mother. "I want you to know, I would never, ever put your remarkable child in any kind of danger. Do you trust me?"

Abby watched a panoply of emotions play across Ginger Mae's face: surprise, distrust, confusion and terror. She reached out quickly to grasp Ginger Mae's hands for reassurance.

"I don't think I like the sound of what you just said, Netty."

Abby could feel Ginger Mae's hand tighten and tremble with tension. "Please keep an open mind, Ginger Mae. This is important."

"My daughter is *always* important to me."

As she trembled, they pulled Ginger Mae around to the back side of the library to face the steel door and watched as her face drained of color.

"What . . . what's going on here? Where's my daughter?" Ginger Mae's voice slid out in whispers. "What is this?"

Netty took a key from around her neck to insert in the door. "This is where your daughter works. This is where she studies." Netty stepped aside to let her enter.

The three women stood together after crossing the threshold.

They gave Ginger Mae plenty of time to digest the incomprehensible vignettes of artifacts collected from around the cosmos. All were protected by sheets of shimmering laser light of rose and amber that emanated from devices attached to the walls. Around the devices flowed a thick coasting of the viscous substance that lined their cavern walls. But this material flowed thickly; ever moving and undulating. Encouraging Ginger Mae closer, Abby directed her to inspect the displays.

Objects of various unidentifiable composition sat on sphere-shaped supports, rising from the rocky ground to be enshrined in the light. Abby still knew very little about where the objects were from, but she knew full well what their awesome purpose was. The objects ranged from tiny to enormous. Some appeared to be transparent, some impervious, some exhibiting movement with flickering characters appearing on the sheets of colored light.

With a smile, Abby beckoned Ginger Mae forward toward one of the flickering objects. Netty stayed off to the side, anxiously searching Ginger Mae's face as she reacted to the foreign objects.

"What is this place? What are these . . . things? Are they for us?"

Abby nodded gravely. "Yes, Ginger Mae. These things are for us. Some of us."

Ginger Mae glanced up at the change in Abby's tone. "What do you mean some of us? And where's Daisy? You said she'd be here."

"She is here. She's studying."

Ginger Mae's eyes narrowed as she pursed her lips. "Pretty strange place for Daisy to be studying. Why does she need to be locked up with all of this stuff? Why don't we go get her, *now*?"

Abby sensed the impatience in Ginger Mae's voice. They couldn't risk alienating her right off the bat, so she turned back to the exhibits. "Here, look." Abby stepped up to an exhibit. Tugging on Ginger Mae, she prompted her forward.

Behind the colored sheet of laser light, there was a tube that protruded from the wall with a wide end facing them. The tube end swirled with red and blue colors with black squiggles. The wall was thick with undulating membrane.

Ginger Mae turned to Netty. "What's this supposed to be?"

Netty came close, her hands clasped behind her back, wings smoothed down gracefully. "It's a book."

"A book? It doesn't look like any book I've seen before."

"That is correct, Ginger Mae. That's because it is not from Earth."

"You gotta be kidding me. Where the heck is it from then?"

Abby's excitement streamed through her voice as she gave Ginger Mae the information she needed to make a fateful decision. Sweeping her hand to encompass all of the vignettes, she began. "These are all books. They are from different planets, different galaxies. Our galaxy, the Milky Way, has over one hundred billion stars. Did you know that? Planets of all composition such as ours, Earth, revolve around the stars." She nodded her head at a blank Ginger Mae. "Did you know our galaxy is over twelve billion years old? How about if I told you our galaxy was just an acorn compared to other galaxies? Ginger Mae, there are over two hundred billion *galaxies* in just *our* universe. We have enjoyed the height of hubris to believe our race was the only life in existence."

Abby strolled around the room like a child who has just been told she can stay up all night and watch her daddy make candy for Santa Claus and his reindeer. She pointed at the sheets of laser light, her cheeks flushed, and her tail twitched in unison with her exclamations. "Do you understand the ramifications? Did you *get* it when we were told months ago that ours was the six thousand, six hundred and ninth intervention by the Womb and the minions? That means the other interventions were on other planets. Planets with life! Can you possibly imagine the adventure waiting out there for us? All we need to do is *grab* at it." Abby turned to face Ginger Mae, watching her struggle to find words.

"Well, that's nice and all, but sorry, I'm not going anywhere. You do what you need to do. I like it just fine here with the animals and my daughter. Now, where is she?"

Crestfallen, Abby walked toward a small door in the wall of membrane.

Netty joined her and placed her hand on the knob. "Daisy is

inside studying. She has been learning languages from life in other galaxies. The wondrous and unique quality of your daughter's brain, never before encountered by any minion, allows her to solve the language complexities of any race. *Any race.*

"Let me explain the significance. It is an ability that the old Elders did not have. Nor the minions. The Womb does not communicate with life forms except for us and, for many reasons, does not travel well, except for the membrane that is merely an extension of the Great Womb. We have so much work to do. It is not always easy or efficient to rely on minions to communicate with foreign life forms using their auras. It is unsettling to many, to say the least. Not all life forms have a discernible brain to reach. Not all life forms are organic. But they *all* manage to communicate in one fashion or another. That's where Daisy comes in. We have yet to discover an existing form of communication that she cannot decipher."

Ginger Mae was stunned. "Oh, my God. She's that good?"

The pride on Ginger Mae's face gave Abby some hope. "Yes, she is *that good.* And she's getting better the more she learns. It's beyond our ability to understand how her brain functions. All language is based on metrics, or numbers. Sound is sound. Repetition is repetition. But not all language has sound. She is able to watch light images of other life—we call them books—and discern how they are communicating. She then learns the breakdown of their language."

Netty swung open the door. "Let us show you."

They walked into a small, dark room, the only illumination coming from the table on which Daisy lay. Her head was encased in a vaguely box-like structure that had a tube from one of the outside exhibits attached to the front where her eyes would face from inside the boxy structure. The container appeared to be supported by a thick column of membrane that ran from the wall of the room that was itself lined with viscous membrane.

Ginger Mae rocked nervously from foot to foot. "I . . . I don't like the looks of this. I guess she's safe. How long has she been doing this?" Abby and Netty remained silent. "You could have had the decency to discuss this with me first . . . but . . . I . . . guess it's okay."

From the tone of her voice, it was clear Ginger Mae wasn't sure. Netty guided them to a wooden bench in the middle of the floor. "Ginger Mae, we have brought you here to ask you permission to do a procedure on Daisy."

"A procedure? You mean an operation?"

Suddenly Baby appeared, startling them all. Ginger Mae cringed. "Where the heck did *he* come from?"

The golden creature approached Ginger Mae, staring directly into her face, his expression solemn. His finger reached out to trace down her forehead to her temple.

"Do you feel his aura probing your mind?"

"Yes, but he does that every once in a while. I thought he might like me and want to talk. But nothing yet."

Netty smiled fondly at the creature. "He is just attempting to understand how you produced such a wondrous offspring. On Oolaha, the minions are all born exactly the same, with the same abilities. To some extent, it is the same here on Earth. Many here are born with different abilities, but it is all within a constant measurable and quantifiable range. Until now."

"Yes, well, when he figures out how I did it, please let me in on it." Ginger Mae rose. "Meanwhile, I'm taking Daisy out of here." She waggled her fingers toward the table. "Please, get her off there. She's coming with me. There will be absolutely no discussion about an operation on my daughter. You have a lot of nerve to even think I would consent to anything of the kind."

As Ginger Mae left with a surprised Daisy, Baby shuffled behind them, trying to keep up. He swiveled his furry face back to Netty and Abby, waving and sending an aura to calm their disappointment.

"Do not fear, Sister Netty, Sister Abby. Sister Daisy will be back. Her mother will relent in *time*. We have much of that." The two visions of feminine beauty and other-worldliness clasped hands, praying that the little creature was correct.

Chapter 11

"Come on, Emma. I need your help." Salina's arms were overburdened with supplies she planned to take to Jennifer and Lorna. "Can you please pick up that bucket of hot water? It should still be warm when we get there. You can bathe one while I do the other."

"But Mama, I have to deliver lunch to the growing fields. And Bonnie's waiting for me."

"Well, she's just going to have to wait a little longer. Dezi is going to deliver lunch today. I need your help. Now let's go."

Shrugging disconsolately, Emma picked up the bucket of hot water to follow her mother to the sleeping quarters, grateful she'd spotted Clyde making off with Seth. She tried desperately to stay out of his way since the day in the bathing caves. So far, she'd been successful, but she dreaded every meal where the power of Seth's covert evil glances seared crystal clear messages into her nerves. Seth's eyes would follow her around the kitchen, causing her to drop dishes, spill hot tea and stumble. Most of the others had noticed, but laughed good naturedly.

Since the day at the caves, Emma had let her appearance go. She no longer brushed her hair in the morning or took pains with her toilet. She found she was too nerve-wracked to eat most of the time, her energy level eroding. She wondered how long she could keep this up. Maybe if she could talk to someone . . .

Salina bustled along at a good clip, Emma struggling to keep up while carrying her big bucket. Arriving at the sleeping caves, they entered the room where the two women lay on their stone dais, healing tendrils from the membrane walls still connected and working hard to bring them back from the brink of starvation and radiation poisoning. She set her bucket down to scoop warm water into the basin they would use to wash the two women. She looked up to see her mama staring down at Lorna.

"Mama?"

Salina glanced at her daughter, pity pouring from her eyes. "What this poor woman must have gone through. She deserves to pull through."

Emma dipped her sponge into the warm water and crossed to Jennifer, wondering if she could discuss Seth with her mother. She carefully sponged off the young girl's face.

"Mama . . . I've been wanting—"

"Emma, come here. Right now." Emma hurried over to her mother's side. She held Lorna's hand in hers, the few tendrils of membrane now thicker on the woman than Emma recalled.

"Look . . . her fingernails are longer. They aren't spilt and cracked like they used to be." Studying the healthy redness of her nail beds, they both searched for improvement in the older woman's face.

"Do you think her face looks fuller, Emma? I don't think she looks the same. She seems filled out. I think she just might make it after all, God bless her soul." Emma saw her mama wipe away a tear from her face, turning away from her daughter.

"I think we need Clyde to take a look. This is the news he's been waiting for. Can you go find him, hon? I'll wait here and finish up. Just leave your sponge in your basin. I'll finish Jennifer."

As Emma backed away from Lorna, she quickly turned to Jennifer. *What the heck?* Emma did a double take as she swore she saw Jennifer's eyes close. Leaning into the young girl, she examined her rosy face. The girl looked healthy. *Why hasn't she woken? Am I seeing things? Is my mind playing tricks on me?*

Her nerves shot, she turned to her mama again to talk. "Mama, I need to talk to you about something. Something that happened a few days ago."

Salina looked up. "I was wondering when you'd get around to this. I didn't want to pressure you, Emma. I knew you'd talk to me when you were ready. I didn't quite buy that explanation for the shiny bruiser you had there." She smiled encouragingly. "Can it wait until you find Clyde? We'll sit down and you can tell me all about it over some tea in the kitchen." Emma glanced down at Jennifer distractedly, and opened her mouth to speak just as Salina came over, holding her arms open for a hug.

"Now you run along. I'll finish up here while you find Clyde for me. Then I'm all yours."

With one last look at Jennifer, Emma kissed her mother and ran out the doorway, feeling the best she had in days.

Ginger Mae tallied her morning list of creatures. Everyone was accounted for except one of Tulip's babies. At this time of day, they usually congregated around their mother before setting out to find Tobi and the rest of the herd. She was positive she hadn't made a mistake. She never did, although today she'd started earlier than normal so she could spend some extra time with Daisy. Taking her along with her for the count hadn't worked. Daisy just wasn't as interested in the animals. She wanted to get back to the library and her studies. *Well, that's not going to happen.*

Ginger Mae still hadn't gotten over the temerity of those women asking for her permission to operate on Daisy. The disclosure of the kind of studies Daisy was immersed in was frightening in itself. What could Daisy possibly gain from learning their languages? It was a good thing she'd nipped *that* in the bud. Daisy would just have to find another interest to keep her busy. Maybe some arts and crafts. If she needed further education, Ginger Mae intended to handle it herself. It couldn't be that hard with all the books available in the library.

Forcing her mind back on the light count, she took another look at Tulip and the piglets. Still one missing. Sighing, she decided to enlist Dezi to help track it down. No sense in alarming everyone. The last thing she needed was dirty looks when they were forced to help find the piglet. When the little rascal turned up, she'd be left looking like a goat, just the way Dezi used to.

Arriving back at the kitchen, Dezi was nowhere to be found. Netty was washing vegetables and Karen was sorting dishes.

She approached Karen, anxious to keep the information from Netty. She didn't know Karen that well. She stuck like glue to Cobby whenever she found the chance, which was usually at meals when Ginger Mae had free time. She wondered idly if she might be jealous of the tall, pretty pilot. It must be easier to attract a man of substance with your brain than your breasts. *Nah*, she thought, laughing to herself . . . *that'll never happen.*

"Hi, Karen. I thought Dezi would be here."

"No, he left to deliver lunches. Salina needed Emma to help her with Clyde's wife and granddaughter. Why? What d' you need?"

"Well . . . I *think* I miscounted one of the piglets and wanted his advice, maybe some help to find it." Ginger Mae watched as Karen's face froze. She turned slowly to see Netty standing behind her.

"You can't find one of the piglets? Why didn't you report this to me immediately? You know the *rules*, Ginger Mae." She untied her apron, tossing it on the table. "Karen, round everyone up and have them meet us by the elephant's watering hole. The keepers and probably Bonnie and Peter will be there. I'll swing around and collect Salina and Emma. Dinner will just have to be late tonight."

As Emma searched for Clyde, she was astonished to find everyone seemed to have vanished. She checked the library and found not a soul. *That's odd.* Swinging back toward the kitchen, she peeked in the supply cavern. Empty as well. Rushing to the kitchen, she realized everyone must have decided to have lunch there. She must have been left out of the loop today when her mama dragged her away to help.

Arriving at the kitchen, she could see it was deserted except for the macaw that Abby and Scotty had rescued from the Big Cat Habitat in Sarasota. Not even a sign of any dogs or piglets. Nothing. She couldn't ever recall a time the place had been completely empty except when Dezi used to miscount an animal and they were all dragged out to help find it. Emma decided to go back to her mama in the sleeping caves. Something must be up and she would want to know about it as soon as possible.

Emma ran as fast as she could to the sleeping caves. Rounding the bend to the cave opening, she slowed to catch her breath. As she stepped through the opening to Lorna and Jennifer's quarters, she was astounded to find Seth bending over Lorna with his hands over her mouth and nose. She could see weak movement of Lorna's legs. Frozen to the spot, Emma watched as Lorna's legs stopped moving.

"How do you like that, you sour old bitch? What'cha gonna complain about *now*? Try . . . *nothing*." Seth wiped his hands down the side of his tunic, giggling devilishly. Suddenly he turned, catching Emma cowering in the doorway.

"Well, what a surprise. My favorite little cocktease." Seth eyes raged with fever; his face was flushed but his voice whispered—calm and relaxed. He began to hum, the tune jumbled and flat.

Abruptly, his voice reached out like a whip, unexpected and paralyzing. "Come here."

As Emma's heart thundered in her chest, Seth bounded across the room, grabbed her arm and, before she could protest, punched her hard in the face. Her head snapped back toward the wall, jackknifing forward as she was engulfed in pain and darkness, urine trickling forlornly down her legs.

Emma woke to the metallic taste of blood in her mouth and a wickedly thrumming headache. She lay flat on a hard surface, her eyes shut. Moaning, she tried to sit up and was shocked to find she couldn't move her hands or feet. Opening her eyes, her memory came rushing back. She attempted to suppress the urge to vomit; failing miserably as she heaved it up, chunks from breakfast gushing over her chin and down onto her neck. Choking, she rolled her trussed body over, discovering she lay on the ground of a huge cavern that cowered over her with its cathedral grandeur.

"For Christ's sake, Emma. You don't expect to kiss me *now*, do you?"

Her heart dropped like an anvil as she located Seth sitting next to what looked like a campfire. The slight hint of grease in the air made her queasy stomach roll again.

"Untie me." She tried to lift herself into a sitting position. Seth watched her struggle without comment. "Why are you doing this?"

Emma suddenly remembered the sight in the sleeping room.

"You tried to kill Lorna. *Whyyyyy?* Why would you do that? You were all like family."

"*Family?* Why would being a family give anyone a pass? What the heck is this stupid sentimentality between a bunch of people that don't even like each other, just because they live in the same house? I don't get it. Do you think that stopped me when I burnt down my parents' house when I was eleven? How else could I stop them from interfering with my . . . *hobbies?* I'm sorry to say we don't have time, Emma, or I would regale you with my exploits with our neighbors' pets . . . or should I say *pests?* Unfortunately, they weren't all as tasty as a fat little piggy I know."

"*Please!*" She began to cry, praying for God to help her. "Where's my mama?"

"Stop bawling, *right now*. You're getting on my nerves. I don't know where your mama is anyway. She's probably out looking for the missing porker. Ha, ha, ha. They should have been looking for him last night."

Seth flipped a rib bone at her and it bounced harmlessly off her shoulder. He stood. "I'm sorry I can't stay to chat, pumpkin. I need to get back to join the hunt before they miss me. This was just the opportunity I was waiting for, but I didn't figure you into it. I can't have you spoil it for me now, can I?"

Seth strolled over to Emma, sliding his hands under her body to lift her high in the air. Emma struggled with her bonds as he carried her close to the edge of the cliff.

"No, *please . . . I won't tell*." Her heart stopped with a gush of panicked adrenaline.

"That's right, baby doll. You won't."

With those words, Emma felt herself airborne. Her young body tumbled over in the air giving her just enough time to sob, close her eyes and whisper "Mama," before she met the lethal embrace of the merciless ground so many stories below.

Ginger Mae walked slowly, quiet and stunned. No one spoke as the dinner was served by Salina, Dezi, Karen, and Billy, who agreed to pitch in to cover for Emma's unexplained absence. Netty and Wil had said they'd be late even as dinner was delayed, due to the unsuccessful hunt for the missing piglet.

Whispers circulated the tables. Urging Daisy along, Ginger Mae moved their seats over to Johno and Crystal's table to listen in on the keepers.

Crystal glanced up glumly as they sat. "Don't be bringing your twisted mojo over here to our table, Ginger Mae." Crystal sniffed then reached out, smiling at Daisy. "But you can stay, Daisy Chain. Just make yourself comfortable."

Johno shook his head at Crystal. "Woman, you should be ashamed. We don't need any infighting. The piglet is missing. We don't know what to expect from the Womb. This is the time we need to hold together."

Ginger Mae gave him a grateful smile as she slid into her chair next to Daisy. All whispers dribbled to a stop as Netty, Wil and Baby entered the room. Netty busied herself at the sink as Wil and Baby sat at their table as if nothing were out of the norm.

Salina looked from one to the other, then scanned the crowd of survivors. Approaching the tables, she smoothed down her hair and nervously clutched at her apron. "Has anyone seen my daughter, Emma? Has anyone seen Emma?"

Necks craned around the room as if they could spot her here.

"Bonnie, when was the last time you saw your sister?" Salina's worried face looked over heads to her youngest.

"I haven't seen her since breakfast, Mama. She was going to meet me before lunch, but she didn't show. I thought she was just being Emma. Then we started the hunt for the piglet. I thought she was looking, too."

"Clyde, did Emma find you and ask you to come to your wife's room?"

Clyde appeared puzzled. "No. Why would she want me to go to Lorna's room?"

"I sent her to fetch you. We were seeing positive signs that Lorna was getting better. I just . . . thought . . . I thought you should know." Ginger Mae could see Salina struggle over the topic of Lorna. Everyone in the kitchen followed the conversation with interest, gossip having placed Salina on the bottom of the romance ladder with the appearance of Lorna.

Clyde stood excitedly. "Seth, did you hear that? I gotta go check."

Seth stood up with his fork poised near his mouth. "Finally. Want me to come with you?"

Clyde eyed the fork in Seth's hand. "No, you stay and finish dinner." Clyde hurried to the kitchen doorway. "Thanks, Salina. Don't worry, Emma'll turn up."

As Clyde left the kitchen, Crystal shouted out to Netty. "Well . . . what about Tulip's missing piglet? That's two disappearances now."

Rumblings started up in the room to be silenced by Wil. "We will give it another day. I must tell you the Womb is . . . *disturbed*. Keep your eyes out for Emma, please. Scotty, will you check the bathing cave before you go to bed? I've noticed she hasn't seemed herself lately."

Kenya snorted from her chair. "Yeah, she hasn't been pestering Kane lately—somethins up for sure." Salina gave her a sharp look. Kenya and Kane looked down, embarrassed. Everyone quietly went back to their dinner.

Ginger Mae estimated only fifteen minutes passed before Clyde returned. She was the first to notice him at the door. He stood quietly as if afraid to interrupt, tears dripping from his eyes. She wondered how long he'd been standing there. As heads turned his way, Jose and Wil got up to go to his side. He appeared not to notice, just kept standing at the doorway.

Wil spoke first. "Clyde? Are you okay?"

Ginger Mae watched as Clyde looked right through Wil, the tears still slipping down his face. Salina slowly made her way toward him. He seemed to see her, finally raising a hand toward her approach. She held out her arms and he stumbled toward her. Everyone in the room strained as his words came out empty, devoid of emotion. "She's dead. My wife died."

112

Seth ate on.

The next few days passed in an uncomfortable haze. Everyone waited for the next bombshell as Emma and the piglet remained missing.

Lorna's funeral was attended by all, even though hardly anyone actually knew her. It was the first unifying moment the survivors had had since the disappearances. Clyde leaned on a gray and drawn Salina through the entire service that was read by Cobby from a book found in the library. No one believed in the Bible anymore, but habits were hard to break and all found solace in the familiar words. As Ginger Mae watched the faces in the crowd, she hung close to Dezi and Daisy. Bonnie stood near her mama, as anxious as the rest of them over the strange disappearance of Emma.

The most difficult reality of Lorna's death had been the disposal of the body. The service was held in the huge cavern where they'd all gathered on their inaugural night in the Hive. Right in front of the spot where Scotty had helped Echo and Baby send Barney's old, cold body into the membrane of the Hive to be reborn. But there would be no rebirth for Lorna, as much as Clyde had begged. Sitting in the back of the cavern, away from the humans, were the dogs, Echo and Barney, Baby, Tulip, Chance, the remaining piglets, and the pair of red foxes. Yes, the foxes that had been healed so quickly one the day Lorna had arrived. They now enjoyed the safety and bounty of the Hive, *unlike* Lorna.

Everyone watched as Clyde's wife, wrapped in a cotton shroud, was lifted by Johno's keepers and brought to the wall where, unlike Barney, she would never be seen again. The survivors shuddered privately as proof of their status in the Hive hit home.

A week passed with still no sign of Emma. Clyde and Salina were certified members of the walking dead, their grief so pronounced it cast a pall over the entire Hive. Even the animals were subdued as their human caretakers mourned.

Bonnie spent more and more time with Tobi, Chance and the lion cubs, feeling the loss of her sister, but unable to discuss it with her mama, who remained in denial, hoping against the odds that an explanation would be forthcoming. Clyde attempted to persuade Seth to let him move in to sit with Jennifer, but he was having none of it.

"I need to be there for her when she wakes. She'll never understand if I'm not, Clyde. I know you understand." Seth sobbed, his face beseeching. So Clyde relented, too emotionally spent to put up a battle. Everyone at the dinner table expressed their wonder at what a great friend Seth was.

Today Bonnie planned to meet Peter for lunch in their usual spot. She had wondered weeks ago why Peter preferred her company. In her teen wisdom, she'd surmised he felt safe from adult pressure. As much as Bonnie was a happy and optimistic person, she had her solitary moods, too. She could see that Peter was a solitary fellow himself. That suited her fine. He didn't bug her with stupid questions like the other adults did. And, likewise, she didn't bug him.

That didn't mean she wasn't curious about why he'd shunned *everyone* in the early days of the Hive. She had heard whispers and seen the glances. And she'd noticed how Ginger Mae went out of her way to avoid Peter who, from time to time, would throw her hateful glowers. Most of the acting out seemed to have dissipated as everyone in the Hive found their niche: Ginger Mae with the animal counting and Peter with the lion cubs and his friendship with her and Dezi. But it had taken a long time.

She waved to Peter as he entered the elephants' bathing cave. He waved back, giving the keepers a shout as he ran over to the rock enclave where they sat to have their lunches. Bonnie followed him to her usual seat as he spread out their lunch.

"So, where's Chance? How come he's not over here begging?"

Bonnie shrugged. "He's not with the herd and the rest of the piglets?"

Peter busied himself with unwrapping his lunch, pushing an extra piece of black raspberry torte to Bonnie as he waited for her answer. She picked it up eagerly, speaking between mouthfuls.

"He must be there, I just saw him ten minutes ago. He likes to hang with Tobi as she fusses over the young female, Namba. I wonder when Namba's baby will come, Johno won't tell me. He had the nerve to tell me he doesn't need me underfoot when the calf comes. But Peter, I want to be here when that happens, don't you? "

"Eww . . . I don't know. I guess I could live without it. I think I'll wait until the messy part is over. Then I'll be here to see the baby. Are we going to see the cubs after lunch?" Peter munched, his attention on Bonnie. "Are you feeling any better today?"

Bonnie stopped chewing and swallowed. "The same. I can't get Mama alone long enough to talk. It's like she doesn't even see me. I feel invisible."

Peter nodded sagely. "I know just what you mean. I used to feel that way too. I was pretty lonely and full of anger. But I worked most of it off."

"The anger?"

"Yeah. I used to walk at night. I needed time to understand what had happened with the Ginger Mae and Armoni thing. Why I was such a dope about her."

Bonnie reached out to pat his hand. "You're not a dope, silly." Bonnie and Peter continued their luncheon chat, making plans for the cubs and avoiding all mention of the recent tragic events.

Then Peter had a proposal. "You know what we need? Some adventure. I have a special spot I like to go to now and then. Tobi goes sometimes too. She brings the herd. Want to go sometime?"

"What? You have a special spot? And you never told me about it? What have you and Tobi been up to?"

Peter laughed. Bonnie thought it was the best sound she'd heard in a long time.

"Ahem . . . excuse me." They whirled around to see Ginger Mae standing there with her clipboard and pencil. She tried to avoid meeting Peter's eyes.

"Hello, Ginger Mae," he said quietly.

Ginger Mae appeared startled, giving a tentative nod. "Peter."

Bonnie interrupted their strained greetings. "What's up?"

Ginger Mae's expression changed instantly. "I can't find Chance.

I would have waited until later to report it, but in view of . . ." Her words tailed off, unwilling to say it out loud.

Bonnie rolled her eyes. "That monkey. He was just here a while ago, right Peter?"

"I didn't see him, remember, Bonnie?"

Bonnie stood up, not worried. "I guess it's possible that Dezi stopped by to peek in. He's done that before and Chance has left with him. It's never been a big deal." She stared at Ginger Mae's stony face. "Until now." She turned to Peter. "Come on, let's go find Dezi. He should be in the kitchen. Are you sure about this, Ginger Mae?" One look at Ginger Mae's raised eyebrow was all she needed. "Okay, let's hurry."

The two of them hustled off as Peter quickly wrapped up the remains of lunch and met them at the exit.

Bonnie's heart began to strum faster as they hurried to the kitchen. Rushing in, they were surprised to see so many of the survivors there: Gloria, Billy, Tucker, Abby and Jose, Karen and Cobby, but no Chance. Emma ran up to Dezi to fill him in while Ginger Mae reported to Jose.

"Netty and Wil aren't going to be happy about this," Jose worried.

Dezi spoke up, his eyes wild and Bonnie held on to his arm. "Come on, everyone. My baby's missing. We've got to find Chance."

Suddenly, Scotty and Kane came running in from the growing fields. "Hey . . . Johno's coming with Tobi. She ran into the field on a tear and then ran back out with Johno and his boys following. He asked me to get you, Dezi."

Kane stood panting as Johno ran in behind them. From the doorway, Tobi's head appeared. She was snorting oddly, her trunk waving wildly. Bonnie and Dezi ran to her, catching her trunk in their hand. As Bonnie unwound her trunk, a small light-gray object fell on the floor. Bending down, Dezi picked it up, holding it out to Bonnie.

"What *is* that, Dez?"

The men crowded around as Clyde walked in the kitchen, heading for Salina. "What's all the excitement about? And who let the elephant in the kitchen?" He smiled at Salina. "Do you realize how funny that sounds?" She smiled back weakly.

Bonnie and Dezi turned to Salina. Stunned and sick faces looked at the object in Dezi hand. He drew a finger across what appeared to be a skull bone.

"Mama, I think it's the piglet." Tears formed in her eyes. "Where's Chance? We need to find Chance." Tobi's head shook from side to side, her trunk waving in the air. Peter stepped forward, his face drained of color. Tobi turned to him, trumpeting loudly. Everyone stared at the display.

Bonnie turned to Peter. "What does she mean, Peter? She's trying to tell you something."

He opened his mouth, but said nothing.

"Peter? Do you know something about this bone?"

Suddenly, everyone was shouting, attention on the bone and Peter.

"Yeah, *Peter*. Where's the pig?"

"Come on, Peter. *What'd ya do with the pig?*"

"Admit it, *you ate* the pig."

Bonnie and Peter shrank back from the hostile voices. Their friends and fellow survivors grew meaner and meaner, louder and louder. Even Dezi stood stupefied. He held up his hand for silence, his pointed face reflecting disappointment and burgeoning anger.

"Do you know something about this, Peter?" He held out the skull, accusation stingingly clear. Peter shrank back, his eyes sad, his posture defeated.

Bonnie stepped up and ripped the bone out of Dezi's hand. "What the heck are you talking about, Dezi? Why would Peter know anything about this?"

Peter coughed; Tobi beginning to thump him on the back with her trunk. "Um . . . Bonnie . . . I think Tobi wants us to go with her." They all turned to Tobi. Peter stepped toward her as she began to back out of the kitchen. Bonnie waved to her mother.

Ginger Mae stood up, calling to Kane, "Where are Kimir and Daisy? Did you leave them in the field?"

Kane turned to answer as Scotty hurried out the kitchen into the caverns. "Don't worry. They're with the girls. Caesar stayed behind with Chloe and the dogs. Kenya will look after them."

"Come on, let's go." Bonnie tugged at Dezi, urging him to follow after Peter, the rest of the survivors tagging behind.

Tobi moved swiftly, Peter following as if he knew where she was headed. As the trip lengthened, mumbles started from the crowd and Karen and Gloria wanted to turn back. Ignoring the women, the survivors trudged on, unease developing as they realized they were in unfamiliar territory. Eventually, they came to a huge boulder in the cavern corridor. Tobi slipped easily behind to disappear.

Peter pulled to a stop, turning to Bonnie. "This is where I wanted to take you. Remember we talked about this at lunch? I followed Tobi here one night, months ago. She was with Echo and Baby. They brought her here. Remember when Tobi was tearing up the fields with her tusks? She needed minerals to eat and couldn't find them. So this is where she takes the herd. It's a magnificent cavern. Come on, I'll show you." Peter led them into the cavern where they located the two paths. The air hung heavy with a dense organic stench. In the dimmer light, Tobi was nowhere to be seen.

The cavern was intimidating, the path to the right rising to a zenith and disappearing into the beyond. The survivors, led by Peter and Bonnie, carefully made their way up. As the elevation rose, they detected the faint odor of grease and smoke. Bonnie felt the hair rise on her arms. Expecting the worst, she caught a whiff of the greasy smell so long forgotten by her taste buds. Reaching the plateau, they heard the sounds of piglet squeaks.

Bonnie dashed from the crowd to behold Seth sitting next to a fire with Chance on the ground, trussed up with his little legs bound.

"Chance."

She ran to the little piglet with Dezi bellowing after her.

"What the hell to you think you're doing, ya dirty piece of garbage?"

Clyde stood shocked and the rest of the survivors were appalled. Clyde's plaintive voice could be heard, soft and confused. "Hey, champ. What in the world are *you* doing here?"

Seth surveyed the crowd, ignoring the surprised angry faces. "Well, well, well, what an unwelcome surprise. If I'd known you'd be joining me for dinner, I'd have prepared something nicer. Oh, and Clyde? Please shut your hole before I decide to cut out your tongue. I've had just about as much of your good ole boy syrup as I can take." Seth grinned, his impudence knowing no bounds.

Kane and Scotty stood glued to the side, watching as Bonnie worked at Chance's bonds. Bones lay strewn around the fire, evidence of the missing piglet.

Kane's face drained of color. "Not cool, bro. You're going to get us in a shitload of trouble with Netty and Wil when they find out."

"They already have." Wil strode forward from the back of the crowd, his wings collapsing to cling to his back. "Netty has a gift for you, Seth. She will be here momentarily."

Dezi squirmed, jumping from foot to foot, unable to take his eyes off Seth who grinned wide with Wil's news. "You piece of garbage. You aren't going to lay a finger on Chance again or any other animal here."

He charged Seth, knocking him onto his back. As Seth rose up, he grasped a dirty knife off the ground, holding it in front of him. A sudden swoosh was felt over the survivor's heads as Echo landed, her wings collapsing alongside her body. The wobbly creature stood there taking in the scene.

Seth taunted Dezi, "So, you need your creepy little pet to fight for you?"

Dezi threw a punch and Seth deftly stepped aside as he landed a painful kick to Dezi's groin. As Dezi tried to maintain his balance, Seth pivoted to the campfire, grabbing Bonnie and backing her up to the cliff edge, his knife to her throat.

"Anyone else have something to say?"

"Let her go." The command came from Wil and Peter at the same time, Peter creeping closer to the pair. Bonnie felt tears course down her face as she tried to be brave. She watched as Dezi limped over to Chance to back him away from the fire and the scene near the cliff.

As she struggled, Seth bent to her ear. "If you don't hold still, I'm going to throw you off this cliff to join your slut of a sister."

Bonnie felt her blood freeze at the mention of her sister. "Emma? You did something to Emma?"

"Emma, you did something to Emma?" Seth mocked Bonnie's words in a high falsetto.

Suddenly, from alongside Seth, a large, dark form emerged. Bonnie felt a huge weight strike Seth from the back, propelling him forward and knocking Bonnie free. Peter raced forward to yank her out of Seth's reach as other survivors pounced on Seth, bringing him to his feet just in time to see the huge form of the magnificent Tobi, the matriarch of the last herd of sentient elephants from the great continent of Africa, slip and tumble off the edge of the cliff into the abyss to her death.

Time stood still as the speechless crowd digested what their unbelieving eyes refused to accept. Johno walked slowly toward the cliff and knelt to pray, his anguish visible in the shaking of his shoulders as he sobbed. Bonnie could hear more sobbing as she wrestled free of Peter's grasp to run to the men holding Seth.

As she beat her fists on him, she screamed. *"You bastard.* You killed Tobi. *I'm gunna kill you!* What did you do with my sister? *You bastard, I'll kill you."*

Seth laughed as Peter gently pulled her off, wrapping the young girl in his arms, shock still on his disbelieving face. Bonnie watched as her mama walked slowly through the crowd, arriving late with some of the keepers. She knelt in disbelief and held out her arms to her daughter.

"Mama, he killed Tobi and Emma. He killed them." Bonnie sobbed uncontrollably in her mother's arms.

Wil tried to quiet the crowd as the survivors called for Seth's hide. "Stop. It will not be necessary."

No sooner did the words leave his mouth than the walls of the great cavern began to undulate. Striations of gold and red flashed over the walls like lightning coming from inside the wall membranes. The pervasive and malodorous organic stench deepened. Panic registered on everyone's face with the exception of Seth and Wil.

Salina clung hard to Bonnie as she shouted to Wil, "Where's Netty? We need her help."

A flutter and collapse of wings answered Salina as Netty appeared, her arms holding a child, her grand amber tail waving as furious as a whip.

Clyde took a step toward them as Netty held up her hand to stop, his voice unbelieving. "Jennifer?"

The young teen, all of a hundred pounds, took tentative steps toward the men who held Seth, her face flushed and intent. The walls of the cavern increased the dramatic movement of the striating colors. From the bowels of the cavern rose the smell of sulfur.

Jennifer stood unsteadily in front of Seth, who squirmed uncomfortably in the arms of his captors. "Hi, Jen. How's my little doll? You look good."

Soundlessly, Jennifer reached into the fold of her smock to pull out a long stainless-steel knife. As the crowd held their collective breaths, she stepped up and stoically plunged the knife deep into Seth's stomach. She left the knife where she'd thrust it, backing away shaking and making low keening noises.

"You ungrateful bitch . . . I should have strangled you when I had the chance." Blood leaked from Seth's mouth as he choked out the words, the knife protruding from his gut, his eyes wide with surprise.

Clyde fought through the crowd to sweep her up in his arms. She turned inward to him, crying. *"Grandpa?* Oh, Grandpa."

Seth's feet buckled under him, held up by the strength of the men who detained him with their backs to the edge of the trail. As they fought to hold him still, the stench of sulfur became overpowering.

A dark cylindrical shape rose ponderously from the bowels of the cavern to loom over the men, striations of light swirling within the gelatinous mass. The horrified faces of the survivors warned Seth of the menace behind him as everyone shrank away. Bonnie shook loose from her mother to take a step forward as her eyes refused to register what was before her. Echo took to the air, her wings fluttering as she flew toward the mass.

"Oh, God . . . *Echo, come back*," Scotty screamed, his voice hoarse and panic-stricken.

The mass was huge; the red and amber lights coalescing in the thickness of the thing that hung in the air; its head bulbous, similar to the Elder and minions' tails. Its body disappeared many stories below. Tears slipped silently down Bonnie's face as she beheld Tobi's broken body wrapped protectively in the gelatinous mass of the thing.

Bonnie felt the presence of Netty at her side. "It's going to be alright, young one. The Womb will provide."

"Provide? Provide *what?* A way to give Tobi back to us? A way to punish the scum who caused this?" She threw herself into Netty's arms.

"Shhh . . . little one. We must say goodbye."

Rising, Bonnie and Netty watched with the fearful crowd of survivors as the gelatinous thing that loomed over them moved slowly toward the cavern wall on the side of the trail. Echo flitted alongside the mass, a golden escort for the beloved Tobi.

Dipping down to the wall, the mass moved through the membrane until Tobi was completely engulfed, Echo letting go of Tobi's trunk as it slipped through her fingers to enter the membrane. As the stupefied survivors watched, Tobi completely disappeared, the huge mass withdrawing to loom over them again. Echo fluttered nearby, alighting back on the ground next to Scotty. He promptly scooped her up to hold her tightly to his chest, as he backpedalled away from the mass that had suddenly dropped down in front of them both, as if it knew them.

Slowly, the thing dipped over toward a petrified Bonnie. She felt Netty's arm around her shoulder, holding her steady. It hung in the air as if to smell her, swaying gently. From over the edge of the cliff, a bulge appeared in the gelatinous mess. It rose high in the air, sucking its way up the neck of the giant entity. To everyone's astonishment, the bulge moved out from the column toward the young girl. They watched the mass reshape itself to carry the bulge to the ground in front of Bonnie. The gelatinous glob then receded, leaving the remains of Bonnie's sister Emma, broken and dead on the ground. Sounds of vomiting and the sharp acrid odor of fear came from the crowd of cringing survivors.

Before anyone could react, the thing moved like a cobra, snatching Seth from the arms of his captors, curling around him like a giant anaconda as Seth's colon released its contents. The last thing anyone heard from Seth was his pleading voice as he blubbered his innocence, cut off abruptly as he was swallowed into the mass. It wavered in the air as if measuring its next victim before it vanished back into the bowels of the cavern stories below, leaving the survivors trembling and in shock.

Chapter 12

Scotty labored in the growing field with Kane, trying to sweat out the effects of the last three days. They were digging deep holes in the rich dirt for the fibrous plugs that Netty said would develop into rich, leafy plants. The plants would give them a natural source to replace the lack of salt in their diet. It could be dried or fresh, chopped in any number of dishes to replicate table salt, one of the luxuries missed by the survivors. The pressure on Netty to come up with this small luxury had produced these brown plugs, a token from the Womb, she said.

"Do you think she just talks to the Womb whenever she needs something? Or is it your little dude over there?" Kane and Scotty turned to watch Echo and Baby planting the plugs. Chloe sat by the hole, filling it in with dirt as the minions took turns dropping in the plug. Caesar lay curled up a few feet away with Barney and Teddy sprawled next to him. The rest of the posse sniffed and cavorted among the groves, tracking mice and monkeys.

One of the white-faced monkeys looked down from her perch with a baby in tow. It had come as quite a surprise to the survivors to discover the birth. The primate was well past the age of producing offspring and the males were well past the age at which they could viably produce sperm. It was suggested that the Hive was at work again in some way. Everyone was wondrously pleased to hear of the birth, but concern over the ability of the elderly female to care for the infant had focused their attention on her, which of course was noticed by the dogs. The new mother took to motherhood with the passion of a monkey decades younger, allowing the survivors' attention to move on to other matters, but not the dogs. They still felt it was their duty to track mother and child from the ground, even as the rest of the troop chattered and dropped twigs and sticks down on the vigilant and harmless pack.

Three days had passed in the Hive since the discovery of the evil they had welcomed into the arms of their naive hospitality. Scotty thought back to the day of Tobi and Seth's deaths as he dug.

No one mourned the passing of Seth and most believed he'd got off too lightly. The sketchy facts revealed by a shell-shocked Jennifer horrified them all. Jennifer haltingly disclosed the truth behind the death of a young teen named Maryann at the maniacal hands of Seth as they lay locked in a bathroom a few steps away; the disappearance of her sister Suzy; and how she had learned during that disastrous day to protect herself by feigning unconsciousness. It was clear to the survivors that Jennifer had no real understanding of where she was or what had happened to the Earth above. Long lapses in her memory indicated her mind protected her still. No one quite knew what to say to her as she vacuously asked any survivor that crossed her path if they knew when her parents would be here to take her home.

Clyde spent every waking hour with Jennifer, leaving little time to console Salina who had been devastated by the loss of Emma. Poor Bonnie wasn't much better. Naturally Salina blamed herself. Scotty, Abby and Jose tried to do what they could to be there for her. But this was the third child she'd lost when you recalled what had happened to Tomas during his involvement with Armoni. Scotty squeezed his effervescent eyes shut with pain as the memories came flooding back. The deaths reminded him of the loss of his mother and Hiro in the accident that had killed them almost four years ago. He sighed to himself, the weight of his wings heavy on his back. So much had happened—it felt more like ten years since they'd buried his mother.

It was safe to say that everyone who had made the trek to the cavern discovered by Tobi and Peter remained in shock. Scotty glanced over at Echo and Baby, well aware they had played a part in the finding of the cavern. Apparently, Peter and Bonnie had kept their roles quiet, protecting the duo for some reason. Bonnie herself had confided in Scotty that Peter had asked her to keep mum about it. *So many secrets.*

Scotty's heart weighed heavily as he thanked the Womb they were all still together. He glanced over at Chloe, who resented having to work with Echo but wasn't bothered by Baby. She moved at only one speed: slow. But he loved her. It made everything easier to have her by his side. He had no trouble picking up the slack and covering for her.

Kane threw down his shovel, dirt encrusted in the lines of his unabashedly handsome face. "I could use a break, bro."

Scotty threw down his shovel, calling out to Chloe, "Want to take a break?"

He felt Echo's aura pricking his brain. "Brother Scotty, Sister Chloe does not need a break. She needs to work. We will not complete our task if she stops. The root stock needs to be planted."

"It's okay, Echo. I'll come over there and give you a hand after our break."

"I do not need your hand, Brother. I need a whole body that will work, and not play at it."

Scotty grinned, shaking his head.

Chloe's head swung his way, then back to Echo, her eyes flashing with anger. "Are you two talking behind my back again? Scotty . . . didn't we agree the two of you would stop that?"

Scotty winked at Echo. "Don't know what you mean, babe."

An aura sprinkled lightly. "Is there something wrong with your eye, Brother Scotty?"

Echo clapped her leather hands together as Chloe huffed, dropping down on the ground, grimacing. "Don't we have more important things to talk about?" Annoyance dripped from her every consonant.

Scotty sent an aura back to Echo as their eyes met, vocalizing at the same time. "Come on over here, you beautiful girl. Let's relax for a while."

Chloe's eyebrow arched at Echo. *"What did you just say, Scotty?"*

Chagrined, he turned to Chloe. "I said . . . I want to relax here with my beautiful girlfriend."

Chloe sent a superior glare to Echo as Kane plopped down next to them. "Would you three please stop it? You sound ridiculous." Kane sighed. "How can you joke after all that's happened?"

Chloe sidled closer to Scotty, dropping her voice. "I'm sorry, Kane. Echo just gets under my skin sometimes."

"Yeah, and I can't erase the feeling that we're being watched now."

They all craned their necks to gaze up at the walls and the ceiling of the enormous cavern draped thickly with the same ubiquitous membrane found all over the Hive. The only difference was they couldn't ignore it now. For ever since the dramatic appearance of what Wil described as a manifestation of the Womb, the membranes all quaked with bursts of light. As Wil and Netty explained, the Womb had been disturbed. But they failed to discuss exactly what that meant, frustrating them all and making everyone fearful.

Scotty watched the posse over in the next field where the fruit trees grew. They were all happy and healthy, keeping their eyes on the hooting primates. From between two trees, he thought he saw a figure moving in fits and starts, then stopping. He stared, attempting to identify the movement, losing interest as Kenya, Daisy and Bonnie climbed the knoll to join them.

Kane rose, quickly helping Kenya attain the knoll. "Hi, girls." He gave Kenya a quick smooch, pressing his hands to her belly. "Any news?"

Kenya rolled her eyes and eased herself down to the ground. "I don't know if I'm gonna be able to get back up on my feet, chickey. You just might have to leave me here."

Bonnie chimed in, her voice empty of her usual animation. "We'll never leave you here, Kenya, you know that."

Kenya tilted her head toward Bonnie, her grateful smile dimmer than normal. She patted Bonnie and Daisy on their legs. "I know, chickeys . . . you're my girls." Kenya had stopped her vocalizing at dinner with the recitation of the events with Seth in the new cavern. The horror of the discovery had chilled everyone to the bone and she was no exception. Ever since, she, Bonnie and Daisy hung out together as much as possible, except for the time Bonnie spent with Peter and the lion cubs or when she helped with the food distribution.

Bonnie had not yet found the strength to visit Tobi's herd,

especially with Johno walking around like a zombie, bereft beyond comfort, to Crystal's consternation. Even the impending birth of the new elephant calf could not assuage their heartbreak. And reports of an edgy herd, agitated over the missing Tobi, did nothing to help the situation. Johno had begged Bonnie to visit the herd, praying her presence would calm them down. She continued to refuse.

Even Kenya herself apologized for any inadvertent responsibility that may have pushed Emma into the clutches of Seth. No one dared mention the unintended consequences that stemmed from Kane's covert affair with Emma and Kenya's suspicions regarding the two. The fact that Kane's subsequent rejection probably exacerbated Emma's flirtation with Seth was left unsaid.

The only survivor who exhibited any happiness in the group was Dezi. His big baby, Chance, was safe and sound, and he had no intentions of taking his eyes off him, doting on his every squeak and squeal. He stuck to his side like a burr, happy to have his daddy to herself.

"I hope we don't have to visit the funeral cavern anymore. The next time I show up there, it better be to climb out of this place," Chloe remarked glumly, casting a quick glance at Bonnie.

Emma's funeral had been two days ago. Scotty wondered how long it would take for the shock of the deaths to wear off. The fact that no one was talking, just skirting around what had happened, would surely cause questions to fester. He felt in his bones that a big explosion wasn't far off. People could only live in fear for so long without cracking.

"I've seen it before." All eyes fastened on Scotty.

"You've seen what before?" asked Kane.

"The thing . . . the gloopy monster."

"It's not a monster. Netty and Wil said it's a . . . ."

"I know . . . a manifestation of the Womb."

Kenya skewered Scotty with her limpid brown eyes. "So, chickey, where exactly did you see this *thing* before?"

Scotty nodded at Echo and turned to Kane. "Remember the night Echo and I snuck out of the house and went into the woods past

Lakewood Ranch, outside Sarasota?"

Kane nodded back. "I know where Lakewood Ranch is. That's where the cops busted the big dog-fighting ring, where they found the skeletons of the dirty scum that were kidnapping pets to use as *bait*."

"That was us . . . me and Echo."

They all looked at Scotty in surprise. "Well . . . and the Womb."

Kenya was the first to break the surprised silence. "And just when were you going to tell us about your chummy relationship with the Womb?"

Chloe rallied to his defense. "He just *did*, Kenya." She rolled her eyes at Scotty. "It might have been a help if you'd brought this up before."

"Honestly, we didn't think of it until the day before, did we, Echo?" Echo stood up and looked at Chloe, then turned away dismissively. Before anyone could comment, a shadow flicked at the edge of the grove, catching the corner of Scotty's eye. He watched as Elias emerged to climb the knoll toward the young friends. As he approached, Scotty could see he wasn't here for tea.

Elias' brow was knitted with tension; his eyes seethed with contempt and were sunk into his rich, dark skin. He made a beeline for Kane with his fists clenched. Landing a blow to the side of Kane's neck, he launched his body on top of him, causing the rest to scatter away. Poor Kenya was left to inch herself and her belly out of the way.

"*You selfish prick.* If you hadn't decided to toy with Emma, she would still be here."

"Whoa there Elias . . . you've got this wrong." Kane rolled away from Elias's punishing fists and jumped to his feet.

"I don't have *nothin'* wrong, white boy. You think you're better than me? You think because you pal around with Golden Boy here, you can have anyone you want? Bet you didn't know he was fuckin' her, did ya Kenya? Yeah . . . and when he was done, he just tossed her away. And that left her open to the other sick fuck. It's all your *fault,* white boy." Elias struck out again at Kane. Scotty could hear

Barney and Teddy barking in the distance. From the corner of his eye, he saw Caesar rise.

Kenya screamed. "Get your filthy hands off him, you idiot." She turned, appealing to Chloe. "Help him." Chloe slowly approached the raving Elias.

Scotty stepped forward. "Stay out of this, babe."

"Look here, there's no need to fight about this. Enough harm . . ."

"Shut up, *bitch*." And before anyone could stop him, Elias lashed out with the back of his hand, sending Chloe reeling to the ground. With an earth-moving roar, Caesar leaped at Elias and bit him on the side of the neck, knocking them both to the ground.

"Caesar, *no!*" Scotty ran to Chloe, picking her up as her face began to swell. Assuring himself she was okay, he rushed over to Kenya and pulled her to her feet. "Get the kids out of here. Ask Wil to find Cobby and get here fast." He ran to Elias where Kane stood gazing in shock. "We need help *now*, Kenya. Bonnie, can you rip off the skirt of your smock?" Scotty pulled his tunic over his wings as Bonnie skirted gingerly around Caesar, who sat there shaking blood from his muzzle and swiping at himself with his paw.

"Jesus Christ, Kane. Can you give me a hand here?" Scotty knelt at Elias' head, blood spurting from his gravely punctured neck with every feeble breath. Scotty wadded up the remnants of cloth as they were handed to him, blood drenching them as soon as he applied pressure to Elias's wound. Kane knelt down to help apply pressure.

"Oh shit." Kane looked up at Scotty, terror in his eyes. "I don't think we can stop the blood. Echo . . . can you help us?" Echo turned to Baby and the two of them rose into the air, their tender wings beating so fast that in an instant they were gone. Scotty and Kane soon found themselves surrounded by the posse, silent and intuitively respectful as the lifeblood drained from the wound at Elias' neck.

His eyes flickered madly. "I'm not gunna make it. It's bad isn't it?" Elias's eyes flickered to Kane for the last time, his voice only whispers. "Why . . . why couldn't you leave her alone? I loved her . . ."

In the next instant, Wil and Netty, Abby and Jose appeared; their wings enclosed over their strumming bodies, tails whipping in the air, and followed by Baby and Echo. As they folded their wings in place, and approached the three men on the hard blood-soaked ground, no words were necessary as Scotty lowered Elias' eyelids over his fixed eyes, hanging his head in despair.

It was a grim atmosphere at dinner. A service had been hastily held for Elias, comforting words provided haltingly by a reeling Johno in Swahili. The other survivors wondered how Johno would recover from the additional shock of losing one of his keepers, all of whom were like sons to him.

Needless to say, Kenya had now had Kane's philandering thrown publicly in her face. Storm clouds and feminine tears laced the dinner Salina served apathetically to the survivors. Hushed whispers and covert glances made the rounds at the dinner tables. Peter sat by himself, feeling ostracized once more as the memory of the accusations that he'd eaten Chance came back to devil him.

One of Johno's keepers stood after dinner, turning to address the crowd. "It is time. We must kill the giant tiger now. He sits outside this very door and still lives. In my homeland, a cat that has killed a man will kill another. We make sure the cat does not live to enjoy another victim. It is the law of the land." African voices broke out in agreement, shiny black faces accepting their duty to their dead countryman.

"We can poison him."

"Yeah."

Before any more could be said, Wil rose from his seat. 'There will be no killing."

The keepers rose one by one to stand toe to toe with Wil, Johno among them. "We must avenge the death of our brother. The cat must go."

Wil whirled on them all, eyes flashing, words cutting like a stiletto. "There will be *no* killing. Do you not see? Caesar was doing the bidding of the Womb. He is here to guard *The One*. It is not the providence of the Womb to explain intentions to you. It is for your own good."

The keepers shouted back at Wil. Johno silenced them with a raised hand. "With all due respect my friend, the giant tiger did not protect Scotty. He was in no danger. The young lady got in the way. She should have left men's work to the men. She had no call to interfere. Her life is not worth that of my best man. The cat made a mistake and must pay."

A hush settled over the crowd as the meaning of Johno's words sank in.

Abby stepped forward. "Johno, I am sorely disappointed in you tonight. There is not one life here that is worth more than another. Your culture is different from ours. Women are just as valuable as a man. But you need to understand something." She scanned the room, making sure she had their attention. "You all need to *understand* something. Wil is trying to tell you that our rules and our cultures are *meaningless* here. We don't matter. We are here for the animals. You *know* that, Johno. You are here for the elephants. That has always been your life. Why change now?"

Wil held up a hand to the protesting crowd, still calling for the death of Caesar. "Let me make this perfectly clear. There will be no more reason to fear Caesar unless there is an attack on The One."

As loud voices tried to point out the fact that Scotty was never in danger, Wil interrupted. "Ut, ut, ut, ut . . . I'm not finished. Caesar is protected. *All of the animals are protected.* They are *not* expendable. Have I not made that clear? Or shall I ask the Womb for a show of support? I can assure you, some of you would not survive it." His glowing eyes traveled around the room, judging the agitation of some, the silence of others. Peter felt eyes rest on him. "Now, let us sit and talk like reasonable men."

Johno and the keepers took their seats, sullen faces forced to accept the law of the Hive, some even showing relief at not having to challenge the big cat.

"Is it safe to say we are all on the same page here? There will be no more trouble?"

"What about the monstrosity in the cavern? How come no one has brought that up?" The accusatory voice came from Cobby. "I need to worry about my son and everyone else in here. Why did you keep such a thing from us? What other secrets do you harbor here?"

Wil remained silent, exchanging quick glances with Netty, who reached for his hand. The exchange did not go unnoticed. Distrust and resentment swirled among the men as the women remained silent. Gloria muttered under her breath.

"What's that you say, Gloria?" Tucker the trucker speared her with his attention.

"I said . . . things could be worse. We could still be above ground and probably dead. I say shut up and don't look a gift horse in the mouth."

"Just like a woman, always the pacifist." Tucker pounded on the table. "Well, I want to know what is going on around here. *We have a right to know.*"

"You have *no* rights here. And no one is hiding secrets." Wil's eyes shifted to Netty again. "There is nothing you need to know right now. As long as you do your duty to the wildlife, the Womb will be satisfied and you will be taken care of. What happened to all the harmony in this place? One man brings evil into our midst and we fall apart? Yes, the death of a loved one . . ."

"*Murder* . . . you mean murder." Salina interrupted, her emotions hanging by a thread.

"Yes . . . the murder." Wil nodded to Salina, his voice softening. "As I was saying, the . . . murder . . . of a loved one is a tragedy . . . as is an accidental death such as that of Elias. But the murderer has been punished by the Womb. You all know the rules here. The wildlife is sacrosanct. If anyone touches them with anything but kindness and respect, the Womb will not hesitate to take appropriate action. You have been given your last chance. Do not bring retribution down on the last of your species. As to secrets, I will decide if there is anything else you need to know."

As everyone absorbed the finality of Wil's words, a lone voice rose above the tension of the crowd. "What about the secrets you *don't* know about?" They all turned to gaze upon Peter, pale and shaky, perspiration dotting his forehead; intense, round eyes staring unblinkingly toward Wil who stood nonplussed.

Recovering, Wil gave Peter a tight smile. "What in the Hive might you be talking about, Peter? As I told you before . . . there are no secrets we are keeping from you. There is nothing in the Hive that we are unaware of." He cast his eyes down, pensively. "Unless, of course the Womb does not wish us to know." He raised his face to Peter. "Why don't you come to the point, Peter? What is it that you are implying?"

Peter peered through the crowd trying to get a gauge on Bonnie. She was his only champion and a source of strength. He had flourished since they'd become friends. He felt like he had a sense of purpose now that she'd awakened a buried empathy for the wildlife in their care.

He still felt a hole in his heart from the absence of the wise and resplendent Tobi. Never again would he climb on her back or wash her in the warmth of their bathing pool. Never again would the glorious goliath fasten him with her eyes of deep wisdom to look into his soul and find him redeemed. Peter squeezed shut his eyes, blocking the gut-wrenching tears that threatened to overwhelm him. Tobi had asked for nothing from him but respect. Yet she'd helped give him back a life. Now it was time for him to go out on a limb and step up. If they were to live without fear all he had learned from his solitary wanderings must be examined. Taking a deep breath, amassing courage from the somber face of his young friend, Bonnie, he plunged on.

"Perhaps you do not know all that Echo and Baby have been up to."

All eyes fastened on the two golden creatures that lounged in their customary spot near the fireplace, each with one arm sunk deep into the membrane of the wall, recharging the energy they called *sustenance*. They slowly retrieved their limbs as they became aware they were now the center of attention.

Scotty's voice rang loud and clear. "Peter, you are out of your mind if you think Echo is up to something. She's with me all the time and she wouldn't do a damn thing to harm a single one of us. And Baby," he turned to glance back at the docile Baby, "Baby is just . . . well . . . Baby—an innocent. How could you even *think* about accusing Baby of *anything*? Echo, come here, girl."

Oddly, Echo remained at the wall with Baby. She turned to her birth minion to cock her head at him, reaching out to touch the little creature's face, tracing slowly down his furry forehead to the golden leather of his mouth. The survivors watched mesmerized as Echo and Baby absorbed themselves in their own world.

"Echo?" Scotty stood up to claim his creature, lifting her off the wall and returning to his seat as Echo's head swiveled all the way around, eyes remaining fixed on Baby. "I don't know why you'd suggest such a thing, Peter. Is the grief and stress of the last few days getting to you?"

Peter scanned the faces of his fellow survivors and the troubled ones of the Elders. Something didn't add up to him. He watched as his old love wrapped her arms around her daughter Daisy as little Kimir sat nearby, a quiet boy who never gave a lick of trouble. *What of their futures?* His eyes rested on the pregnant loveliness of Kenya with her dependence on Kane and concern for her unborn baby overcoming the revelations of his unfaithfulness. *What of the future for the budding family?* He turned to the strong yacht captain, knowing full well Cobby's heart still rested with the unrequited longing he had for the courageous Abby, even as he tried to forget her in the arms of Karen, the willing navigator of the plane that had flown them to New Jersey.

Moving on he spied a somber and devastated Johno, an unlikely match for the redneck and vocal Crystal, a loving mom to their resident oinking and over-indulged porker, Tulip, and her beloved litter of juvenile piglets. He observed Dezi in the background, trying to entice Chance to eat a morsel off his plate.

Dezi had come far, no longer looking for validation through his supposed prowess with women. Red-headed Billy and the dark-skinned, newly svelte Gloria, the survivors' mixed-race lovebirds, looked fearfully up at him, their fingers entwined, wondering at his revelation. He glanced over the table of sullen keepers who sat with trucker Tucker, realizing he knew little of them except for their penchant to love their elephant charges and the easy way they had with wide smiles for everyone. The careworn Salina sat with young Bonnie, a table away from Clyde and the newest member of their collective family, Jennifer . . . still damaged but with a good prognosis if the tendrils of the Womb could continue to work their magic.

As Peter observed the still-mourning Salina glance over to the pair, he wondered if the Diaz and Preston matriarch would every find the happiness she so richly deserved.

And what of me and my happiness? He glanced back at Ginger Mae, remembering the exquisite joy he'd felt as he fell in love for the first time in his life. He loved his elderly parents that had no doubt perished in the aftermath of the bombs, but he didn't recall seeing signs of passion in their steady affection for one another. Little did he know such passion existed. To be offered a taste, and have it so brutally yanked away by the revelations of a disgusting and sick man such as Armoni, had damaged him irreparably. He had doubted he would ever heal from the deep injury. But now he had his perspective back. He understood one could live with other types of passion if denied the love of a good woman. How much did he owe this motley group of people who were still learning how to be a family? What challenges faced them as they waited for the Earth to be ready for them? Peter still smarted from the quickness of those who had turned on him and accused him of consuming the lovable Chance. *And what of Scotty?* He kept his affection for the boy to himself, but he was always aware of the designation of The One anointed on him by the unusual attention of the great Caesar, whom just a few moments ago some wanted to kill. What was the meaning of The One? Was Scotty portended to change their lives in some meaningful way? Peter's emotions warred, flickering across his bland, yet more confident face, as the survivors shuffled with their restlessness.

"Peter?" Scotty tried again to get his attention.

As Peter warred with his decision to challenge the Elders, he gave them one more dispassionate reflection. *Is that a look of fear on the faces of Wil and Netty? Why is that? Do they have something to hide? What's going on behind the large, heavy door with the robed figure and the shrieks that follow as Wil and Netty continue their constant trek with the food wagon?* Peter weighed how much information and how much more stress the survivors could handle, seeing the glimmers of strength in their faces that had taken them all this far. Deciding that they couldn't fall any farther, he decided that the best medicine would be to exorcise anything that threatened their safety.

"I would like to ask a direct question to Echo and Baby. I will trust that, as Elders, you will convey the truth of their answer to us?"

The crowd rustled uneasily with the weighty significance of Peter's words.

"Of course," answered Netty. "We would not do otherwise."

Peter took a deep breath and prayed for the correct words. Glancing into the worried eyes of Bonnie, he found the strength to be blunt. "Echo and Baby have someone or something caged up in another cavern far from here, and they are periodically torturing it. I would like them to explain."

"*What?*" The crowd erupted in fearful astonishment.

Tentative auras assailed the Elders simultaneously as their faces revealed communication with the creatures. "My Brothers and Sisters. You know a minion has not the capability to harm life. We are about the furtherance of all that is good and balanced. But we *do* have the ability to intervene when there is no balance. You know that also." The ominous suggestion of Echo's words was not lost on the Elders.

Netty cried out to Baby with her aura. "Baby? Do you know anything about what this man speaks of?" Baby fluttered down from the wall to stand as though cornered. "Baby?"

Without warning, Baby took to the air, wings beating swiftly. He hung in the air over Wil and Netty, poised for flight.

The moment was hushed as Netty slowly raised her hand to her mouth. "Baby? What is going on? Please . . . you *know* I love you. What is this man speaking of?"

Then Baby was gone. Netty reached out to grasp Wil's arm for support. It was clear there must be some merit in Peter's words. She forced her attention back to the survivors as they peppered Peter with questions and demands.

Netty watched as Peter stood as if he was a creature frozen in front of a hunter not knowing where to run for cover. The sound of a chair scraping over the stone floor drew her attention as Bonnie rose and made her way to Peter's side. She slid her hand over his, her quiet courage all he needed to gather his own strength.

"Well, Netty . . . Baby's behavior appears incriminating. I suggest we get to the bottom of this, don't you agree?" Peter's unwavering focus sent a premonition down her spine.

"I do not know *what* Baby's behavior portends, but I can assure you it is nothing untoward. Perhaps you can show us what exactly you are referring to, Peter?" Netty regarded the survivors. "Who cares to accompany us on this journey? You did say it was a distance away, did you not, Peter?" Again she exchanged worried glances with Wil.

As the survivors sorted themselves out, Wil spoke in low whispers. "Do not worry, Netty. *No one* could know about Father. This is not the time to visit them with another shock. I do not know what this could possibly be about, but Baby's behavior is odd." Wil turned to Scotty. "Do you know anything about this, young man?"

Bristling at the tone of Wil's voice, Netty examined his expression as Scotty defended Echo, believing she knew nothing. Echo herself remained silent, all the more incriminating. With a heavy heart, she made her way to the door of the kitchen. "If you are coming, Scotty, I would like all of the dogs and Caesar to stay behind. If Caesar refuses to leave your side, we will be forced to go without you. I do not want any more creatures put in jeopardy in the event we encounter any . . . danger."

It was decided all the women would stay behind with Kenya, Daisy and Kimir and the creatures. Unbidden, Caesar crept quietly inside to take a place near the posse. No one said a word as the giant cat made himself comfortable near Teddy, the tiny dog no bigger that the tiger's front paws. Netty laughed to herself as she observed Teddy eyeing the big cat, then making his way up the cat's back to introduce himself to its fluffy ear. The levity of the moment lightened her spirits as she set off with the men, Peter in the lead, with Jose and Scotty bringing up the rear and Echo riding on Scotty's hip.

The crowd quietened down as they made their way through the unfamiliar passageways, the constant specter of membrane-enshrouded walls with streaks of lightning reminding them of potential danger even as they forged ahead in search of truth.

Netty worked at her fingers, picking her skin with random nervousness as she wracked her mind about what this could possibly mean as they trekked deeper and deeper into the cavern. *How could Baby, of all of them, play any part in something so diabolical?* she wondered. She glanced constantly at Wil, relishing his quiet, confident air as they made their plodding way, relentless and tiring.

Peter slowed to a stop as they came to an unobtrusive opening in a corridor wall. Netty estimated they were at least two miles from her kitchen. The air felt warmer here, but the small cave in front of them remained shrouded in dimness, making it difficult to see inside. A rancid odor drifted from the cave, redolent of spoiled meat and the metallic scent of blood. Netty bravely squinted into the unknown cave unable to discern a thing. She faced Peter.

"If this is it, where is Baby?" The sudden sound of her anxious voice echoed unnaturally off the walls of the small cave, as if it were empty. To dispel that notion, an unexpected whimper emanated from the cave, followed by a groan as if the very dead had been awakened by the sound of her voice.

Everyone froze, panic in the eyes of most of the survivors.

Cobby spoke up. "There's something in there. It must be hurt. Clyde, did you bring it?"

Netty started as Clyde unwrapped the sledgehammer that had hung on her wall to remind them of what King and Queenie had been through at the hands of the criminally evil dogfighters who had brutally crushed their skulls. *When did he remove that?*

As if he had read her thoughts, Clyde remarked, "We needed something for protection. This was the only thing handy."

Johno turned to Netty and Wil, his voice shaded in whispers as another moaning whimper drifted out to them. "Ms. Netty, I think if you know anything about this, now is the time. It will be hard enough to face what may be waiting for us."

Netty spread her arms wide as they looked from her to Wil. "I assure you, gentlemen, we know nothing of this. I am as curious as you are. Please . . . proceed carefully. And *Baby*. Keep your eyes open for my Baby . . . I beg you. He is fragile and needs to be looked after." She clutched her smock obsessively. "I just do not understand . . ."

Wil circled her shoulders with his arm, puzzlement in his eyes, their golden hue dimming. "Shhh, it will be okay, Netty. Baby will turn up. Let us permit the good men to investigate and we will handle whatever it is."

She smiled as his words brightened her. "Yes, you are correct. I will just wait out here. Call if you need me. Echo . . . would you like to stay here with me?"

Scotty stepped up to transfer his golden creature to Netty, Echo remaining completely silent. Netty gave the hushed minion a quick glance as she nestled her comfortably on her hip, her wings rustling nervously as she snaked her tail around them both for comfort. She stepped back to observe the gathering of men as they took a valiant collective breath and moved forward on the heels of another whimper.

Netty held her breath, the silence of the men ominous. A slow minute passed as she listened. Suddenly she heard something. She craned her neck, the better to hear. Netty could tell they had found something, but their exclamations were indistinct. A new sound assailed her. *What?* She could recognize the sound of retching anywhere. She started to pace, Echo squirming out of her hands to wobble into the cave after the men.

"Echo . . . *stop!*"

Peter crept carefully into the cave, the temperature rising as the heat from their adrenaline fueled bodies mixed with that of the bloody sides of beef that had once been men. He cringed as he grasped the fact that amazingly, the men were still alive. They hung suspended from the walls, their arms engulfed in the protruding undulating mass, essentially acting as a manacle. Beneath the men lay prodigious hills of dried and fresh blood and feces collecting on the flat rock floor.

"Holy Mother of God . . . ." Gasps from Peter's fellow survivors were augmented with tremors of pity and horror. The stench was overpowering. Trailing his eyes over the men, he kept his hand to his nose. He could clearly see that they were being kept alive by the familiar tendrils that ran from the walls directly to the veins of the men who appeared to have been flayed almost to death, leaving only their macabre faces untouched. A large tubular swath of membrane drove directly into their stomachs, providing what appeared to be nutrition.

Cobby and Wil crept closer, peering through the dimness. Wil's tail began a steady swatting in the air, his fist pounding into his thigh as he stared uncomprehendingly at the man in the middle.

"Do you know these men, Wil?"

Wil continued to stare, ignoring Peter's question as Netty's voice carried to the front of the little cave.

"*Echo* . . . stop."

Before Peter realized it, Netty stood next to Wil. His arms held her back as she stood in disbelief to survey the hapless men. The moment was frozen in Peter's mind as he heard Netty gasp then shake her head, hair cascading as she bent at the waist as if in pain. She looked around, a woman crazed.

"Baby . . . uggg . . . where is my Baby?" Tears fell from her eyes as her groans matched that of the man in the middle. Just as suddenly, she vomited. An unexpected sound emanated from the sufferer in the middle. Peter strained to hear. A whisper. Netty froze as Peter crept closer to hear.

"Whore."

Did I hear that correctly?

Netty snapped out of her malaise, whirling around frantically.

"Baby . . . *where is Baby*? He must be here. We must find him. Wil . . . *where is my Baby*?" Her voice rose to a scream and Wil never took his golden eyes off the man in the middle.

Peter rushed to calm a hysterical Netty, while the other survivors remained rooted in place, overwhelmed by the tableau, their minds unable to process.

"Hey, can I have some *help* here?" Scotty blinked as if waking from a trance to turn to Peter who stood with his arms wrapped around a screaming and crying Netty. "Come *on*, I need some *help* here."

Finally, Johno and Cobby ran to Peter's side. Johno lifted Netty in his strong arms and carried her outside the cave to sink to the ground with her in his arms. The other men followed them out of the cave to cluster around Johno and Netty, leaving Wil like a stone statue in front of the hunks of hanging flesh.

Netty clutched at Johno's arms, her face turned up to him beseechingly. Clearly not in her right mind, she began to beg. "Johno, where is Baby? Please . . . we must find *my Baby*."

An abrupt sound, like rock scraping on pebbles, begged their attention. Craning their heads toward an overlooked boulder about the size of a chair, they were astonished to discover Baby crouched down, plastered tightly to the rock and curled up in a fetal position.

"What? *Baby*." Netty scrambled out of Johno's arms to stand unsteadily. Peter watched, keeping everyone back as she approached the shivering creature, her tears now happy ones as a relieved smile split her face. "My precious one. Why are you hiding there?" Netty crouched down, holding her arms out to the creature as he slowly unwound his tail and crept over to Netty's waiting arms. She held him to her breast, folding her wings to enclose them in an intimate embrace. Peter could hear her crooning and murmuring to the shivering creature as they all waited for an explanation.

Within moments they were joined by Wil, who gulped deeply of the clearer air before peeling back Netty's wings to lift Baby from her arms. He held Baby close, muttering to the creature as they swayed together. Peter could hear snippets of reassuring words. "It is okay, Baby. We love you, don't you know that? That is all right, we understand. You could have told us. No, no . . . you did it for *all of us*. We are the same way. Retribution is part of the human condition. It makes sense, we got it from you. We are part of you. You are our creators. Yes, yes . . . shhh, maybe we can find a better way."

Netty stood close, nodding as Wil spoke to the creature. A sudden whimper from inside drew everyone's attention back to the contents of the cave.

Wil, Netty and Baby turned to face Peter and the rest of the survivors. Netty spoke first, crestfallen and contrite. "Well, Peter. I sincerely owe you an apology. I pray you will accept it."

Confronting the rest of the survivors, she took a deep breath, shuddering as she shook away the effects of her momentary hysteria. Smoothing her hair into place, she raised her hands to her face, whisking the last residue of tears away and squaring her shoulders. Then she hung her head silently.

Peter whispered her name. "Netty? Are you all right?"

She continued to hang her head. Peter heard her take another deep breath then she raised her face to meet theirs, her eyes brightening, and her chin proud. "I am sure you are wondering who those . . . men . . . are in there. I have not seen them in over one hundred years." She blinked at the puzzlement on Peter's face, and then dropped the bomb. "The man in the middle was . . . is . . . my former husband, Robert Doyle."

Netty's voice stopped as she closed her eyes, the strain evident as she visibly gathered strength. "The other two are his lackeys, Eli . . ." she exhaled, "and Sheriff Hudson. They are murderers most vile."

Netty reached for Wil, her hand trembling, her voice catching. "They are . . . they are the evil that took our lives out of greed for money."

A hush fell over the dazed crowd as Peter realized they were in the midst of an account of a very personal human tragedy.

Netty carefully sank to the hard rock floor, gathering her wings close, her tail limp and quiet. "Wil, may I please have Baby?" Wil passed the little creature over to her. She smiled gently at the creature, stroking and comforting him. With one more embrace, Baby settled down to curl up in her lap, Wil and the survivors settling down on the ground to listen to her explanation.

As Netty haltingly related the horror of her life with Robert Doyle, Peter watched the emotion pour like blood from a wound. Periodically, Baby reached up to place his fingers on her face. Netty would stop to pause as they exchanged communication, prompting a smile or an embrace from Netty. Wil sat quietly, his face tight, eyes dim.

Netty's life sounded like something from a horror movie: ripped from the comfort of a sheltered home to be abused unmercifully by a rapacious fiend, then murdered for her inherited farmland. After Netty stopped speaking, Wil picked up the story, eulogizing the fruits of their hard work on their farm and the love they had shared as a family, until he'd been framed and thrown in jail, where he'd been murdered by an assassin engaged by Robert Doyle. His voice drowned in bitterness, with the exception of his tender memories of his horse, Maggie. Peter was appalled by the description of Maggie's wanton death by the loathsome monsters.

As the story came to an end, Peter's analytical attorney brain begged a few questions. "But Netty, if you don't mind, can you please explain to us exactly how you came to be here?"

Netty nodded, anticipating the question. "Upon our burial, the Womb sent its manifestation to recover our bodies. You have seen the power of the beast. We call it the Kreyven. It cannot do anything other than fulfill the dictates of the Womb. It can travel anywhere underground and retrieve anything the Womb desires. It can travel under the floor of any body of water, even oceans. The Kreyven can excavate tiny tunnels or entire cities if the Womb desires."

Netty smiled tightly. "How do you think we were able to supply this place? And the library? The Kreyven simply created a wide tunnel under the building in Washington that engulfed it. As Washington quaked about the bombs, who was left to care about the shambles of The Library of Congress and the missing books? That is why we have been forced to spend so much time cleaning and reorganizing. The room in the back, where Daisy studies, is what was left of the tunnel the Kreyven used to bring material and books here. The same goes for everything you have found in the supply room. It was a simple matter to retrieve our bodies the same way. The extraction of our DNA and our memories were child's play to the minions that regrew us."

Peter nodded slowly, unfazed by the science behind the obvious cloning. From behind him, he overheard more muttering. A distant sob from the cave set the rest of the men off; Johno's keepers were the most vocal and the most frightened, fearing what they failed to understand.

Cobby sounded a question. "But what of the men in there? We can't just let them hang there like that. Even murderers are treated better than *that*. We are a country of laws. You just can't take matters into your own hands like that."

Wil fixed Cobby with his withering scrutiny. "Where is your country of laws now? I thought you understood: The law is what the Womb wants it to be. The conscience of the Womb dictates the level of reasonableness and we have never had any reason to test how far that may go."

Peter could hear the doubt in Cobby's voice. "But you are a man. How could you condone such monstrous treatment?"

Wil fixed the yacht captain with his stare, lips compressed in anger. "Yes, I *condone* this. This is what they deserve. Did you not hear the psychotic deeds they have done to us? *They stole our lives.*" Wil slammed his hand on the stone floor in anger, his eyes flashing and his tail high in the air, snapping as if ready to flagellate them on his command.

Peter raised his hands in a supplicating gesture. "It's all good, Wil . . . relax. Cobby didn't mean anything by it."

"The hell I didn't."

Peter shot him a silencing look and continued. "So, you're saying you knew about this? Did you set this up?"

"Hahahaha." Startled by Wil's laughter, Peter looked to Netty. Baby sat up and tried to right himself, slipping off Netty's lap to scurry back to the rock to cower.

"Please . . . can we please just have some quiet? No, Peter . . . we did not . . . plan this. Nor did we know of it until . . . today." Netty sounded exhausted, her words slowing.

"Well, then?" he asked.

Her voice was hesitant and low but the survivors heard her all the same. "It was . . . Baby."

Peter's astonishment mirrored that of the entire group.

"Well, the little fucker." A voice from the back.

Wil went wild. *"No.* Don't you even *presume* to malign Baby. *How dare you?* If it weren't for Baby, your bones would be nothing but crumbled ash and *don't you forget it."*

"Well, what are we going to do with the men in there? We cannot leave them like that." Johno's reasoned tones were like cream to a starving cat. Wil sobered quickly as they all watched Netty coax Baby out from under the boulder, Echo standing silently by. After a moment of communication, the duo approached the entrance to the cave. Baby turned, his eyes flashing, his demeanor animated unlike anything Peter had ever seen. The golden creature suddenly looked menacing. He stood as tall as his small body would allow, tugging on Netty's hand.

Wil slipped to their side as Netty spoke in low emotional tones. "He did this for *us,* Wil, *for us.* Baby was so filled with hate and anguish over what happened to us that he orchestrated this with the cooperation of the Kreyven." Her eyes glittered with love and pride for the devoted creature. "They have been here for at least fifty years." She looked up wondrously. "They must be quite mad by now."

Peter heard gasps from the crowd as they reacted to Netty's revelation.

"What . . . your God was not an avenging god? Remember of

whom we speak. They are one and the same," she added with raging indignation. Netty placed her hand in Wil's and turned back to the men. "It is time. They will be given one last chance . . . *if* there is anything left in their black souls." Turning back to the cave, the tiny family entered and stood in front of the meat hanging from the walls.

The survivors crept behind, not anxious to confront the beastly odors, but curious none the less. Peter covered his mouth with his sleeve as he watched Netty, with Baby in her arms, approach the first man. The man rustled, sensing something different. His eyelids actually opened, squinty and bloody under his hairless pate. Peter could hear the fractured gurgling deep in the man's throat. Netty stood, unmoving.

"Eli." The man did not respond. "Eli." Netty's voice rose, her anger showing. Still no response; the gurgling diminished. Netty stooped to Baby, the creature nodding his head.

From the cave walls a tendril extended to each side of the men, embedding themselves in the open flesh of their throats. It took a few minutes, but Eli's tendrils then receded back into the wall.

"Eli." Netty's call was followed by the gurgling and then a swallow.

"NNNNNN."

"Eli."

"Nnnnneey?" The man was incomprehensible.

Peter glanced at the other two men and saw the tendrils had visited them as well; viscous evidence protruding from the walls to disappear into the men's necks. Feeling dizzy, Peter reached out to steady himself with Clyde's arm. That was all it took to send Clyde crashing down to the floor in a profound faint.

"Neeetty?"

"Yes, Eli, it is me."

"Get me . . . me oooutta here."

"I would like to ask you a question, Eli."

"Outa here." Eli's head rolled forward, the stench from his mouth forcing Peter to step back. Retching sounds filled the little cave again.

"Eli." Netty's voice exuded ice, her face like marble

"Out nowwww, bitccccch." Slobber from Eli's mouth dripped down, spattering Netty's arm and still she didn't move.

"Fuuucckin bitccccch, out noooow or I'mmm gunnnna keel you."

"Is that all you have to say to me, Eli?"

Eli's eyes leaked blood, rolling back into his head as he responded with gibberish. Netty moved on to stand in front of her former husband.

"Robert."

Apparently Robert's throat had received a better dose of healing because he wasn't as unintelligible as Eli. His voice whispered clearly. "Whore."

Netty didn't blink. "Do you have anything to say to me, Robert?"

"Get me . . . down from here, Netty." Robert had begun to drool, his body twitching madly. Netty stood, unmoved. "Now . . . get me down, *now*."

"What if I tell you that is not going to happen?"

Robert's head jerked back, his eyes flashing in their sunken sockets. "How *dare* you defy me, you gutter snipe? Hey you . . . over there. Get me off this wall *right now*."

Netty gazed up at Robert, disgust on her face tempered with what Peter thought was tired resignation. She inspected every inch of his face and found him wanting. With a shake of her head, she moved on.

"Sheriff Hudson."

The man gazed down on Netty. "An angel?"

Netty shook her head. Peter remarked on the man's calm, clear tone even as the blood dripped into his mouth from his nose.

"No, Sheriff. I used to be Netty Doyle. Do you remember me?"

"You cannot be Netty. She died. She died with her creature."

"Do you see what is in my arms, Sheriff Hudson? It is the creature. *My Baby*."

"You had . . . you had a baby, Netty?"

She closed her eyes and bowed her head. "Sheriff, do you have anything to say to me?"

Sheriff Hudson moved his head from right to left, blinking down at her. "My Lord, it . . . it really is you, Netty?" His voice lowered, soft and labored, his strength waning.

Netty shook her head and turned away.

"P . . . le . . . ase. P . . . le . . . ase, Netty . . . forgive me . . . ."

Netty froze. She turned slowly to the man, approaching him to position her hand softly on his bloody chest. As Peter watched, her fingers started to glow, activating the tendrils to swell, and the skin on the sheriff's torso healed before his eyes. Lightning streaks flashed from inside the membrane that clung to the wall. Fearfully, the men pulled back to the opening of the cave, not anxious to meet the Kreyven again. Netty turned away as the membranes released the sheriff, dumping him to the ground, his body landing on the noxious hills of blood and waste.

Netty crooked her finger at Peter and Cobby while Jose attended the feeble Clyde. "Bring him."

With relief Peter signaled Scotty as Johno and Cobby lifted the tortured man, two of them taking an arm and throwing it over their backs to drag him outside the cave. Jose and Tucker lifted the queasy Clyde, helping him to fresher air as Billy shambled behind, vomit strewn down the front of his shirt.

"Hey, where you all going? *Netty*. You get back here right now. Get me out of here." Robert's voice rang out strongly.

"Yeah . . . come on back here, baby. Let your ole buddy Eli down, nice and friendly like. Ya know what I mean?" Eli leered obscenely.

The last thing Peter saw was the vision of Netty's resplendent beauty, with wings open wide as her crystal horns swirled with red and black streaks. Her regal face remained calm and resolute as her horns split, sending minute red and black projectiles to the men, cutting their voices off in mid-scream. Netty held out her hand to Baby, lifting him to her hip where he clasped his little leather hands around her neck and tucked his golden head onto her shoulder. She then slipped her other hand under Wil's arm and proceeded resolutely down the cavern trail back to her kitchen as Peter took a last peek at the bare skeletons that hung swaying from the gelatinous walls of their half-century home. May the Womb rest their black souls.

Chapter 13

Ginger Mae kept her eye on Daisy and Kimir as she stroked the tresses of Kenya's long, dark, curly hair. Everyone tried to relax as they waited for the men to return. Anxieties ran high as the women prayed everyone would return safely.

"*Ouch*. Chickey, if you keep pulling like that on my hair I'm gunna give birth just so I can send the baby back there to show you a thing or two."

"I'm sorry, Kenya. I was just daydreaming."

"What's ya dreaming about, chickey?"

Ginger Mae's face took on a far-away expression. "You know . . . I was pretty happy here. My life wasn't what I wanted it to be in New York City or Sarasota. God knows it was my own fault I got mixed up with Armoni. And every time I think about what he did to hurt Daisy, I want to cry. But before that monster Seth appeared we were all pretty happy, weren't we?"

Kenya started to relax again under the touch of Ginger Mae's brushing. "I know . . . don't I know . . ." she sighed. "I guess my idea to go back to Sarasota was pretty lame. Musta been the hormones."

"Yeah, Kenya. It must have been the hormones." The two women burst out laughing.

"I guess some things never change. We'll keep using that lame excuse as long as we still have men around." Kenya rubbed her abdomen, a pretty smile curving her lips. "I think I need to work on Abby and Netty. I think they can help me birth this baby a mine. Whatcha ya think, chickey?"

"I think if they could, they already would have."

"Nah, I think they're just testing me. I think they have their reasons. I just need ta git on their good side. You know me, Ginger Mae. Sometimes I can just wear ya right down." She sobered, biting a finger nail. "I think that's what I did to Kane. Why else would he have been toying with Emma behind my back?"

"Sweetie, that's not why men do what they do. It probably had nothing to do with you. They just can't help themselves. You best be making damn sure you're good to Kane, so he sticks by you and this baby. He's a good boy and you're going to need him."

Salina walked by with a cup of tea in her hand, giving the girls a pasty smile.

"Miss Salina . . . come right here, chickey. You sit right here with us. Put yer feet up here in my lap, there's still some room. I'm gonna give you the foot massage of your life."

"That's very kind of you, Kenya. But I'll take a rain check." Salina's face looked wrinkled and old, her eyes still full of pain. Even the healing powers of the Womb had failed to erase the vestiges of her mourning.

"Mind if we join you, ladies?" Karen and Gloria made their way to the fireplace to pull up chairs, Clyde's granddaughter, Jennifer tagged along and crouched on the floor next to Kenya. Karen sat crossing her long limber legs after giving them a good stretch. "You sure look good, Kenya. I know it's not fun for you, but pregnancy really agrees with you."

Chloe plopped at their feet next to Jennifer, tired of playing with Teddy and Caesar. Chiming in, she squeezed Kenya's hand. "I can't wait for the baby to come. We need some distraction around here. I always wanted a brother or sister. This will be the next best thing."

"Jose's your brother, young lady," Salina chastised Chloe.

"But I didn't grow up with him. It's not the same at all."

"Well, chickeys . . . ." Kenya waggled her eyebrows. "We've been here getting on close to a year now . . . what's it been . . . eight months? And I know you all aren't sleepin' alone."

Snickers from the women encouraged Kenya's knowing assertion. "I don't think it's a stretch to expect a tucker or two ta keep my baby company."

Karen grinned anxiously. "I sure would love to have a baby with Cobby."

I bet you would. You're going to need something like that to bind his eye for Abby back to you, darling. Ginger Mae felt a pang for herself as she realized she didn't have a man to love. *Am I jealous of Karen?*

Gloria spoke up. "Billy and I have talked about having a little redhead of our own." She frowned as she spoke. "I'm surprised it hasn't happened, it's not like we use birth control."

Chloe weighed in. "Scotty and I have discussed it, too. I think we're just a little young for that now. But we don't know how to prevent it either." Her voice took on a conspiratorial tone. "And what would happen to the baby? I mean . . . uh . . . Scotty's an Elder. Would my baby be alright?"

Ginger Mae turned to Chloe, slipping a loose wisp of her short hair back behind an ear. "That might be a good question for Netty." Ginger Mae glanced across the kitchen where Abby busied herself with cleaning. "Kenya wants to pin her down about the baby's delivery, too. Maybe you could both have a talk with her."

Chloe's face flushed. "I couldn't. I'd be too embarrassed."

The women snorted, Crystal's hoots the loudest as she came in on the tail of the conversation. "You're just a baby yourself, little one. If ya want to be a mommy, ya better toughen up. It ain't for the faint of heart. Right, Kenya doll?"

A sudden noise at the kitchen door drew Ginger Mae's attention. *"They're back."* The women rushed to the door, recoiling as the stench of the men preceded them.

"Eww . . . what the heck?"

"For heaven's sakes, guys."

They stepped back as Netty entered, Baby on her hip, her face a mask, effervescent eyes averted, her tail and wings clasped tightly to her body. She was followed by Wil, stony and silent. The women exchanged quick glances, fearful and confused.

Behind the Elders came Johno and Tucker with Clyde between them. They set him in the nearest chair, hollering for water.

"I need something stronger than water, boys," Clyde remarked.

Gloria embraced Billy, jumping back as the source of the stench greeted her from the front of his shirt. "What the . . .?" Her words were cut off as Peter and Cobby dragged in a strange figure; Scotty,

Jose and Kane bringing up the rear. Echo jumped from Scotty's arms to run to the fireplace, burying his head in Barney's curly fur.

Johno began to shout orders. "Ms. Salina, we need bandages and warm water. Boys, lay him out here." Johno cleared the closest table, sweeping out with his arm, sending utensils crashing to the floor. "Ms. Abby, can I impose on you for some of Netty's hot potage? *Hurry now*. Soap . . . we need soap too, Ms. Salina." He glanced up to see Ginger Mae hovering nearby. "Ginger Mae, can you round us up some blankets and clean clothes?"

She nodded her head as she examined the tall stranger on the table. His eyes were shut and gunk covered him from head to toe. He was buck naked with what looked like trails of dried feces stuck to his withered legs. Johno met her eyes. She relaxed visibly as she recognized the placid urgency in his African orbs. Not fear.

"Ginger Mae . . . today, please."

She jumped, snapping back to the task at hand. Rushing to the kitchen doorway she threw a quick glimpse at Daisy and Kimir. "You stay right where you are, okay Daisy Chain?" Her eyes moved to Abby who spoke up, making her way to Daisy to place her hand on the child's shoulder as she smoothed Kimir's thick, dark hair. "Don't worry, Ginger Mae. I'll take care of her. She'll be fine with me."

Dashing out of the kitchen, Ginger Mae bristled. *I bet you'd just love to take care of my daughter, wouldn't you? Well, that'll be over my dead body, Miss Hot Stuff.* And off she ran to the supply cave, returning as quickly as she could. The kitchen had quieted down as everyone hovered over the stranger, peppering the men with questions about Peter's discovery. Wondering why he'd kept it to himself for so long, Peter stood, flushed and grinning like a fool as he found himself the man of the hour.

Well, I guess that's an improvement. Maybe now the bad blood between us will cool. Looks like he's coming out of his shell. Ginger Mae glanced at Bonnie, who hovered nearby with Dezi, clapping her hands in awe, as Peter regaled them with details of their adventure.

As she handed Johno her supplies, she observed Crystal gathering the dirty cloths from the floor that had been used to clean the stranger. The man lay clean and naked on the table as Johno, assisted by Tucker, attempted awkwardly to dress him in the clothes she'd retrieved.

"For Pete's sake, you two. Let me." They gratefully turned the chore over to her capable hands. *It's not like I haven't seen a naked man before.* Carefully she threaded his arms through the shirt and, propping his head up with her shoulder, slipped the garment over his shoulders to smooth down over what looked like tissue-paper red skin, tracings of blue veins showing prominently through the epidermis. She carefully set his head atop a pile of blankets she'd retrieved from storage, noticing not a strand of hair remained on his tender scalp. She could witness the man's heartbeat, weak and thready as the pulse of his blood, showing clear under the red skin of his skull. Lifting his hand to anchor on his chest she noticed the lack of fingernails, her stomach doing a flip-flop as she cringed with the knowledge of how painful it must be. Another glance at the man's face and she wondered if he was with them enough to even *feel* pain.

She moved away as Salina approached with some water. She watched as Salina slipped her arm under the man's head to attempt to force the liquid between his misshapen and horribly crusted lips. The water ineffectually dribbled down his neck.

Leaving Salina to her task, she scanned the room, deciding to join a table that held some of the men, after assuring herself with a little wave that Daisy was fine by Kenya and the dogs at the fireplace.

Now that Scotty had returned, Caesar had apparently returned to his customary position in the hallway, all thoughts of killing the big tiger forgotten.

With relief, Ginger Mae sank down in a chair to catch up on the gossip. Before she could even ask a question, the table was approached by Wil and Netty, Baby clinging tightly to her as if modeling the behavior of a real human child.

Wil opened his mouth to speak, both the Elders looking drawn and defiant. Ginger Mae knew something was up. "Gentleman, we realize you must share our . . . adventure . . . with the rest of the survivors, but we ask for your understanding and to keep the details to a minimum." Wil gave them a weak smile. "Do I have your assurances?" Heads bobbed rapidly as the men swore they understood . . . and he could count on them.

What the heck is going on? Ginger Mae watched as the unhappy twosome left the room.

It took Ginger Mae an entire six minutes to pull the story out of them. Within another half hour everyone had the details, all the way down to how many of the men had barfed.

The survivors spent another hour sipping tea, gulping down prodigious amounts of Netty's green-crust fruit pies and having a surprising uplift of spirits from the sensational peculiarities of their latest exploration. Nothing like some ole fashioned prurient interest in someone else's pain to allow you some respite from your own. Even as they feasted, the men all fearfully agreed that they had a newborn respect for Netty and her powers.

Cobby finally rose, pointing to the man who still lay unconscious on the hard table.

"Johno, Scotty, Kane. Any of you want to give me a hand with this guy? What do you say we bunk him in Seth's old room. You're not using it anymore are you, Jennifer?" A quick shake from Jennifer was all they need to cart him off.

Ginger Mae collected Kimir and Daisy. "Come on you two, time for bed."

As they made their way through the corridors, Daisy turned to her mom. "I'm trying to estimate the probability of the strange man being a psychotic extrovert like Seth, Mommy."

Ginger Mae looked with pride and surprise at her precocious six-year-old. "Don't worry your head with things like that, Daisy Chain. Forewarned is forearmed, I always say. I am darn sure the men won't even *think* of taking their eyes off this varmint."

So it came as quite a surprise when the next morning Netty informed her of her new assignment. In addition to her other duties, she would be in charge of monitoring the health of their new guest. *Guest? I thought the man's a murderer?* All eyes turned expectantly to her as her mind floundered from one weak excuse to another. She spied Daisy eating some strange concoction Netty had put in front of her: her brilliant, innocent child. She looked back at Netty. *No, she wouldn't do that, would she?*

Shrugging her shoulders as she realized her time with Daisy would be severely limited with an added responsibility, she accepted. It would only be for a while, until they decided what to do with the man. Maybe they would send him on his way once he was healthier. Or let the Kreyven have him. She knew for damn sure that tending to a murderer might not be that hard, but she had no intention of allowing this to become a long-term thing. She had her animals that needed her. She sipped her tea, glancing back at Daisy for reassurance in time to catch Abby brushing her hands through Daisy's thin hair as they shared a private laugh.

After breakfast, Ginger Mae headed for the stranger's room. Netty was kind enough to tell her the man's name was Hudson, but no more than that. Setting down her pail of warm water, Ginger Mae tied back her hair with a band. She dipped a cloth into the water, taking an extra minute to let her hands luxuriate in the warmth. Wringing out the cloth, she negotiated around the healing tendrils that remained to cleanse the man's skeletal face. The warm cloth rode over his jutting cheekbones and down to his neck. He began to twitch, startling her. *Must be the warm water.*

The stink of the man held fast, even as she gave him his second bath since his arrival. Examining him closer, she decided she had nothing to fear. Stepping back to survey her work, she considered he looked like a mummy someone had taken the time to unwrap, even with the tendrils hanging from his pores. She bet he couldn't even stand. Who could, after hanging from a stinking wall for fifty years? *Hmmm . . . why fifty years? Why not a hundred? That's how long Netty and Wil have been here.*

Ginger Mae quickly concluded Hudson's bath with a fresh smock to cover his bony frame. Whistling happily, she eventually made her way down the corridor with her clipboard to inspect her animals. The best part of her day had just begun.

*

Three weeks passed quickly. Ginger Mae found herself feeling as fit as she had when she was a young women in her twenties. With her newfound vigor, her capabilities sharpened, her disposition improved, and her annoyance over the care of Hudson diminished. He slowly regained some body mass as the tendrils did their intricate magic. His skeletal frame no longer curled itself into a fetal position and his body relaxed and found its own resting point. Now he merely looked like a recovering cancer victim with stubble appearing on his skull to suggest his hair would regrow. Examining his nail beds, she could feel ridges that would become fingernails. His skin was flushed with the activity of healthy blood cells, rushing oxygen to the parts of his body under repair. She stepped in to change his linen three times a day now as his body regained more normal waste removal functions. Large cotton cloths worked well as adult diapers. *Where are those wonderful Pampers when you need them?* She laughed to herself. Hudson remained comatose, the twitching having escalated to being accompanied by periodic groans.

The rest of the survivors had slipped back into a quagmire of frightened mourning; Salina, Clyde, Bonnie, and Jennifer the most affected. They all recognized that Salina and Clyde needed a great deal of time. The respite they'd felt on the night they'd rescued Hudson was now a distant memory. They prayed that in their grief they'd be able to find their way back to one another.

Bonnie and Jennifer were another matter. Both were healthy young girls with long lives ahead of them. Nature had a way with youth. The problem with Jennifer was that she was in need of professional help. They could only speculate on the tendrils' healing of the mind, a much more complicated process. Judging from the uncorrected damage to Baby during his death and subsequent mind transfer, the survivors speculated avidly on the finite powers of the Womb.

Dezi and Peter devoted themselves to the task of supporting Bonnie, who still refused to visit Tobi's old herd. The elephant behavior was not what one would call normal, but their restlessness had abated with small signs that one of the juvenile females might be ready to assert a claim to mini-matriarch.

The herd's excitement over the impending birth of the first calf since they'd left Africa boded well. Nothing brought a herd of elephants together more than a calf in their care. Calves became so important to the mental health of a herd that in the wild, some older elephants were known to attempt kidnappings of babies from other herds. The few calves they had now were so well adjusted to the Hive that everyone hoped they would more than make up for the missing Tobi.

Today, Ginger Mae found herself late for the count in the cat and bear bathing cave. As her body became healthier, her muscles developed more strength. She no longer had difficulty controlling their enthusiasm at her appearance. She now received less bumps and bruises, and had learned how to bob and weave as they jumped up at her for their brand of kitty love. Her fondness for the majestic cats ripened and deepened. Caesar's constant presence had served to desensitize her to their frightful power.

As she entered their cave, she took note of Bonnie and Peter playing with the lion cubs, the mother nowhere to be seen. She breathed deeply the rich aroma of wet felines as she began her count. An occasional chuff from a bear, or a low roar, told her all was well as they played hide-and-seek among the boulders and jutting outcrops over the water, soaking her to the skin as usual. *Oh well, it's only water.*

As she finished the count, she could hear laughter floating along the water's edge. Glancing back at Bonnie and Peter, she wondered at their relationship. She'd been aware of its budding months ago and had witnessed its miraculous effect on Peter. She reflected on his tale of a lonely childhood when they'd dated. She could certainly understand the attraction Bonnie would represent. Almost a return to the childhood he'd missed out on. A chance to develop a few of the social life skills we learn as children that had eluded him. He would be surprised to know she was happy for him.

Ginger Mae's thoughts returned to the time she first met Peter, smiling inwardly. She hadn't initially been attracted to the nebbish lawyer, but when he'd smiled, his face had transformed. He had that boyish, clear-eyed honesty—almost an innocence—compared to the world she was from. She shook her head, reminding herself that those days were long gone, leaving only the scars they all shared from their encounter with Armoni.

She decided to stroll over to the lion's pen to check off the cubs, having located their mother on a rock ledge within eye sight of the pen. Peter looked up as she approached, a subtle tightening around his eyes and the flat smile serving as a reminder of their current cordial but cool relationship.

"Hello, Ginger Mae." He stood up, leaving Bonnie flat on the ground with two of the four cubs stretched across her back and entangled in her hair. Teeth and claws mauled her unmercifully as the happy cubs moaned in ecstasy.

"HHHi . . . hey, don't leave me down here. Get these monkeys off my back. Come on, you two." Bonnie flayed her arms back awkwardly, trying to knock the now fifty-pound cubs off her back. Breathing heavily she rolled over, dumping them to the ground and taking her head with them as a paw remained tangled in her hair.

"Ow . . . owowoo."

Peter laughed and leaned down to help her disentangle.

"It's nice to see you having fun, Bonnie." Ginger Mae gave her a warm smile.

"Thanks." Bonnie eyed her from head to toe. "I wish I could say the same to you. I guess the cats have been at you again?"

Ginger Mae smiled ruefully at her drenched and sodden appearance. "I don't mind. It's become fun for me. They don't mean anything by it."

Conversation stopped as Peter just stood there wordlessly. She began to feel the strain when shouting came from the other side of the pond near the entrance. They could see lovebirds Gloria and Billy with two of the keepers, waving their hands. As the threesome made their way over, Ginger Mae saw excitement and grins splitting their ruddy faces.

"Come on, come on . . . ya gotta see." Gloria grabbed her arm.

"Come on, we don't want to miss it. Everyone else is over there." One of the keepers put his hands together in supplication.

"It is the baby. She is coming. The baby ele is coming."

As they were swept up in the exultant tide of observers, Peter murmured to Bonnie, her posture stiff and resistant, confusion in her eyes. "You okay, kid? You don't have to go if you don't want to."

"Will you stay with me if I don't go?"

"Ha, ha, ha, ha. Heck *no.* I want to be there for this. The whole Hive is probably there now. Come on, you can do it." With those words they hustled Bonnie down the rock corridor to the elephants, barging in as the calf made the beginnings of her momentous slide out of the snug shelter of young Namba's womb.

They were greeted by cheers as the other survivors spotted Bonnie.

Johno rushed to her side. "I am so happy to see you here, little one. Your friends have missed you."

The celebration dampened as Bonnie surveyed the herd, the elephants leaving the side of the birthing mother to barrage Bonnie with their welcoming trumpets and questing trunks. Johno held her tight as they threatened to knock her over with their exuberance. Ginger Mae saddened as Bonnie wiped away a tear, valiantly attempting to rise to the occasion. Everyone could see her trembling. Ginger Mae reached out to squeeze Bonnie's hand. She nodded gratefully.

Soon everyone's attention focused back on the calf still struggling to break through the last barrier of its journey, to let gravity announce its arrival with the customary thud to the ground. They made themselves comfortable around the little herd, some finding the piles of browse from the growing fields, others just sitting on the cold stone floor.

Making their way in slowly for the benefit of the perennially pregnant Kenya; Scotty, Chloe and Kane joined the crowd. Of course, with them came the accompanying posse of excited dogs. Kane placed the chair he carried from the kitchen in a good spot for

Kenya. Ginger Mae looked around, failing to see Netty, Daisy, Baby and Echo. Dismissing them from her mind, she watched Kenya try to adjust herself to a comfortable position.

"All right, all right. Stand back." Kenya waved her demanding arms to the crowd of survivors. "I don't want *nobody* to get in my way, understand, chickeys? Ain't *no way* this big mama is gonna have her baby without me catching every move. If she can do it, I sure as hell can too. *Now watch out.*"

It took another hour before they were rewarded with the sight of the Hive's first elephant calf. Everyone oohed and aahed as the baby dropped with the expected thud. Their clapping hands frightened the skittish mom as Johno hushed them, explaining his concern that the mom now had no experienced female model from whom to learn how to care for her calf. They couldn't afford to have the young mom reject the infant. It needed that critical drink of its mother's first milk to ingest the lifesaving colostrum that would pass on precious antibodies to the newborn. Without them the calf would not survive when they resurfaced. It would be protected by the benefits of the Hive, but that would cease when their tenure underground ended.

"I think it is time for everyone to return to their day. Mama needs to be stress free, now," Johno decreed, his face ashy and tired. They all turned as the wobbly calf made a squeal; its tiny trunk, hardly longer than a man's arm, searched for its milk as it struggled to keep its balance on the hard rocky floor, getting no co-operation from Namba. To everyone's dismay the confused young mama ran to the fringe of the herd, looking back at the calf as if it were a foreign object. Conversely, the rest of the herd met the baby with excitement and trunk sniffing, examining its pliant, wrinkly skin from head to toe. Sadly, none could give the hungry calf what it so desperately needed from its own mama.

Ginger Mae watched Bonnie carefully as she detected further wretchedness weighing the teen down, the dejected air of the keepers infecting everyone. *Just what nobody needs right now.*

Suddenly, the air filled with feathery flutters as Echo and Baby decided to put in an appearance. They alighted on the floor near the elephants, delighting the pachyderms that had missed their playful buddies. Barney broke from the crowd to scurry as fast as his legs would take him, asserting his usual place at Echo's side, the minion's hand dipping possessively around Barney's neck.

As everyone gawked at the creatures, in walked Netty and Daisy. They approached slowly, Daisy holding a ribbon around the neck of a newborn baby elephant, considerably more stable on its legs than the first calf. In silence, they made their way to the herd and the survivors. Netty wore a satisfied smile as Daisy danced her way across the rock floor with the strange tiny calf in tow.

"*Surprise,*" she shouted, her glee uncontainable. The new calf waved its trunk wildly, sounding little squeals and snorts. The herd froze in place, intent on the strange second calf, which began to scratch at the floor with its miniscule legs. As it let loose another ear-shattering squall, the herd made a mad rush to its side, trunks a-quiver, accompanied by the deep rumblings they employed to communicate.

Ginger Mae could feel the timbre of the rumblings in every fiber of her body. Wearing a look of astonishment, Johno approached the herd. The elephants parted as he approached, leaving the baby to stand alone fearlessly. It lifted its baby head into the air, its trunk sounding out an improbable screech that pierced Ginger Mae's eardrums. It rested then rushed headlong for the dumbfounded Johno, who squatted as the strange baby calf threw itself at him to bowl him over. The unexpected calf eagerly ran its trunk over every surface of Johno's body and, inexplicably, into the small empty pocket sewn into the head keeper's shirt high on his shoulder where he was known to hide treats for only one special elephant.

Bonnie stepped from the crowd, her head pitched in puzzlement, her mouth moving, but with no words. The calf sniffed the air with its trunk . . . searching . . . smelling Bonnie as it issued an identical screech, blasting forward to throw itself against the young, astonished teen.

Daisy skipped her way over to Johno and Bonnie. Jumping up and down her face lit up with knowing excitement. "So . . . *what do you think?*"

Johno and Bonnie frowned, shaking their heads, clearly at a loss.

Netty approached soundlessly, sweeping her delicate arm to rest her hand on the inexplicable infant. "*Tobi.*"

Daisy clapped her hands together and spun around. "I'm *very* sure you're surprised. I have learned to keep secrets, right Netty?"

Netty beamed at the child and turned back to the flabbergasted survivors.

Ginger Mae felt a jealous twinge deep in her belly as she observed her child with the imposing Netty. She glanced at Bonnie to discover a slow dawning on the teen's face.

"You . . . cloned . . . Tobi." It was a statement not a question. "You *cloned* Tobi. *My God!*" Bonnie's voice hushed with awe. Kneeling down by the exuberant calf she wrapped her hands around its neck and cried.

Johno stood tall, his eyes wet with tears, as he made the sign of the cross.

Netty quirked a golden eyebrow. "I'll let that pass, in view of the circumstances." She turned to Bonnie. "My dear child. Do not expect too much from Tobi. Yes, all her memories are intact. But she has a severe displacement dysmorphia. She has not had the luxury of a century to . . . *adjust* . . . as we have. And we had the added advantage of looking much the same as when we died." She fluttered a wing. "At least mostly. Those that die before we can reach them must be reborn. *Cloned* as you call it. Her brain is much more complex than one such as Barney's. A dog has no great perception of self, so adjusts quite readily. An elephant, especially one as old as Tobi, is a complex sentient being. She has a very clear awareness of whom and what she is. Or . . . what she *was*. She is now the size of an infant and will have some trouble adjusting when the pleasure of being reunited with her herd wears off. She will undoubtedly act out."

Netty turned to Johno, giving him a small smile. "Just prepare for it. I know you realize extra TLC goes a long way. "

And with that pronouncement, Netty swept out of the cave, Baby fluttering at her side, leaving the survivors with their mouths hanging open as usual.

Chapter 14

It took another month, but the survivors in the Hive finally began the healing process. Bonnie's distraction with the new calves and her obvious joy at Tobi's resurrection helped put the beginnings of a smile back into the heart of Salina as she watched her only remaining natural child come back to life.

The fear of the Kreyven diminished as the survivors accepted Netty's assertions, that as long as they continued to work in the best interest of the creatures, there would be no reason for it to appear. Many felt Netty's behavior that night in the small cavern where they'd found the men made the beautiful, remote Elder more human . . . more identifiable. It served to unite them once again back to the former camaraderie the Hive had enjoyed before the introduction of the deranged Seth.

Clyde found himself at a loss with Jennifer, who really needed the company and support of a female in her life. He began including Salina in his plans for his granddaughter, hoping a relationship with the older Bonnie would be a benefit. Salina welcomed the role, but everyone could see how deeply Clyde's defection had wounded her. But . . . time heals all wounds and God knows . . . er . . . Womb knows, they had plenty of that in store for them.

Scotty made an effort to get the facts from Baby and Echo regarding the three men in the cave, discovering that Baby had simply done it out of hatred for the men who had murdered his family. He had felt he was honoring his love for Netty and Wil. As the truth of Baby's motives circulated the Hive, many agreed they would have wanted to do the same thing had it been *their* families. Some deeper thinkers privately understood the similarity of emotions that undoubtedly evolved from their early ancestors: the minions themselves.

Johno had wonderful news at dinner one evening, as he reported the presence of two more expectant moms: the female grizzly and one of the camels. He also reported unusual behavior in one of the turtles that led him to believe it must be a female looking for the proper material in which to build a nest. On consultation with Wil, he got permission to remove sand from the bottom of the elephants' pond to build a nesting area for the frustrated turtle before she decided to use the elephants' browse pile, which would spell disaster for her eggs.

Netty, Abby and Ginger Mae finally worked out their territorial issues regarding Daisy's 'education', with Ginger Mae's admonishment that if she caught them touching her daughter with anything other than a loving hand, she 'would rip every feather from the backs of their wings and pound Netty's crystal horns to nubs with her own sledgehammer'. Daisy renewed her studies with a reluctant Kimir joining in to further his more traditional education.

Kenya ramped up her campaign to convince Netty that the Womb must help her deliver her baby, to no avail. Mealtimes often became a comedy hour with Kenya's tears, Johno's consoling and Crystal's demands for Kenya to shut up. Kane smiled unabashedly through it all.

Ginger Mae noticed that Captain Cobby spent more time looking into the blissful Karen's eyes then he did searching for a glimpse of Abby. A man can only take so much before he gives his all to the available female who's asking for it.

Her ministrations to the stranger, Hudson, had become non-eventful. At least he was still alive, but it was clear to her that his recovery would take an indeterminable amount of time. She'd been able to eliminate the stink that emanated from his body and it was clear his body functioned well; converting calories into fat had made him look human again. But other than the superficial cosmetic changes she made note of, the man lay unresponsive.

And the wondrous Echo. She never took her eyes off Chloe as the young girl continued to guard her position in Scotty's life with jealousy.

And in the background . . . always . . . the relentless, iconic Siberian tiger, Caesar, who never, ever took his eyes off The One.

Epilogue

Wil paced restlessly in the corner of the library, his feet kicking dust onto the two small caskets of seed that sat ready.

"Wil, please sit down. You're going to knock the seeds over," Jose complained. Flailing his arms about, Wil shook his head, frustration drenching his face, his tail flexing like a whip, staccato to his words.

Netty rose from her chair to stop him. "This isn't helping. Please just sit, so we can come to some kind of decision." She pulled him to the table where Baby and Echo sat waiting for them to make up their minds.

"It's one thing after another. Can't we have a time of peace for a while?" Abby drummed her fingers on the wooden reading table, glancing at the piles and piles of books that still remained to be sorted.

"You all know this can't wait. I realize the thought is frightening, but we *must* put a stop to it. And this is the only way we can be effective without revealing ourselves."

Abby rubbed the top of her head where it was sorest, her horns taking their good time to grow in. "I think we have to do it, Wil. I can't bear the thought of what they're doing."

Wil slapped his leg, sighing deeply. "I think we are making a mistake that everyone could live to regret. Are you with me, Jose?"

Jose shrugged; looking from Netty to Abby's horrified and determined face. "I'd like to stand with you man, but I'm with the girls. We can't just ignore it."

"What if it meant our survival? Would you ignore it *then*?" The three Elders met each other's eyes, knowing Wil could be right. He persisted. "This could put us right back where we started. You know that, don't you?"

Netty stood to look at Wil, a stray tear making its way to her chin. "It would be the end for sure. I don't think I could live with this knowledge, Wil. Nor with doing nothing." Her shoulders shook as the tears increased.

Holding out his arms, Wil swept his eternal love onto his lap where she sobbed on his shoulder. "Instinctively, I know we are making a grave mistake and it could be our undoing. But alright . . . We'll do it."

Netty sat up, rubbing her arm across her wet face. "Thank you, Wil. I know you understand. I'll ask the Womb for assistance." She stood, smoothed down her skirt, and took a deep breath. Auras soothed her mind as the minions chimed in.

"We are ready, Sister."

Jose lifted the seed caskets, handing one to Wil as everyone stood, resolute and fearful.

"Okay. Let's do it."

The End

Dear Reader,

I want you all to know how heartfelt my appreciation is that you have taken the time to read my books. Being an author is one of the most torturous professions out there. Many of us live on the thanks of our readers alone. If anyone cares to leave me an honest review on Amazon.com, Goodreads.com, Smashwords.com, Kobo.com or Barnes and Noble, I would be ever so grateful. Some of you are unaware that Amazon, in particular, promotes books based on the amount of reviews a book gets.

Don't be afraid to make suggestions or criticize the writing. How else is one to improve? I look forward to your comments!

Yours fondly,
J.K. Accinni

Introduction to
Species Intervention #6609
Book 6

The One

Synopsis for Book 6: The One

One hundred years pass. The Earth is ready for habitation. But it is a far different Earth than the one last seen so long ago. New plants and new forms of wildlife populate the planet, from different worlds as the Womb saw fit.

The survivors, as expected, have not aged a day since the bombs dropped. New alliances have been made; relationships that should have led to the birth of children flourish unhappily without babies. The original wildlife is still with them, along with their generations of offspring. Every human now realizes their role is to support that of the animals.

And what of poor six-year-old Suzy, as she is mourned and forgotten by her grandfather and her sister?
Scotty is hailed as The One to restore domination by the humans, even as they all fail to realize how. Struggles ensue as the survivors discover the perils of the new and amazing life delivered to the planet by the Womb. They fight to eke out a role in the new ecosystem that has put them at the bottom of the food chain.

As the survivors begin to develop a new civilization for themselves above ground; the new natural order thrusts women into positions of power. Will the softer of the species spell success for what is left of the human race? Or are the mistakes of the past doomed to be repeated?

Chapter 1
2058 AD

The library resonated to echoes of their footsteps on the dusty rock floor as they made their way through the silent makeshift stacks of books; the classics rubbing spines with zombie and vampire paperbacks from 2013.

Jose and Wil carried the treasured seed in two crocks, while Abby and Netty guided Baby and Echo to the back of the library.

"It's just off the tunnel that was used to get the books here."

Netty opened the door to Daisy's classroom, where they quickly passed the artifacts from other planets. Planets that existed in other solar systems, in other galaxies.

"Ah, the possibilities." Netty spoke low, and Abby smiled and nodded as if she herself had been thinking the same thing.

"As Daisy becomes more proficient, I have great hopes she'll convince her mother to let her have the procedure. I think we can leave it in her hands. There's no point in trying to persuade Ginger Mae ourselves. She'd only fight us. Besides, there will come a time when Daisy is an adult and can make her own decisions. Even though she'll still look like a child, her mother will not be able to interfere," Netty announced.

As the Elders reached the back of the room, Netty swept away the camouflaging debris that masked a diminutive opening into the beginnings of an endless tunnel.

Baby and Echo entered first, accepting the containers of seed as Wil and Jose knelt to squeeze themselves through the opening. After wrenching their prodigious wings painfully through the hole in the wall, they stood, smoothed their bent feathers and healed the unfortunate broken ones.

"Are the two of you all set?" Netty's voice carried from the other side. Abby's heart tripped as she weighed their risk. Auras calmed her mind as the minions reassured her.

"Sister Abby, fear not. We have a big task, but we will be back safely. And we will destroy the tunnel behind us when we are clear. Brother Wil and Brother Jose will depart as soon as they have secured the seed. Trust and have faith. The Womb is with us."

"The Womb be with you," Abby and Netty murmured together.

The foursome didn't have to wait long before they found the tunnel branching off in the direction of their destination.

Turning south, they started the walk that would take them most of the night. Wil and Jose found they could make better time if they carried Baby and Echo. Unfortunately, the tunnel wasn't large enough to allow them to fly.

The fact that they had never been there before was an additional handicap; they could only will themselves there if they could encapsulate themselves with their wings and envision a location they had once visited.

Using their luminous eyes to light their way, they walked throughout the night. Arriving at their destination, they stood before a dead end. Jose approached the wall.

"This is it?"

"Yeah, we should be able to kick it in." Instructing Baby and Echo to stand back, they set aside the casks of seeds and began kicking.

Little by little, a hole developed in the wall. They worked hard to widen it until it was big enough to allow them to slip into a large cavern, similar to the one they had gathered in on the survivors' first evening in the Hive, almost a year ago.

Helping Baby and Echo scramble through the hole, they set down the seed casks and decided to do some exploring first.

"We must proceed carefully, Jose. If we are discovered it could be the end of our own safety and comfortable existence in the Hive. The Womb will not tolerate any possible threat to the animals. There is no telling what would happen."

"Yeah, yeah, I know. We'll just be a few minutes. Echo, you and

Baby stay here and get started. You remember where everything goes?"

"Brother Jose, this is not our first time. Did you not see the growing field that Brother Scotty and Brother Kane are so proud of?"

Jose grimaced. "Sorry, guys. I forgot. I know you'll do a good job. We'll be back in a while."

Wil and Jose crept quietly out of the cavern. Weaving their way around obstructions on the dirt floor, they found a tunnel leading away from the cavern. Signs of long-forgotten mining abounded; old-fashioned timbers still shored up the walls and ceiling, although some had dropped to the ground.

"Do you think we need to make this safer, Wil?"

Tripping over a fallen brace, Wil steadied himself. "I guess I could have the Kreyven check it out."

The two Elders poked around some more, wondering how far off the beaten path they were.

After thirty minutes of exploring, they picked up the smell of smoke. Following the acrid scent, they were led to a fire pit in a small cavern not far from where Baby and Echo worked. Piles of debris had been swept to the side to create a clearing. Burnt-out torches lined the walls. Bowls sat on the floor alongside hand-hewn beams which had been placed around the fire, perhaps to serve as a place to sit.

Wil picked up a bowl and sniffed, upending it to have liquid drip to the dirt floor. A rudimentary spit was suspended over the blackened fire.

"Looks like someone's been cooking here. And not too long ago."

Jose kicked around the debris pile, his foot hitting something with a crunch. He bent down to investigate, freezing as the round shapes came into focus.

"You better come here, Wil," he said, swallowing tightly.

Wil made his way to the debris pile as Jose pushed one of the objects with a toe.

"Oh, good Lord. It's true. We'd better get out of here. Come on, Jose. There's no telling how often they use this fire."

Wil and Jose hurried back to Echo and Baby, leaving behind the evidence of boiled human skulls from the most vulnerable in all species: the newborns.

Echo finished digging in the newly-arrived fertile soil. As she dug a hole, Baby would drop in a seed and lightly cover it over.

The Kreyven worked hard and fast, filling the cavern with the smell of sulfur as it carved more efficiently than a modern-day steam shovel. The basin for the waterway began to fill with water that trickled down the wall of the cavern from the new hole the Kreyven had punched in the ceiling. Before long, the trickle had turned into a nice, steady flow, having been directed from an underground spring through a new pathway created by the Kreyven through solid rock.

Wil and Jose appeared, watching as the minions and the Kreyven finished their miraculous creation: a brand new and productive growing field.

Once Baby and Echo had emptied half the caskets, Wil and Jose joined in the planting. The Kreyven sent solid ribbons from its body along the freshly-planted rows to create trenches, which the trickles of water sought out hungrily, bringing lifeblood to the waiting miracle seeds.

After laboring long and hard, the two Elders and golden minions made their way back to the small hole Wil and Jose had kicked through the wall. They turned back to the new growing field to watch the Kreyven conclude the life-giving construction.

"This is taking longer than I thought, Wil. We need to get out of here." Jose's anxious whispers made them all jittery.

"Calm down. We're almost done. If someone shows up, the Kreyven will take care of it."

"But Wil, we can't have that. They would never return to discover the new groves."

"Look, Jose. We're almost done. Relax, would you?"

The Kreyven hovered over the new field from its position in the cavern wall. They watched as it appeared to puff itself up, increasing its monstrous size. The odor of fresh organic loam combined with sulfur to make the air unbreathable.

They backed away as the Kreyven let loose with a black substance, spraying it over the new soil. It then began to shoot a mucky flesh-colored substance onto the walls of the great cavern. As the substance hit the walls, it spread, changing color and lighting the cave with ultraviolet light that would, in time, take on all the properties of the wondrous membrane that lined the walls of the Hive.

The Kreyven turned to the hole in the wall where the foursome huddled. It slowly descended from the heights of the cavern to suspend itself in front of the opening.

Echo wobbled out from behind Wil and Jose to peer at the creature. The Kreyven swayed to the left and to the right, appearing to assess the minion.

"Echo, I think you need to back away." Jose slipped himself in front of the little creature. The Kreyven jerked back up to the highest point of the cavern. Echo's aura pricked Jose's mind.

"It is not necessary, Brother Jose. The Kreyven is just curious. It is in the service of the Womb. It is time for us to go. It needs to seal up this hole and remove all traces of our visit."

They backed away just in time as the Kreyven gathered itself to attack the hole, leaving the growing field silent but charged with miraculous activity under the blanket of extraordinary earth.

Chapter 2

Ginger Mae and Daisy finished breakfast, the remains of Netty's delicious purplewort loaf lying in crumbs on their plates.

It had been three months since Seth's justified death by the Kreyven. From the looks of the rest of the survivors, that was now a distant memory; camaraderie was back in boisterous force.

They ducked as flying food sailed over their heads from another table, accompanied by hoots and sniggers.

Ginger Mae breathed a grateful sigh as she realized most of her confidence regarding their safety sat firmly back in place.

"Momma, it's time for me to begin my lessons. I'll have Kimir accompany me to my lab."

"Oh, you will, will you?" She smiled at her seven-year-old precocious daughter. "Since when is it your lab?"

"Silly you, Momma, you know I alone use the lab, hence the possessive pronoun."

Ginger Mae rolled her eyes at Daisy. Her daughter dribbled water from her mouth onto her plate, watching it splatter. She stuck a finger to her tongue and sucked, watching her mother from the corner of her eye, a suggestion of mirth tugging at her lips.

"Don't put your fingers in your mouth, Daisy."

She slapped the finger away from her child's lips. Her head swam with the realization that Daisy's powerful mind was robbing her of the joys normal children experienced.

Yes, the Hive did present limitations to a child's growth, but they truly had everything they needed for productive childrearing. Trees to climb in the growing fields while the pollinators slept, water to splash in the bathing caves, corridors upon corridors to play in, creatures to further the development of responsible compassion, a huge and diverse family of caring adults to model after, healthy and unusual foodstuffs to delight the most finicky child, and a first-rate library to expand the mind.

Ginger Mae tapped her work-reddened finger on her smooth cheek as her eyes tracked Netty and Abby's figures, wings tightly molding their backs, tawny tails flexing naturally as they moved around the sink washing bowls.

She couldn't help but wonder what exactly they had planned to do to Daisy if she had been willing to relent and give permission for this procedure they wanted her to have so badly.

She glanced again at her unusual daughter, assessing the likelihood that she would eventually demand the procedure herself.

Daisy's hair hung thin and lank, no matter what she did to it. Her pale skin shined with an unblemished translucence, giving her a fragile appearance. But her light-gray eyes; they sparkled with unbridled curiosity and intelligence. She could identify a spark of raw determination that had not been there a mere year ago.

And how was it that Daisy had miraculously learned to speak upon her first meeting with Abby?

"Sorry." Ginger Mae nodded hello as Peter and Bonnie squeezed by in their perpetual hurry to assist with the animals. Sighing over the mystery of her daughter, she rose to carry their dirty plates to the sink so her day could begin.

First up, bathing the stranger; then off to start the daily census. Parking Daisy in a chair, she crossed back to Abby to question her.

"Will she be with you all day?"

Abby gave her a gentle smile. "If that's okay with you. I have work to do in the library, and Netty will set up her lessons."

"You mean hook her up to those weird contraptions."

The young Elder ran her hand up and down Ginger Mae's arm, the warmth of her golden touch soothing her.

"I'm sorry. I know she's only learning things. It's just that she's my only child. The only child in the Hive if you don't count Kimir. That makes her the youngest."

"You can trust me, Ginger Mae. She's in good hands. And she's so happy. We all want that for her. I know you do too. Even if her path is meant to be different."

Ginger Mae nodded, giving Abby the suggestion of a smile.

"Let's just make sure it's not *too* different, okay?"

With her firm tone, she had made it clear to Abby that she was the one in charge. Waving to Daisy and picking up her clipboard, towels and small bucket of hot water, she said goodbye and left the homey seductiveness of the kitchen.

Lumbering along the stone corridors, careful not to slosh her hot water, she unexpectedly caught a glimpse of Gloria and Billy sneaking into the sleeping caves. *Hmmm, bet I know what they're up to.*

"Hi, Ginger Mae." Captain Cobby and Karen passed her in the corridor, hand in hand, Cobby nodding as Karen gave her a blissful beam.

What, I'm the only one working today? Smiling back, Ginger Mae turned and entered the chamber that held the man called Hudson.

Dipping her cloth back into the cooling water, she finished rinsing Hudson's now dense, long, dark hair. She contemplated a haircut but decided, why bother? Except for the occasional visit from Netty, she was the only one who ever saw him. She suspected that most in the Hive barely remembered he was here.

As she dressed the now healed and reasonably fit man, she surveyed his body for signs that might prevent him from regaining consciousness.

A few months ago, she had gathered from Netty that the man was in his late fifties. He certainly didn't look that old to her now. Maybe forty five? She had come to accept that most in the Hive no longer looked their exact age due to the health benefits from the nightly tendrils.

She brushed up against the one that disappeared into Hudson's ear; watching it ripple as if to say excuse me. He was obviously responding well to the effects of the tendrils, yet still remained in a coma.

Brushing the wrinkles out of his new, clean smock, she slipped it over his head, lifting him to brace his upper body with her shoulder as she smoothed it down over his naked healthy form.

Hudson let out a sigh. She raised an eyebrow as she hadn't heard such a sound from him before, only groans.

Now it was her turn to sigh as she laid him back down, dropped her cloth into her bucket and lowered herself to the hard floor, overcome by a sudden wave of loneliness.

Sitting cross-legged, she took her face into her wet hands and held her head. An unexpected tear coursed down her cheek as the memory of the two couples in the corridor flitted across her mind.

By no means was she jealous, but she couldn't shake the unexpected feeling that had just blindsided her. *Since when have I ever felt so lonely, except for the time I waited for Daisy to be born? And even then, it had felt different than it does now.* She lifted her hands to rub them hard into her scalp, then massaged the bridge of her nose while her mind searched for the source of her discomfort and loneliness.

"Can I give you a hand with something, miss?" Ginger Mae's heart missed a beat as she looked up to see the man she had been nursing for so long sitting upright, his feet over the side of his dais, all traces of the tendrils evaporated, and with a kind smile on his rugged face.

She slowly rose to her feet, not taking her eyes off the man. Her mouth dropped open, astonishment muddling her senses.

The man struggled to stand, finding himself very unsteady. She rushed to his side, slipping his arm over her shoulder as he became aware of the uniqueness of his surroundings. It was his turn to open his mouth to speak, but he became overwhelmed with the sensory strangeness.

"What . . . I . . . miss, who . . . I don't . . ."

"Shh . . . it's okay, sir. Please, why don't you just lie back down?" She eased him back onto the dais, where he remained in a sitting position, bewilderment his sole expression.

"I don't understand. Where am I? Who are you?"

His hands roamed over his body, he flexed his extremities and found himself sound. "Why am I not dead? I don't feel . . . pain." His eyes closed tightly. Waiting a beat, he opened them to expose her to the agony that lurked on the surface.

"Where's the angel? I remember a beautiful angel." His eyes roamed over her face and body.

"You're the angel, aren't you? But your wings . . . where are they?"

His eyes rested on her forehead. "No, I guess not. She was golden with horns . . . she had horns that sparkled in the dark. Please . . . can you not speak to me? Miss? Can you tell me your name?"

"Oh, yes . . . I'm so sorry. I just don't know where to start." They stared at each other as the seconds ticked away. He slowly extended his hand.

"Well then, lovely lady, let me start first. My name is Hudson. My friends call me Hud."

She rose to take his hand, finding it warm and strong despite his weakened condition. She looked into his eyes as a feeling tickled the back of her stomach.

"I'm pleased to meet you, Mr. Hudson. My name is Ginger Mae Shrute."

News of Hudson's awakening raced through the Hive. Some were frightened, all were curious. Most of all, Netty was forced to come to terms with the finality of her former life resurfacing in the form of the cowardly sheriff who had failed to honor his badge and prevent her greedy, psychotic and unrepentant ex-husband from having them all killed.

As much she had been touched by his plea for forgiveness when he became aware of her identity the night they had discovered Baby's brand of retribution, she planned to weigh his every move in the Hive.

As life would have it, Ginger Mae wouldn't take her eyes off Hudson for months to come as he slowly integrated himself into the Hive, after first coming to terms with the fact that he was still alive and his own family long dead.

He retained no memory of the decades Baby had held him hostage in the tiny cavern with the other two men. And he apparently no longer recognized Netty, Wil or Baby. To him, they were the rulers of the underground sanctuary where he found himself after being awakened from the dead.

All of the survivors, with the consent of the Elders, agreed to let the past remain the past until Hudson himself felt the compulsion to inquire.

Loading the recovered man up with just the facts of the war above, the current year of his existence, the life in the Hive, an explanation for Baby, Echo, the Elders and a huge tiger that skulked in the background without eating anyone was more than any one mind could ever hope to process.

Even the existence of the Womb was held in abeyance until Wil decided Hudson could handle the facts.

The dishonored sheriff naturally chose Ginger Mae to attach himself to; joining her at meals, helping her with the census, and taking delight in her daughter.

Daisy and Hudson fast became buddies as he professed an interest in her studies at the library, joining her from time to time and gaining a growing awareness of the insignificance of man and his planet.

The tall, quiet gentleman of wisdom and firm voice became someone to rely on as he took turns helping everyone with their projects, including a stint in the growing fields, yet always coming back to Ginger Mae and her creatures.

It was no surprise to anyone when Hudson and Ginger Mae fell in love . . . except to them of course.

It was only one year later that Ginger Mae and Hudson, now called Hud by all, were married in the first official wedding held in the Hive.

At the lovely ceremony, Ginger Mae was given away by a somber Dezi. The best man was none other than Wil, who had incongruously developed a great friendship with Hud. The ceremony was officiated with all necessary gravitas by a benevolent Netty. The two flower children, who preceded the beautiful bride and her handsome groom down the makeshift aisle in the great cavern of the survivors' beginnings, as well as a few sad endings, was none other than Daisy, hand in hand with Baby tottering alongside.

Baby considered it a great honor as he continued to be mesmerized by Ginger Mae's position of mother to the wondrous Daisy. Privately, it was astonishing to all the survivors that Baby's bloodthirsty streak of revenge no longer deviled him, allowing him to peacefully accept Hudson's presence in his life.

Behind them minced baby Tobi, adorned in a wreath of fragrant greenery picked and woven by Kenya and Chloe. Tobi stole the show as she ran from guest to guest glad-handing or, shall we say, glad-trunking?

Crystal's mother pig, Tulip, attended, adorned with made-over fragments of her long-discarded tutu. Caesar melted into the background with the dog posse, never taking his eyes off Scotty, who stood stoically while Chloe cast pensive eyes from her beau to the bride and groom.

Only the Womb could tell how many women cast wishful musings toward the men whose arms they clung to as Netty pronounced the happy couple, man and wife.

Needless to say, a great time was had by all as the festivities carried on merrily into the night.

Chapter 3
2066 AD

Suzy carefully ran the clippers through ten-year-old Tandy's hair, relieved to find lice. She knew some of the men in the vast camp were not above checking through the mass of discarded hair in the dirt to confirm their presence, trying to catch her in a lie to discredit her with Doc Benjamin.

When she was lucky enough to find lice in one head, she found she could get away with claiming a dozen. The men were so squeamish about the bugs, no one checked further. She found it a great advantage in her efforts to keep the younger girls safe as long as possible from the sexual advances of the men who owned them.

"There you go, Tandy. You might want to mention you've come down with scabies if you're bothered again. I'll speak to Doc Benjamin for you. He needs to know the men aren't honoring his laws about the age of consent. I'm sorry they tried to force themselves on you. This should help. You have a good three years yet before you have to submit."

Suzy lowered her voice as a group of grungy men trudged by, their boots clanging loudly on the boards that lay on the floor of the cave, lifting them a few inches off the cold, muddy floor.

She kept her glance conciliatory and vague, forcing her natural intelligence and bitter resentment to stay well concealed.

She was fully aware of the festering anger against her as she insidiously influenced Doc Benjamin to the benefit of the women in camp, even at her budding age of fourteen. For her, it was all about surviving until she could find a way to escape.

Her and Liz's idea to shave off the hair of the younger and most vulnerable of the female children was showing encouraging progress. Little girls hardly look seductive with shaved heads, discussions of lice, nasty clothes, and surreptitious applications of feces to their shoes and the backs of their leggings.

Whatever it took to keep the little ones safe from the perverted sexual advances of their common enemy was a necessity. The fact that she herself would be at risk if not for the occasional protection of Doc Benjamin made her more determined to give the others every edge she could dream up.

Little Tandy scampered off after a timid hug for Suzy, looking like an emaciated scarecrow. She had felt Tandy's bones protruding under her layers of rags, her skin shuddering with the perpetual chill of their makeshift temporary home.

She set the heavy clippers down, shutting off the electrical connection that Avery maintained for her on Doc's orders. She dropped her aching arm down across her lap to rest as she struggled to massage the tired muscles. Tandy was her fifteenth cut today. Not all new shaves, some just touch ups, but holding the heavy metal razor was very tiring nonetheless.

She breathed in heavily, feeling a hitch in her chest even as she sucked in the too-common stench of feces and sweet, ripe sweat.

Most of the tribe only bathed occasionally. There was only so much you could do with one bucket of water per person each day for cooking and cleaning. At least Doc Benjamin had decreed drinking water would be limitless.

Straightening up, she quickly packed up her precious razor. It had taken her months to wheedle it away from Doc Benjamin. Her constant complaints of lice in her own hair had finally worn him down, but she knew she couldn't take her eye off it or it would disappear. Slipping it into its box, she tamped it down to the bottom of her worn backpack for safe keeping. Her fingers searched, reassuringly patting the pilfered medications she needed to deliver to the other side of camp.

Scanning the makeshift construction of hodgepodge tiny hovels strewn around the main cave, she waited for the right moment to begin her difficult errand of tracking down Liz. She unfortunately lived in one of the other caves reserved for the men held in less esteem by Doc Benjamin.

Liz was in her late twenties. The only reason she hadn't been discarded by her man was because she was so smart and funny. Their lives were so tragic that anyone who could maintain a gentle humor was valued. To have the ability to make one of the men laugh was priceless. Her man kept her in his hovel with the other females he bedded simply because she made him feel good in a different way. She was an Insider.

The discarded women typically slept outside with what comfort they could fashion from cast-off and surplus materials. They were the Outsiders.

Of course, nighttime was dangerous. That was when the weaker of the men prowled the discards of the stronger. Many of the women were claimed and dragged to the front of the cave where the undesirables slept, exposed to the unspecified dangers of the cold winds which blew through the opening to the entrance of their home; low in status, lower in wealth.

Yes, wealth. Females were coin. To be traded, awarded, loaned or sold.

Females did 70 percent of the work in the camps and all of the cooking and cleaning. They never stopped, not even at night. And lo, to be the lucky man with plenty of females. Remember the old expression, the rich get richer? The old practice of barefoot and pregnant now took on a more useful meaning. And if what Liz and the older woman suspected was true, a very sinister one indeed.

Her squinty brown eyes, alert as a bird of prey's, watched for her chance to cross through the council square in the middle of the cavern, with the huts ringing the clearing based on Doc's own private ranking system.

She was haunted by the verbose claims as the men congregated in the square after dinner with Doc Benjamin to scream about what they would do if they managed to find the lost shelter of Suzy's grandfather.

The current wisdom was that it was filled with all the gold from the U.S. Treasury. Suzy wondered what gold looked like and what one would do with it. To her mind, the only thing of value she could recognize was freedom. *Or maybe a fresh juicy peach,* she thought wistfully.

She retained little memory of her old family. Just two names, Lorna and Seth. He had either been a friend or relative; no one seemed to be clear anymore. She thought she remembered having a sister, but she wasn't sure. Frankly, she didn't have much time to think about it as her life was consumed by frantic plots and subterfuge, all meant to keep her safe.

Liz was the center of the well-guarded subversion the women tried to keep alive in their ranks. But they had to be careful. There were spies everywhere. Some of the women would sell out their sisters to curry favor with the man that owned them. Especially the older ones as their looks faded quickly in their new, unhealthy environment.

The sickness in the air from the war nine years ago had robbed everyone of their vitality. Oddly, it had taken a bigger toll on the women. It shouldn't be a surprise that some would turn on their friends, hoping for an extra morsel at dinner; their only real meal, if you could call it that. But it was more nourishing than the unleavened flatbread dispersed by the communal kitchen every morning.

Suzy had once overheard Doc and Avery whispering about the fact that their flour supplies were dangerously low. It forced her to wonder why most of Doc's inner circle looked so much heftier than everyone else. The only tribe members who ate extra rations were the myriad of expecting women and the scouts. Doc was forced to bribe the scouts with extra grub to motivate them to do their jobs.

Facing the winds, pregnant with an assortment of hot bugs, came at great risk to anyone's health. Unfortunately, someone had to do the nasty job of combing the countryside for anything left alive that could be eaten.

They labored to locate vacant grocery stores which might have something left in their cellars or storerooms, even breaking into homes to salvage what may have been left behind. And pharmacies. Not that much was ever found.

They usually had better luck with medicine cabinets in the vacant homes. When you're fleeing for your life, you just don't think about what's in your medicine cabinet. Although other thugs and marauders had usually picked the houses clean from the year of the bombs, they hit jackpots often enough to keep Doc supplied and make the risk acceptable. Everyone knew that if they ran out of the critical medicines scavenged by the scouts, many would sicken further and die.

The fact that all of the original members of the scouting teams were now dead, failed to discourage the younger members of the new teams. No doubt, the extra rations and periodic borrowing of the camp women to help them relax and enjoy their week's rotation off, served to obscure most thoughts regarding their probable early demise.

She looked down on her own frame, poking her bones under their layers of rags and salvaged clothing retrieved by the scouts. She felt her tender skin stretched taut over bony ridges that stood out in deep relief. Her bald head sprouted scabs all over its sallow surface.

She was lucky that Doc Benjamin shared his creams and medicine with her, or her sores would weep and stink like the rest. She never failed to catch the resentful glances at her dry head. Doc's favoritism did not go unnoticed.

Now that she was no longer a child, the men thought she should integrate into the community like the rest of them. She knew she was referred to as Doc's house pet, even though she did her share of work around camp.

But the truth of the designation made her very useful to Liz and her group of defiant women. And that was the only thing that mattered to her. She vowed to do all she could to participate in the growing female insurrection, with the fervent hope that it could somehow lead to her freedom.

You see, Suzy Calloway had a secret. Years ago, as Doc Benjamin treated her with inexplicable kindness, she had re-emerged from the distant, deep blackness her mind had chosen to hide itself in. Her psyche slowly sparked; a tiny ember that flickered in the shadows, desperate for the nourishment that would allow it to burst into a tangible flame capable of sustaining itself and allowing the traumatized child to live again.

It had taken a few years, but Suzy's mind had healed. She wasn't quite as good as new, but better. They say if life doesn't break you, you grow stronger. Regrettably, Suzy had been broken. The sweet, innocent and sheltered child from a happy prosperous home with doting grandparents was forever gone.

Funny how nature sometime hands you exactly the tools you need to survive as circumstances blindside you. Some fail to adjust and perish, while others discover a buried capability.

For, in the place of the naïve victim of a brutal kidnapping, a cunning and secretive creature had emerged, wise beyond her years in the art of manipulation. Her education had been fast-tracked over the days and months she had studied everyone in camp as her recovery afforded her the unexpected opportunity. From Doc Benjamin's elite hovel, she watched, absorbing everything. Her survivor's mind calculated who had the power; both real and perceived.

She marveled in her cunning virgin's mind as the men fashioned a makeshift town of bastardized abodes, using the paraphernalia looted from so many small towns and cities, purloined from the cold hands of so many murdered folks.

And then the time came to mutely witness tribe members sickening and disappearing, her thoughts refusing to accept the silent ride on their death trolley as one of the men wheeled it down the deep burial tunnel to dispose of. Oh, no. That was not going to happen to her.

Over time, she celebrated silently with the rest of the boisterous tribe members as Avery harnessed the mystery of their water source alongside the western wall of the enormous cavern.

It rose a dozen stories to the pinnacle of the astonishing launch of their life-saving waterfall. The fall dropped powerfully past the floor of their cavern to disappear deep within the serpentine faults of the mineral-laden boulders and walls of their ancient refuge. It allowed them to fill their buckets with a system of lines rigged by the ingenious Avery.

The mist from the thunderous falls drenched the surfaces of the rock walls and cold floor, intensifying the bitter cold and creating a dangerously slippery environment. Therefore, Doc restricted the water gathering to the necessities. Baths were not considered necessary, of course.

The women managed the best they could. Liz drummed it into them all that a clean body was a healthy body. Their bodies were the only currency they could attempt to control. If they were to obtain their freedom, above all, they must stay healthy.

Eventually, the tribe obtained fully-functioning electricity, thanks to the mechanical genius behind Avery's huge ugly mug and their lifesaving waterfall. Candles no longer burned to add smoke to the widening cloud of pollution that gathered high in the cavern ceiling like a malignant tumor from the numerous individual fires that burned for warmth and cooking.

As the pollution cloud increased, Doc's council members wisely decided a central cooking arrangement would be of great benefit. Preferably in an unexplored tunnel they could test for a possible ventilation source to remove the deadly smoke.

A location was selected and the demands on the woman increased as they staffed a huge cooking facility created to feed the several hundred members of the tribe.

Before long, under Avery's direction, the men rigged up enough kerosene and gas heaters to make the perennially-chilly cavern livable. Suzy shut her eyes tightly, willing her mind not to remember the flames and agonizing screams of the dead tribe members, mostly women who had catastrophically fallen victim to a poorly-built gasoline heater in the dead of night. The explosion hadn't been huge, but the sound still echoed in her nightmares to this day.

Funerals were considered a waste of time and energy. No one complained as the tribe was only together out of necessity. It wasn't like they were family, after all. No opinions were ever solicited from the women who mourned their sisters' deaths in silence. Swift memorial words were said with all in attendance, crushed tightly, as close as they could around the Council Center. The mess was disposed of and life went on.

Suzy's thoughts of her earlier metamorphosis tapered off as she revisited the nugget that kept her warm at night and fueled her determination to flee. Her secret. One that was so dangerous, she refused to share it even with Liz until she knew the time was right.

For Suzy knew exactly where her grandfather and his wondrous shelter were located.

Her Grandma Lorna's words had inexplicably flowered in her mind when she had emerged from the pit of devastation brought on by her frightful kidnapping.

How she might determine the correct time was far beyond her ability to calculate. That part she had failed to work out. Yet. The monumental task of escaping with a hundred women and children in various stages of weakness and pregnancy loomed on her limited horizon like an approaching cyclone determined to bear down on her. At this moment, she just couldn't locate a safe path around the deadly obstacle.

"Psss . . . Suzy." A hunched-over young woman stepped close to the doorway of the hovel, dropped a folded note, then scurried away. Suzy scrambled over to the doorway to snatch up the note. Reading slowly, she sounded out the words, identifying the author as her friend Liz who begged for her presence.

Ripping the note into bits, she stuck the tiny pieces inside the pillow on her messy bunk. It wouldn't do to let Doc find the pieces. Women were forbidden to communicate amongst themselves except when sharing a task. Male eyes watched every move they made, making organized insurrection difficult to get off the ground.

She shivered with the knowledge of what would happen to both of them if the note were to be discovered. It didn't take too many hammered and mangled fingers of the women around camp who had been disciplined, for the rest of them to fear the risk. The note must be very urgent.

Checking to make sure her backpack looked innocuous with its load of purloined drugs, she made a dash across the council square, well aware she was being watched as men of all ages dropped what they were doing to observe Doc's house pet and wonder what she was up to.

Dodging nimbly around piles of garbage, serpentine aisles of hovels, bastardized bedrolls of the Outsiders and pathetic children all under the age of five, she made her way like a darting lizard toward the passageway leading to a smaller cave that housed the lower-ranked men and their women.

She stopped in her tracks as a female child of around three squatted in her path to move her bowels, naked as the day God made her. Snot ran from the girl's nose to mix with the food from her last meal that had dribbled from a mouth she was unable to close. Her acute hair lip, one of the common deformities of most of the newborns since the war, assured the poor girl a life of misery. What man would want that at his table?

Most of the mothers learned quickly to keep them out of the way of the men who raged at the sight of them. The toddler flashed an arm from behind her back, displaying further evidence of the damage done to her mother's DNA from the fallout of the bombs that had spread on the cold virulent winds before they had found their present shelter.

Eying the distorted limb with its missing hand and flattened forearm, she cringed. Suzy had heard unconfirmed whispers that the men found these babies such liabilities that a movement was underfoot not to waste resources on them.

Oddly enough, the male babies born with abnormalities were hailed a success, no different than an unmarked one. Her resentment simmered at the unfairness of it, but the women were powerless to do anything except attempt to hide the little girls from sight.

Sighing, she squatted in front of the child, removed a rag from her backpack and cleaned her off as she scanned the women in the area for the missing mother. Worried about the time, she tugged the child up into her arms.

The toddler's enormous eyes stared at her unblinkingly. As Suzy watched, the child screwed up her face and let out a wail. Spewed mucus and saliva splattered the teen's face as she ducked down with the child, trying to hush her.

"What do you think you're doing with that kid?" From out of the crowd of milling tribe members, shot Avery's hunk of a hand.

The giant's ugly face leered down at her, his shaved head with its knobby protrusions, blocking her escape. He wrenched the toddler from her arms as she frantically tried to twist away. Her voice growled back at him.

"Get your hands off me, you piece of garbage."

He laughed, tossing the toddler to the ground. Craning his neck over his massive shoulder, he shouted to another man.

"Get this worthless meat out of here. It shouldn't have been allowed to get this old. Go find out who it belongs to and report it to Doc. I want the mother to be made an example of at council tonight. We can't be having these monstrosities draining us anymore. You know what to do."

Avery's henchman bent to retrieve the child, distaste evident on his dour, scabby face as he held her by one callused hand, dangling the frightened toddler by her good arm.

Suzy watched the women from the crowd surrounding the spectacle quickly cast their eyes down in an effort to hide their burning hatred and frustration at their own impotence. Not a one dare come to the defense of the toddler as she quickly disappeared from sight, her fate unimaginable.

Avery turned his attention back to her. His hand on her upper arm tightened as he fumbled at the layers of rags on her chest. Squeezing a young breast, his eyes glazed feverishly.

"This should belong to me, bitch. Don't you even think I've forgotten. Doc can't protect you forever. He owes me."

Avery leaned in, his rancid breath a menace of its own. Trying hard not to cry or scream, she kept her face neutral.

All predators needed to see was one sign of weakness to know they had you. Summoning up the nerve, she spat in his face. Avery recoiled in surprise, titters from the crowd inflaming him.

Suzy didn't see the fist coming until it sank into her abdomen, the pain robbing her of the ability to speak as it forced up what was left of her last meal. Avery dropped her to the ground and turned to scream at the crowd, his thick meaty cheeks throbbing with indignation.

"What the fuck you all lookin' at? Move on before I give you something you wish hadn't asked for."

Avery wiped the spit from his face, distracted enough by the crowd to allow Suzy to crawl on her elbows and melt away. She heard the giant roar his anger as he discovered her escape.

Quickly, she hobbled the rest of the way to Liz's hut, grateful that Avery hadn't noticed her backpack. That would have been the end of her. Doc wouldn't have been able to save her had the contents been discovered. She realized that, sooner or later, the situation with Avery would explode. She chafed at her powerlessness, dispirited by the inequities of her miserable life.

The lingering nausea from Avery's punch swept over her in waves, acerbated by the heavier collection of unwashed bodies and slop buckets that awaited collection in Liz's section of the tribe's quarters. In her own cavern they had several locations to relieve themselves. Doc insisted on strict sanitary conditions. But the further away from the main cavern you traveled, the laxer the sanitation became.

Approaching her friend's hovel, she found Liz sitting, her enormous belly laden down with her own pregnancy; nothing new, since over half the women were pregnant at one time or another. Liz struggled to rise as she approached, getting assistance from two other young women that stood nearby, their expressions of frantic anxiety telegraphing the urgency of Liz's note.

"For heaven's sake, Suzy. What took you so long?" Liz hissed as she stood, her hand pressed hard to her back to message the aching muscles that invariably accompanied pregnancy and hard work. Thick clumps of coarse, dark hair escaped the elastic that swept the rest of her long mop back from her appealing face.

Signs of Outsider women, relegated and out of favor with Liz's owner, littered the surrounds with their scavenged mattresses. Liz's generous lips tightened as she swept them all into the relative privacy of the ramshackle quarters she shared with the man that owned her with his other two women.

The women helped lower Liz onto her bed, her delivery only a few weeks away.

"Well, did you get it?" Liz shook her hands with impatience, panic seeping into her expression to mirror that of the other women. They suddenly heard the sounds of a wounded animal not far away. Deep ragged coughing, a choke that morphed into a guttural scream filled with long agony. Suzy's heart almost stopped.

"Oh my God. Is that her?" Liz closed her eyes and silently nodded.

Suzy dove into her backpack, extracting her critical cargo. She unwrapped the towel that hid the lifesaving box of antibiotics and pain pills filched from Doc Benjamin's cache.

Rarely did any women have access to the drugs that often saved the life of a man felled by a formerly common infection. Infections that could now spell death if allowed to come into contact with any of the unknown microbes that strayed into their shelter on the dangerous winds that harbored them from as far away as New York City.

Dense suburbs of the onetime financial center were known to have spawned several outbreaks of diseases unseen in this country in centuries.

Suzy's shaking hands withdrew syringes from her pack. She noted the expiration date on the box of antibiotics, but said nothing, knowing that most medication viability lasted long after the recorded expiration date. *Here's hoping it's the same with liquids.* Her fingers absorbed the vital coolness of the antibiotics. For once, she thanked the chilly temperatures found in the mines. The medicine had been in her backpack and out of their refrigerated storage for well over twenty four hours.

"You know, if it's more than an infection, this won't help."

"I know, I know. But it's not like we have a doctor to take her to. And if it's a virus, wouldn't others have caught it by now?"

Suzy tried to reassure Liz. "I don't know. She's had this for almost two weeks now. I don't know how long viruses take to incubate. I think it varies. I don't even know what she has. But if the men find out, you know what they'd do." One of the other women stifled a sob.

"And Janie's overdue. What will this do to the baby?" Another coughing scream filled the air. The four women froze, blood draining from their faces as they heard men shouting.

"Oh, my God. I have to get over there." Suzy was close to panic. Liz clutched her arm.

"No. You can't go, Suzy. You'll draw too much attention. You know we can't have that. It may be too late as it is." They listened as male voices carried into the shelter, well into the throes of discussion.

"Kimmey, you and Liselle get over there. Now! Take this. Don't get caught with it, no matter what. There's no telling what would happen if the men find out. Give her a double shot. And try to muffle that noise the best you can."

Suzy passed the medicine to the other women and watched as Liselle stuffed it under her rags, failing to obscure the telltale bulge. Kimmey reach over and readjusted Liselle's layers and they hurried off.

Suzy sank to the ground and rested her throbbing head on Liz's comforting leg. The older girl reached down to stroke Suzy's bald head.

"It's okay, hon. We wouldn't stand a chance without all you've done to help these last few years." Liz turned Suzy's face toward her with a worn hand. "You all right? Something happen?"

Suzy's mouth turned down. "It's just Avery again. He cornered me on the way here. But not before he had a chance to remind me of how he feels." She rubbed her stomach, not needing to explain further. Liz sighed.

"I don't know how much longer some of the women can go on like this. We seem to get weaker and weaker as the men still look fit. The only thing we have in common is the sores that devil me so.

Uurr." Liz picked at a particularly evil one on her arm that refused to heal.

"Let me put a bandage on that, Liz. You need to keep it clean."

"And just where will I say I got the bandage when he sees it tonight?" Suzy reached for her backpack to pull out an adhesive bandage for Liz.

"Don't worry, I can tie a rag over it. He won't even know there's a bandage underneath."

Nodding, Liz held out her arm.

"Did you hear Deborah, the redhead over in the next area to this one, killed herself yesterday?"

Suzy stopped working in surprise, a hint of fear budding in her already delicate stomach. She lowered her voice as she continued to bandage Liz's arm.

"I guess she never really recovered after her last was born . . . God, I can't even think about what the poor thing must have looked like without a skull. Does it seem to you that the younger girls have more babies born with defects that the older girls?"

"Ummm . . . I've noticed the same thing. It must have something to do with the damage done by radiation at a more tender age. Most of the girls that deliver the worst of the babies were captured at an early age." Liz's voice faltered. "Just like you were."

"There . . . you're done." Suzy acted like she hadn't heard Liz, stashing her scissors back in her pack.

Liz continued. 'You were such a sweet, little girl. Lucky too. You might be dead by now if it wasn't for Doc. I can almost see the person you would have been if this hadn't happened." Suzy picked up her pack and slammed it down, startling her friend.

"What the heck is the point to all this? I'm not that little girl. I'm a different person. I care about only one thing." Her face lit up with a ferocious determination. She grabbed both of Liz's hands in hers. "Come with me, Liz. We need to get out of here. You can't have your baby near a bunch of sick bastards like this. We can just walk out. Together."

Liz stared, stone faced, her voice flat and empty. "And where exactly would we go? With me ready to deliver in a couple of weeks?" She shook her head slowly. "I'm surprised at you, Suzy. You know I can't just walk out on the other women and leave them at the mercy of the men. What do you think would happen to them if we disappeared? I wouldn't give some of them more than a day with Avery's machete always itching for a chance to teach someone a lesson."

At the strange look on Suzy's face she stopped. Suzy noticed and turned away.

"Hey, what's really wrong with you? This is too out of character."

Silence.

"You gunna talk to me or do I have to drag it out of you?"

Suzy moved restlessly, not knowing where to start. "It's Doc."

"What do you mean, it's Doc? Something wrong with him? Is he sick or something?"

"No, no, nothing like that." She swallowed, suddenly shy and embarrassed with the attention on her. This was something she had hoped to avoid even as she knew it was impossible. "Eh . . . Doc . . . has been . . . eh . . . looking at me."

"Looking at you? What the heck are you talking about, girl? He's been like a father to you."

Suzy cast her eyes down and mumbled, "That's what everyone thinks. But he only cares to make me remember where my grandfather's shelter is. He's convinced I'll remember someday . . ." Her voice trailed off.

"Well, that's no big deal. It's not like he raped you."

As Suzy sat unmoving, the silence thickened.

"Oh . . . my sweet, little Suzy girl. Come here and sit next to me, hon. He did rape you, didn't he?" Her horrified voice reduced Suzy to tears and she quickly moved to the bed to be swept up in the capable hands of her best friend, mentor and surrogate mother. Her hot unshed tears finally emerged to gush unchecked onto the flannel smock of the only one in the whole tribe that could give her the kind of comfort she so desperately needed.

*

Two weeks passed in the Franklin Mines. Suzy managed to elude Avery, but her evenings became a nightmare. Even though she always knew the time was bound to come, she was revolted by the sick expressions dancing across Doc's face now every time he looked at her.

Often, they would sit outside their hovel to share the food she brought from the master kitchen. Suzy could always tell from the look on his face when she was in for another bad night, another assault. That's what she called it. That's what it was.

During the moments he demanded she disrobe, she could feel her spirit slip back into her secret black hole, piece by piece, as he caressed her barely-developed breasts and moved on to his beastly satisfaction.

She felt branded by the initiation. Branded and humiliated, positive everyone could see and mock her. No longer did she venture out into the cavern on her mercy errands, Doc's trove of medicines now safe from her sticky fingers. She missed her moments with Liz, but couldn't risk the exposure, and who had the strength anyway?

The last time Liz had sent someone to get her, she lay flaccid, unwilling to listen to the summons for help that was sure to bring more stress and pain at a time she overflowed with horrors of her own.

That's where she lay today. On the same shabby altar Doc Benjamin had first used when he raped her. Wondering why he had waited this long to do it, she could only imagine that he must have given up on the hope she would reveal the whereabouts of her grandfather's bomb shelter.

As she lay drifting in and out of her fugue, she suddenly felt the jarring of her bed. Opening her eyes, she realized Doc was back.

"Are you just going to lie there all day, missy? I'm not going to put up with much more of your prima donna conduct. You know I can't afford to let the tribe see you disrespect me like this. You're my woman now."

Suzy weighed the merits of rising, but was unable to rouse the energy. She watched Doc as he paced, his long, greasy hair tied back like the rest of the men, unable to disguise his now receding hairline. His once-straight legs had a decided bow to them, shortening his stature. Between his scabs, the blisters in his face, and the tooth loss they all suffered, he no longer retained the aura of a confident able leader she had once thought he was.

No. He just looked like a common man with an evil core; the core of a slave owner who abused his slave.

And now that she was a woman, Doc was treating her the same way the rest of the camp women were treated.

From inside Suzy's dark space, a burst of bitter bile illuminated her pain, crystalizing a shred of reality. She slowly lowered her feet to the floor of the hut.

"That's better. Now go get me something to eat, woman."

Fourteen-year-old Suzy stood, eyeing Doc's machete that lay in the corner of the hut. The bile from her dark space began to rise, tentative and unsure. She let her eyes again flicker to the machete. Smoothing down her tattered clothes and reaching for a cloth, she rubbed down her bald head as if preparing to leave.

Her feet slowly inched closer to the machete, sweat trickling down from under her arms in the coolness of the hut. Her right hand made contact with the handle of the machete as she continued to slowly and methodically rub her scalp.

They heard a commotion outside the hut. Doc moved to the entrance, peeling back the privacy blanket.

"Ladies? To what do I owe the honor of this unusual visit?" His voice thrummed with the message that served to remind the visitors their presence clearly was not an honor.

Two women belonging to Liz's man ducked inside, tears and red faces on fire as they gushed out the news.

"Please, Doc. Please. You must come. They're dying." Kimmey sank to her knees to blubber her entreaties while Liselle sidled up to Suzy with a low hiss.

"Suzy, you must come quick. It's Liz. Where've you been? There's blood everywhere. It's the baby."

As if emerging from underwater, Liselle's dire news pushed Suzy through to the land of the miserable living as her spark was released from where it hid and shocked her into action. Her eyes regained focus.

"Liz?"

"Yes. Now get us some help!"

Suzy moved to a chest filled with freshly-rolled bandages, reaching in to pass them to Kimmey and Liselle as Doc Benjamin laughed.

"Just what the hell do you women think you're doing?"

Suzy stopped, turning her bald head to Doc. She motioned to the women.

"Go . . . I'm right behind you."

Doc laughed again; scorn his flavor of the moment. "I don't recall giving you permission to go anywhere." He stood with his arms crossed, relaxed and appearing not to take her intentions seriously. Looking him in the eye, Suzy demanded the keys to the medicine cooler.

"You must be joking, dear girl."

She moved in closer, her face a mask of heinous intention and something else . . . something snake-like that flickered across her face. Something new that she understood frightened them both. "One more time. The keys." The intonations of her voice promised nameless misery as Doc removed the keys from his chain. His unexpected capitulation emboldened her.

"You're coming too." Wordlessly, with a shove from Suzy, they were out the door and on their way to Liz. Doc's medical bag with an assortment of chilled vials and capsules from the locked cooler stayed clutched in her white-knuckled hands.

The screams could be heard the second they stepped into the cavern, cutting through the thickening miasma of stench.

Hurrying, they followed the sounds of commotion until they reached the large crowd around Liz's hovel. Men and women surrounded the entrance, fear and terror in the posture of the women as they hung on to each other, praying for the woman who meant so much to their sanity.

Suzy fought her way through the crowd, which finally parted as they realized Doc was with her. Ominously, the screams stopped.

Suzy crept up to Liz's blood-soaked bed, struck dumb by the copious amount that couldn't possibly have come from one boney pregnant young woman. *Not my Liz.*

Casting her terrified eyes around the crowded hut, she watched Kimmey sobbing softly, curled up in the corner. Liselle stood motionless, her eyes wide and unseeing. Liz's man, Surrel, knelt at the side of the bed covered in blood as he tried to rub life back into the cooling hand of his favorite woman. Outside women clustered meekly at the foot of the bed, one holding a bundle in her arms.

Doc sized up the situation, before ducking back out of the room to return with three other men who began to roll up their sleeves.

"She died." The words dropped like stone . . . cold venom filling the room. Liselle turned to face Suzy. "She died. And where were you when she needed you, little girl?" Liselle launched herself at Suzy, arms flailing, blows landing ineffectually on the teen's head and shoulders.

Surrel stood up as Doc and the other men subdued Liselle. She stood shaking, fear in her eyes as Surrel slapped her hard across the face.

"What the hell's gotten into you tonight? I said to bring Doc not his useless pet." A quick glance over at Doc. "Beg your pardon there, Doc, don't mean no offence, now."

"No offense taken, Surrel. Why don't you let the boys get her out of here so the women can clean up this stinking mess?" Doc's tone was dismissive and impatient. He reached out to liberate his bag from Suzy's limp hands.

"You've got five minutes. I'll be waiting outside." Doc's voice sounded sure and commanding, the momentary control achieved by Suzy long departed.

As Doc left the hut, the men pushed Surrel aside and began to wrap Liz in the bloody sheets and blankets.

No one even heard Suzy whisper as they lifted her spent body from the bed. "Noooo, please God, give her back. I beg you . . ."

Evil Among Us: Species Intervention #6609

"Move aside there now, girl." Surrel began to take control of his hut and his women. "Kimmey, for Christ's sake, stop your sniveling and get off the floor. She's gone. It's not like she's not replaceable. Now get this place cleaned up. I want my dinner."

The Outside women brightened noticeably at Surrel's words, hoping one of them might be the lucky replacement, enabling them to sleep safely inside, well removed from the nightly marauders.

As Suzy numbly turned to leave, she heard the unmistakable sound of a newborn cry. Turning back to the Outside women, all eyes fastened on the bundle held in the arms of one of them.

The tallest man carrying Liz out the door stopped.

"You want to throw it in with this, Surrel? Or you gunna keep it?"

Surrel scratched his head, looking at the dirty floor. "I don't rightly know, boys. I'm of a mind to let you take it. I have enough little ones running around right now. His eyes lit up with a feral gleam of cunning.

"Don't suppose any of you boys might trade me for it?"

"Is it a boy or a girl?"

Surrel turned on the salesmanship. "It's a boy. And not in bad shape. The foot looks a bit turned, but no bad lip. Cauliflower ear, but that ain't nothing." The men looked at each other, a silent message flowing between them.

"Na, we'll take a pass. He won't be good for much with a turned leg. He'll just be a gimp. Doc don't want no more resources spent on unproductive outcomes. Ya know what that means. If it had a been a girl, we coulda worked something out."

Suzy watched everyone nod their heads as if they understood; the women all agreeing while Suzy could see they were plainly paralyzed with fear and horror at the new policy.

"Okay, just throw it on top here and we'll be getting out of the way." Surrel took the baby bundle from the woman and dropped it on top of the rubbish that was no longer Liz.

Weak cries came from the bundle as the infant hit the dead body of his mother. The men lifted the pile, moving out the door; just another disposal job to finish so they could get on with dinner and some relaxation.

"Wait," Suzy shouted after the men, running after them and out the door. She scooped the infant up from Liz's lifeless body, holding it against her chest, her heart thumping violently.

As one of the men tried to pull the bundle from her arms, the infant's cries increased.

"Suzy, what the hell's going on here? Let the men do their job." Doc pulled on her arm as the baby was wrenched away from her.

"Please." Suzy made a pitiful meow. Her face shriveled with emotions, panic paralyzing her. She cast a quick glance at the men with Liz's body and her baby, feeling that her essence lay under the bloody sheets with them.

Her life was over. All hope of freedom had died with Liz. Her love for the young woman that had protected, nurtured and educated her in the subtlety of patience, threatened to tear her in two. *And what of the other women in the tribe? What of their hopes of freedom and safety for their children, far from the brutality of Doc and his men? How could they replace Liz?*

Sure that her own strength came from the spirit of Liz, she knew she had to save the baby. Liz's baby. It was a sign. A glimmer of a lifeline. A wisp of hope.

She felt strength of purpose galvanize her into action. She threw herself at Doc's feet, wrapping her skinny arms around his legs.

"Please, Doc. The baby. I'll do anything. I'll take good care of him and keep him out of the way." Her beseeching words, so uncharacteristic, made Doc pause. Suzy noticed and pressed her advantage.

"I promise. I'll do anything." Jumping up, she ran to the men and made another grab for the infant.

"Hey. Doc said . . ."

Doc raised his hand silently, waving the men off. With resignation, they shrugged, mumbling under their breaths and moved off through the crowds with Liz's body.

Suzy walked slowly back to Doc, his expression unreadable. His silence made her nervous as she began to stumble and rush the words she hoped would persuade him.

"How will you feed it?"

Suzy's heart missed a beat. "I can get the milk he needs from any number of women in the tribe. Some have had their babies . . . eh . . . taken." Might as well call it with the truth. "They'll be happy to allow the baby to nurse."

Doc's expression remained unreadable, but Suzy could see calculations behind his eyes. She held her breath.

"If I let you have this babe, I don't want to see any more sulking. You will take your proper place in the tribe like any other woman. You will come to my bed when I call and you will do it eagerly. Is that clear?"

The innocent child in Suzy was stung, her face drained of blood. Her thoughts warred with themselves as she considered the evenings of pain and humiliation it would take to save the baby. Her voice was a whisper. "Noooo. I cannot."

Doc moved forward to take the baby, his face darkening with anger. The infant suddenly calmed in her arms, a sweet musical squeak that muffled its way to her ears.

"Wait, wait." Sometimes pain can be bearable when done for the sake of love. Suzy didn't know this, but she did know she loved Liz's baby. Without it she would die anyway.

As Doc placed his hands on the bundle in her arms, she reached out to place her fingers on his arm, his sweaty maleness invading her nostrils. She pressed down on his arm, sliding her fingers up to his shoulder in an attempt at a caress. "Okay, I agree."

Doc looked stoically in her eyes. The seconds ticked. Then his broken smile declared his acceptance; possessive and knowing as he slipped his arm around her. "All right now. Let's go home. And no more nonsense."

Anxious over the deal she had just committed herself to, Suzy followed Doc through the stinking mess that Liz had called home.

Approaching their own cavern, they could hear screams of laughter and cheering. Suzy wondered at the sounds, unusual in their nature for they included the sounds of women's voices. As they followed the boisterous clatter, it became clear that something was occurring in the Council Center.

Weaving their way through the deafening crowd, Doc pulled her and the baby to the center where some of the men stood dancing.

Their faces were smeared with fruit juices and flakes of crusty green bits. The tribe members around them squatted in supplication, hands reaching out to beg as everyone stared at the impossibility of the giant fruit and vegetables piled high near the fire, the flames turning the healthy vibrant colors to jewels.

Stunned, Doc and Suzy approached. Doc reached down to pick up a three-pound peach, heavy with ripe juices. The fragrant smell of freshness made Suzy dizzy. Doc took a sniff, his eyes still unbelieving. He held the peach out to her, inviting a bite. She looked around at the cheering crowd then down at the bundle in her arms. She hesitantly bit down into the soft juicy meat of the mythical fruit, liquid running down her chin.

And Suzy smiled.

You can read more by going to Amazon or Barnes and Noble and clicking on The One, Species Intervention #6609 Book 6

Author's Page

J. K. Accinni was born and raised in Sussex County before moving to Randolph, New Jersey, where she lived with her husband, five dogs and eight rabbits, all rescued, and currently resides in Sarasota, Florida. Mrs. Accinni's passion for wildlife conservation has led her all over the world, including three trips to Africa, where ten years ago she and her husband fell in love with a baby elephant named Wendi, who had been rescued by a wildlife group. That baby is the inspiration for the character Tobi, the elephant featured in *Hive*.

The character of Caesar is inspired by a real life iconic tiger from the Big Cat Habitat and Gulf Coast Sanctuary in Sarasota. A portion of the proceeds from her third book, *Armageddon Cometh*, will be donated to the sanctuary in support of the enormous expense required to house and feed the displaced wildlife in their care. Mrs. Accinni invites her readers to visit bigcathabitat.org to view the astounding facility and plan a visit with your family.

Mrs. Accinni also invites you to visit her webpage at www.SpeciesIntervention.com, where information on the Big Cat Habitat and Gulf Coast Sanctuary can also be viewed. Readers are encouraged to comment about the book or your own creature experiences.